Nightmare in Berlin

Nightmare in Berlin

HANS FALLADA

Translated by Allan Blunden

SCRIBE

Melbourne • London

Scribe Publications
18–20 Edward St, Brunswick, Victoria 3056, Australia
2 John Street, Clerkenwell, London, WC1N 2ES, United Kingdom

First published in English by Scribe 2016
First published as *Der Alpdruck* by Aufbau in 1947

Copyright © Aufbau Verlag GmbH & Co. KG, Berlin 1947 and 2014
Translation © Allan Blunden 2016

Typeset in 11.5/16.5 pt Adobe Garamond by the publishers

Printed and bound in Denmark by Nørhaven, Viborg

Scribe Publications is committed to the sustainable use of natural resources and the use of paper products made responsibly from those resources.

9781925321197 (Australian paperback)
9781925228380 (UK hardback)
9781925228915 (export paperback)
9781925307382 (e-book)

CiP records for this title are available from the British Library and the National Library of Australia

scribepublications.com.au
scribepublications.co.uk

CONTENTS

GERMAN PUBLISHER'S FOREWORD
TO THIS EDITION

Hans Fallada's penultimate work, *Der Alpdruck* [*Nightmare in Berlin*], appeared under the Aufbau imprint in the autumn of 1947, but the German publisher's warm commendation and sustained international lobbying elicited only a handful of foreign-language editions — in French, Norwegian, Italian, and Serbo-Croat — despite the countless translations that had been brought out earlier by Fallada's various foreign publishers. Contemporary publishing houses reacted to this novel in much the same way as Britain's Putnam had to *Jeder stirbt für sich allein* [*Alone in Berlin*]: it was felt to be a weaker product from a once successful writer, the author of *Little Man – What Now?* and other global bestsellers, whose demise was widely mourned, as he might well have produced further masterpieces had he been granted a longer span of life.

In the case of *Alone in Berlin*, posterity has already come to a very different conclusion. Sixty years on, this last work, which initially met with a rather muted response, has become what is probably his biggest international success, which has moreover significantly altered the perception of Fallada and, to some extent, of Germany itself. So the question is whether the same can be claimed for *Nightmare in Berlin*, the book that Fallada was working on in the immediate aftermath of the collapse of Nazi Germany, from February to August

Leabharlanna Poibli Chathair Bhaile Átha Cliath
Dublin City Public Libraries

1946 (for some of that time as a patient in various sanatoriums and hospitals), and which by his own account he needed to 'get out of the way' first before he could tackle the subject matter of his next book. He had already started to study the Gestapo files from which he drew the material for *Alone in Berlin*, but it was only after writing *Nightmare in Berlin* that he was able to turn these shocking and extraordinary documents into another novel.

But why, after the sensational late success of *Alone in Berlin*, in which Hans Fallada, through the story of the seemingly futile resistance of ordinary people, paints an unsparing picture of the moral ambivalence of an entire society, would one want to re-issue a book (or indeed read a book) which, in the words of reviewers at the time of its first publication, 'is a kind of thinly disguised autobiography which it is difficult to read with any great pleasure' (*Schwäbisches Tagblatt*), and which was seen as 'a confession of his own human weakness and a picture of life in Germany in the wake of its downfall' (*Leipziger Zeitung*), and as an 'account that is perhaps not yet sufficiently distanced from the horrendous events of Hitler's war' (*Freie Presse*)?

Well, Cossee for one, the distinguished Dutch publisher of Fallada's works, did not even ask itself this question prior to the recent publication of *Der Alpdruck* in a Dutch translation, along with the other important late works with which the book belongs by virtue of its subject matter and genesis: *In meinem fremden Land (Gefängnistagebuch 1944)* [published in English as *A Stranger in My Own Country: the 1944 prison diary*], *Der Trinker* [*The Drinker*], and *Jeder stirbt für sich allein* [*Alone in Berlin*]. Cossee's initiative is to be applauded: for with the directness of its observations from a long-suppressed phase of German history — that time between the end of the evil old order and the gradual emergence of a new one, when life was on hold, abandoned by the past and still in search of a future—this book fills a gap that far more comprehensive and ambitious works such as Kasimir Edschmid's *Das gute Recht* (published in 1946) had not been able to fill. This is true of provincial life (Mecklenburg, in this case), which was more or less marginalised anyway in the literary treatment of these times; but more especially is it true of Berlin, the setting for the last months of Fallada's life: the city punished for its historic guilt, where the local population and the author were both fighting for their survival—lost and adrift to begin with, but then increasingly with a single-minded determination born of necessity.

More especially, this child of his times, this writer caught up in a private battle for survival, for a firm stance, for a clear perspective on his own guilt, achieved something unique, which has perhaps been best summed up by his obituarist Johannes R. Becher (who appears in this book in the guise of Doll's advocate and champion, Granzow): 'The contradiction that he embodied was not just private and personal. He embodied and represented, in his mental and spiritual crises, a general German condition.' Nowhere in Fallada's work is this more true than it is here, in *Nightmare in Berlin*.

When the protagonist, the writer Dr. Doll—easily recognisable as a figure based on Fallada's own experience—tells us that he is filled with a 'feeling of utterly helpless shame', 'the malady of the age, a mixture of bottomless despair and apathy', this private mentality shared by Hans Fallada represents that of German society at large, which found itself in a state of crisis. It is hard to imagine a more striking or immediate insight into the psyche, the dawning realisation of a German living in those times who had not been a supporter of the Nazis, but who had also not done anything to oppose them, who had come to an accommodation of sorts with them, than the following scene. Doll thinks he can welcome the occupying Russian troops joyfully as long-awaited liberators, only to be confronted with a different reality: 'He was a German, and so belonged to the most hated and despised nation on earth. [...] Doll suddenly realised that he would probably not live long enough to see the day when the German name would be washed clean in the eyes of the world, and that perhaps his own children and grandchildren would still be bearing the burden of their fathers' guilt.'

Tragic episodes like the story of the chemist and his family who had survived all kinds of horrors, but now tried to take their own lives because they were afraid of the Russians, alternate with more mundane observations, such as the fact that nobody who had not seen Berlin for a while could find their way around any more, since all the familiar landmarks had disappeared under a uniform landscape of rubble. Fallada directs a pitiless gaze at the all-encompassing misery around him, which was also his own: 'But what Doll had not foreseen was a new loss of self-esteem. [...] They would be left naked and empty, and in letting go of the lies that had been drip-fed to them all their lives as the most profound truth and wisdom, they would be stripped of their inner resources of love and hate, memory, self-esteem, and dignity.' He paints a frank picture of Doll and Alma's drug addiction, clearly drawing on his own experiences in a series of touching, sometimes pathetic, and at other times supremely comic descriptions, as when Doll and Alma, cunning and brazen by turns, are forever angling for fresh supplies of their 'little remedies' from hospital doctors or GPs (and here Gottfried Benn puts in a guest appearance as Pernies, 'the doctor with the papery skin').

With the unique capacity for empathy that characterises his work, Fallada also describes the 'little people' here, such as the kindly and ever-helpful Mrs. Minus, who ('just this once') packs up bags of groceries for him in her shop when he has no ration cards to pay for them, while elsewhere he displays a no less typical penchant for euphemism, especially when it comes to Alma. On one occasion early on in the book, for example, she goes to get her 'medication for her bilious complaint' (in other words: the morphine addict goes in search of her next fix).

At the same time, this tendency to whitewash, which runs through virtually all of Fallada's quasi-autobiographical works, stands both the novelist and the reader in very good stead. The latter will certainly enjoy the little scene where Doll and Alma are on a tram together, and Doll is doggedly refusing to speak to his wife, who instead of trying to kick her drug habit is determined not to deny herself anything. The two of them find seats across the aisle from an old lady, who starts to get worked up because Alma is casually smoking on the tram. The old woman's remark—'They're all the same, these dolled-up little tramps!'—is parried by Alma with: 'And they're all the same, these dried-up old bats!', whereupon the whole tram erupts in laughter, and one passenger is so tickled that he even drums his feet on the floor with glee. Then we read: 'After this little interlude, everything was sweetness and light again between the married couple.' Fallada's natural talent for storytelling finds an outlet even amidst the squalor and misery of a devastated Berlin.

What he does here is to make the depressing reality more bearable — for the reader, and perhaps for himself. There's no doubt that these times were hard for Fallada, hard for Doll to endure: 'We're probably going to die soon anyway, but you can do it more discreetly and comfortably in the big city. They have gas, for one thing!' Fallada is able to turn even this into a little tragicomedy: *How would we do it? We don't have access to poison. Water? We both swim too well. The noose? Couldn't face that! Gas? But we don't even have a kitchen with a gas stove any more.* And yet a little later, despite all this, a gleam of hope appears briefly on the horizon, a tiny shred of optimism: 'But the world out there, this vast, sprawling, chaotic Berlin, is so weird and wonderful, so full of wondrous things!'

Qualities of this kind, unique to Fallada, the qualities of a strong book about a weak human being, earned him the respect of contemporary arts reviewers, who were starting to find their feet again. Berlin's *Tagesspiegel* wrote: '*Nightmare in Berlin* is emblematic of what went on in Germany after the capitulation.' The *Berliner Zeitung* noted: 'A piece of concentrated contemporary history whose value transcends the personal [...]. It need hardly be said that the writing is both gripping and vivid.' The *Frankfurter Neue Presse* wrote: 'A supremely honest book, a human testament.' And the *Norddeutsche Zeitung*: '*Nightmare in Berlin* is the quintessence of Fallada's realisation that the ruins are not important, that the only thing that matters is life and living.' It is best summed up by the journal *Der Zwiebelfisch*: 'In his excellent book *Nightmare in Berlin*, Hans Fallada paints a picture of the despondency and apathy felt by Germans. The final months of wartime life are portrayed in masterly fashion, along with the end of the war, the entry of the Russian troops, the "respectable" bourgeois world as it adjusts to the new environment, and the moral decline of the population.'

Fallada himself achieved one of those wondrous things that Berlin, by his own account, was full of. In one last push he succeeded in producing the two late works, *Nightmare in Berlin* and *Alone in Berlin*, that have cemented his enduring literary reputation. But before these last two books could appear, the man behind the writer, Rudolf Ditzen, died of heart failure on 5 February 1947, his strength finally exhausted.

The *Schwäbisches Tageblatt* lamented the fact that when *Nightmare in Berlin* was first published, the moving obituary penned by Becher for his writer friend appeared at the end of the book: 'It would have been better as a foreword.' The present brief introduction is an attempt to make good that deficit—even if the passage of time has made it easier for today's reader to judge the book's merits and its place in the canon. The personal directness of this 'strong book, which tells us so much about the author' (to quote the then director of Aufbau Verlag, Erich Wendt), bridges the time gap as only literature of enduring relevance can do. It would be wrong to deny the reader access to such literature—even if it means that he or she may learn more about the dark side of an admired author than he or she is comfortable with. For this is the only way we can learn real answers to the basic question: how can we build a happy world again on the ruins of a world that has been defiled?

Berlin, April 2014
Nele Holdack & René Strien

AUTHOR'S FOREWORD

The author of this novel is far from satisfied with what he has written on the following pages, which is now laid before the reader in printed form. When he conceived the plan of writing this book, he imagined that alongside the reverses of everyday life—the depressions, illnesses, and general despondency—that alongside all these things which the end of this terrible war inevitably visited upon every German, there would also be more uplifting things to report, signal acts of courage, hours filled with hope. But it was not to be. The book remains essentially a medical report, telling the story of the apathy that descended upon a large part, and more especially the better part, of the German population in April 1945, an apathy that many have not managed to cast off to this day.

The fact that the author could not alter this, and could not introduce more elements of levity and gaiety into this novel, is not simply due to his own outlook on life, but has to do much more with the general situation of the German people, which today, fifteen months after the end of hostilities, remains grim.

The reasoning behind the decision to place the novel before the public despite this shortcoming is that it may perhaps be of some value as a *document humain*, a faithful and true account (to the best of the author's abilities) of what ordinary Germans felt, suffered, and did between April 1945 and the summer of that year. The time may soon come when people are no longer able to understand the paralysis that has blighted this first post-war year to such disastrous effect. A medical report, then, and not a work of art — I'm sorry to say. (The author, too, is a child of his times, afflicted by that same paralysis.)

I have just called the book 'a faithful and true account'. But nothing that is related in the following pages happened exactly as it is described here. For reasons of space alone, a book such as this cannot possibly record everything that happened; I had to be selective, to invent material, and things that were told to me could not just be set down verbatim, but had to be recast in a different form. None of this means that the book cannot — therefore — be 'true': everything related here *could* have happened in the manner described, but it is nonetheless a novel, or in other words a product of the imagination.

The same is true of the characters who appear here: none of them exists outside the pages of this book exactly as they are portrayed here. Just as the events described had to obey the laws of narration, so too did the characters. Some are pure invention; others are amalgams of several different people.

Writing this novel has not been an enjoyable experience, but to its author the book seemed important. Amidst the changing fortunes of life, the upturns and the reverses, what remained important to him throughout was what people went through after the end of the war, in mind and in body. How nearly everybody lost faith, yet in the end rediscovered a little bit of courage and hope — that is the story that these pages tell.

Berlin, August 1946

PART ONE

Downfall

CHAPTER ONE

The first illusion

Always, during those nights around the time of the great collapse, Dr. Doll, when he did eventually manage to get to sleep, was plagued by the same bad dream. They slept very little those first few nights, constantly fearful of some threat to body or soul. Well into the night, after a day filled with torment, they stayed sitting by the windows, peering out onto the little meadow, towards the bushes and the narrow cement path, to see if any of the enemy were coming—until their eyes ached, and everything became a blur and they could see nothing.

Then someone would often say: 'Why don't we just go to bed?'

But usually nobody answered, and they just carried on sitting there, staring out, and feeling afraid, until Dr. Doll was suddenly overcome by sleep, as if ambushed by some bandit clapping his great hand over his whole face to smother him. Or else it was like some tightly woven spider's web that went down his throat with every breath he took, overpowering his consciousness. A nightmare …

It was bad enough, falling asleep like that, but, having fallen asleep in this hideous fashion, he was immediately visited by the same bad dream—always the same one. And this was Doll's dream:

He was lying at the bottom of a huge bomb crater, on his back, his arms pressed tightly against his sides, lying in the wet, yellow mud. Without moving his head, he was able to see the trunks of trees that had toppled into the crater, as well as the facades of houses with their empty window openings, and nothing behind them. Sometimes Doll was racked by the fear that these things might fall down deeper into the bomb crater and end up on top of him, but not one of these dangerously precarious ruins ever shifted its position.

He was still tormented by the thought that a thousand water veins and springs would inundate him and fill his mouth with the sloppy yellow mud. And there would be no escape, because Doll knew that he would never be able to get up out of this crater by his own strength. But this fear, too, was groundless; he never heard a sound from the springs or the trickling water veins, and all was deathly silence inside the huge bomb crater.

He was haunted by a third fear, and that was an illusion, too: vast flocks of ravens and crows flew in a constant stream across the sky above the bomb crater, and he was terrified that they might spot their victim lying down there in the mud. But no, the deathly silence continued unbroken; these vast flocks of birds existed only in Doll's imagination, otherwise he would at least have heard their cawing.

But two other things were not figments of his imagination, and he knew for certain they were true. One of them was that peace had finally come. No more bombs came screaming down through the air, no more shots were fired; peace had come, and silence reigned. One last huge explosion had flung him into the mud at the bottom of this crater. And he was not alone in this abyss. Although he never heard a sound, and saw nothing except what has been described, he knew that his whole family was lying here with him, and the whole German people, and all the nations of Europe—all just as helpless and defenceless as him, all tormented by the same fears as him.

But always, throughout the endless hours filled with anguished dreams, when the busy and energetic Dr. Doll of the daytime was obliterated and he knew only fear — always in these harrowing interludes of sleep he saw something else. And what he saw was this:

Sitting on the edge of the crater, silent and motionless, were the Big Three. Even in his dreams he called them only by this name, which the war had seared into his brain. Then the names Churchill, Roosevelt, and Stalin came to mind, though he was sometimes tormented by the thought that something had changed there recently.

The Big Three sat close together, or at least not very far apart; they sat as if they had just turned up from their part of the world, and stared down in silent grief into the vast crater, at the bottom of which lay Doll and his family and the German people and all the peoples of Europe, defenceless and defiled. And as they sat there and stared, silent and full of grief, Doll knew with absolute certainty in the innermost depths of his heart that the Big Three were ceaselessly pondering how he, Doll, and everyone else with him could be helped back on their feet again, and how a happy world could be rebuilt from this ravaged one. They pondered this ceaselessly, the Big Three, while endless flocks of crows flew homewards over the pacified land, from the killing fields of the world to their old roosts, and while silent springs trickled inaudibly, their waters bringing the sloppy yellow mud ever more perilously close to his mouth.

But he, Doll, could do nothing; with his arms pressed tightly against his sides, he had to lie still and wait, until the Big Three, deep in mournful thought, had come to a decision. This was perhaps the worst thing about this bad dream for Doll, that although he was still threatened by many dangers, there was nothing he could do except to lie still and wait, for an endless eternity! The empty house fronts could still fall in on him, the flocks of crows, hungry for carrion, could still spot the defenceless figure, the yellow mud could still fill his mouth; but there was nothing he could do except wait, and maybe this waiting would make it too late for him and his family, whom he loved very much ... Maybe they would all perish yet!

It took a long time for the last traces of this haunting bad dream to leave Doll, and he did not really break free until a change in his life forced him to stop brooding and busy himself with useful activity again. But it took a great deal longer for Doll to realise that this entire bad dream, rising up from within like a ghostly apparition, was only there to fool and delude him. As painful as this dream was, Doll had believed it was true.

It took a very long time for him to grasp that there was nobody out there who was prepared to help him up out of the mire into which he had plunged. Nobody, not the Big Three, much less any of his fellow countrymen, was remotely interested in Dr. Doll. If he died there in the wet mud, too bad for him — but only for him! Not a heart in the world would grow heavier on his account. If he really had a desire to work again and write things, then it was up to him and him alone to overcome this apathy, get up on his feet again, brush the dirt off, and get down to work.

But at that time Doll was still a long way from understanding this. Now that peace had finally come, he thought for a long time that the whole world was just waiting to help him back on his feet again.

CHAPTER TWO

The second illusion

On the morning of 26 April 1945, Doll had finally woken in a good mood again. After weeks and months of passively waiting for the war to end, the hour of liberation now seemed nigh. The town of Prenzlau had been taken, the Russians could arrive at any moment; in the morning, planes had been circling over the town—and they were not German planes!

But the best news had come to Doll's ears in the late evening: the SS was pulling out, the *Volkssturm* had been disbanded, and the little town would not be defended against the advancing Russians. That took a huge weight off his mind: for weeks now he had not ventured out of the house for fear of drawing attention to himself. Because he was absolutely determined not to fight in the *Volkssturm*.

But now, after this welcome news, he could venture outdoors again without worrying about what the neighbours would say—three of whom, at least, overlooked his house and garden. So he stepped outside with his young wife into the glorious spring day. The sun felt warm, and its warmth did them a power of good, especially down here by the water's edge. The leaves and grass were still fresh and bright with all the myriad hues of the season's first growth, and the ground beneath their feet seemed to heave and tremble with urgent fecundity.

As Doll was soaking up the sun outside the house with his wife, his gaze fell upon two long borders planted with shrubs, which lay either side of the narrow cement path that led to his door. There was new growth sprouting in these borders, too, and the first grape hyacinths, primroses, and anemones were starting to come into flower. But welcome as this sight was, it was spoilt by a tangle of wire, some of it hanging free, some of it still attached to ugly wooden stakes, which formed an untidy mess that was an affront to the young growth, while the loose ends of wire, dangling where they could catch you unawares, made it dangerous even to walk along the footpath.

No sooner had Doll's gaze taken in this untidy mess than he exclaimed: 'I've got my work cut out for me today! That hideous tangle of wire has been annoying me for ages!' And he fetched his pincers and mattock, and went to work with a will.

While he busied himself in the sun, he was finally able to see into his neighbours' gardens again. He soon noticed a lot of unusual activity there. Wherever he looked, there were people running back and forth, lugging suitcases and furniture out of their houses and into sheds—or the other way round—and others wandering about aimlessly (or so it appeared) with spades, which they drove into the ground here and there, seemingly at random.

One neighbour ran out along the jetty and then stood still, hands in pockets, as if he suddenly had all the time in the world. Then something plopped into the water, and after the neighbour had looked around in an elaborately oh-so-casual way to see if anyone was watching—Doll carried on swinging his mattock the while—he sauntered back to his house with a rolling gait, as if deep in thought, and then promptly threw himself into another round of frenetic activity.

Then, all of a sudden, everything came to a halt again. Groups of people gathered at the fences dividing their properties and whispered conspiratorially among themselves. Large packages changed hands over the wire, and then everybody scattered again, looking furtively about them, intent on more secret business.

Doll had only been living at this property, which belonged to his second wife, for a few months, and as an 'outsider' he remained excluded from all these busy comings and goings, which suited him just fine. The fact was that most of the people engaged in this blatantly surreptitious behaviour were women or very old men, which gave him licence to dismiss it all contemptuously as 'women's stuff'.

But he was not able to enjoy his isolation for long, because two women, ostensibly friends of his wife, now turned up at his property. These women, whom he had never been able to stand, hung around next to him and acted all surprised that he had time for that sort of work on a day like this—when the Russians would be arriving any minute!

Dr. Doll had now been joined by his wife, and with a slightly mocking smile he explained that that was just the point: he was clearing the paths for these long-awaited visitors. The ladies inquired with astonishment if he was planning to stay here and wait for the enemy to arrive, because that was surely not advisable, with two children, an aged grandmother, and a young wife? The people living out here on the edge of town, at any rate, had all got together and agreed to cross by boat to the other side of the lake when dusk fell, and to hide deep in the forest and await the next turn of events.

Doll's wife replied for her husband: 'Well, we won't be doing anything like that. We're not going anywhere, and we're not hiding anything away; my husband and I are going to welcome the long-

9

awaited liberators at the door of our house!'

The two ladies urged them strongly to reconsider, but the more forcefully they argued, the more they wavered in their own resolve, and the more doubtful they seemed about the safety of the forest retreat they had just been commending so warmly. When they finally left, Doll said to his wife with a smile: 'They won't do anything, you'll see. They'll poke around aimlessly for a couple of hours, like the hens when there's a storm brewing, picking things up and putting things down. But in the end they'll just flop down exhausted and do what we've all been doing for weeks: just wait for the liberators to arrive.'

As far as her friends were concerned, Alma was in complete agreement with her husband; but as for herself, she felt neither exhausted nor disposed to wait patiently. After lunch she told Doll, who planned to lie down on the couch for a while after his unaccustomed morning's labours, that she just wanted to cycle into town quickly to replenish her supply of gallbladder medicine, as there was unlikely to be much opportunity to do so in the coming days.

Doll had some concerns, as the Russians could arrive at any moment, and it would be best if they were there at home together to welcome them. But he knew from past experience that it was a waste of time to try and dissuade his young wife from some course of action by pointing out the possible risks. She had proved to him a dozen times—during the heaviest air raids, battling the firestorms of Berlin, under attack by low-flying enemy aircraft—that she was utterly fearless. So he gave a small sigh and said: 'If you must. Take care, my dear!', watched from the window as she cycled off, lay down on the couch with a smile on his face, and fell asleep.

Meanwhile Mrs. Alma Doll was pedalling hard uphill and

down, heading for the local small town. Her route took her initially along quiet tracks, where there were hardly any houses, then along an avenue lined on both sides with villas. It struck her here that the streets were completely empty, and that the villas—perhaps because every single window was shut—looked unoccupied and somehow ghostly. *Maybe they're all in the forest already*, thought Mrs. Doll, and felt even more excited about her little adventure.

At the junction of the avenue and the first street of the town proper, she finally encountered a sign of life, in the form of a large German army truck. A few SS men were helping some young women and girls to climb on board. 'Come quickly, young lady!' one of the SS men shouted to Mrs. Doll, and it sounded almost like an order. 'This is the last army vehicle leaving the town!'

Like her husband, Mrs. Doll had been very pleased to learn that the town was not going to be defended, but would be surrendered without a fight. But that didn't stop her answering back now: 'That's just like you bastards, to clear out now, when the Russians are coming! Ever since you've been here, you've acted like you owned the place, eating and drinking us out of house and home; but now, when the going gets tough, you just turn tail and run!'

If she had spoken to an SS man like that only the day before, the consequences for her and her family would have been very serious. The situation must have really changed dramatically in the last twenty-four hours, because the SS man replied quite calmly: 'Just get on the truck and don't talk rubbish! The leading Russian tank units are already up in the town!'

'Even better!' cried Mrs. Doll. 'I can go and say hello right now!'

And with that she stood on the pedals and rode off into the town, leaving behind the last German army truck that she hoped to see in her life.

Once again, it felt as if she was riding through an abandoned town—perhaps those few women by the army truck really were the last people living in the town, and everyone else had already gone. Not one person, not even a dog or a cat, was to be seen on the street. All the windows were shut, and all the doors looked like they had been barricaded. And yet, as she cycled on through the streets, approaching the town centre, she had the feeling that this creature with many hundreds of heads was just holding its breath, as if at any moment—behind her, beside her—it could suddenly erupt in a hideous scream, tormented beyond endurance by the agonizing wait. As if living behind all these blind windows were people driven almost mad with fear for what lay ahead, mad with hope that this horrendous war was finally coming to an end.

This feeling was reinforced by a few white rags, barely the size of small towels, that had been hung over some of the doors. In the ghostly atmosphere that had enveloped Mrs. Doll since she entered the town, it took a moment for her to realise that these white cloths were meant to signify unconditional surrender. This was the first time in twelve years that she had seen flags other than ones with swastikas on them hanging from the houses. She involuntarily quickened her pace.

She turned the corner of the street, and that sense of a pervasive unseen fear was gone in an instant. And she had to smile in spite of herself. On the uneven street of the small town, moving in all directions in a seemingly random way, were eight or ten tanks. From the uniforms and the headgear worn by the men standing in the open hatches, Mrs. Doll could tell at once that these were not German tanks; these were the leading Russian tank units she had just been warned about.

But this didn't seem like the sort of thing you needed to be warned about. There was nothing menacing about the way these tanks drove back and forth in the fine spring sunshine, effortlessly mounting the edge of a pavement, scraping past the line of lime trees and then dropping back onto the roadway. On the contrary: it seemed almost playful, as if they were just having fun. Not for one moment did she feel herself to be in any kind of danger. She wove in and out between the tanks and then, when she reached her destination, the chemist's shop, she jumped off her bicycle. In her sudden mood of relief she had failed to notice that the houses in this street, too, had been barricaded and closed up by their fearful occupants, and that she was the only German among all the Russians, some of whom were standing around in the street with submachine guns.

Mrs. Doll dragged her gaze away from this unusual street scene and turned her attention to the chemist's shop, whose doorway, like those of all the other houses, was securely barricaded and shut up. When banging and shouting failed to raise anyone, she hesitated only for a moment before walking straight up to a Russian soldier with a submachine gun who was standing close by. 'Listen, Vanya', she said to the Russian, smiling at him and pulling him by the sleeve in the direction of the chemist's shop, 'open up the shop for me there, will you?'

The Russian returned her smiling gaze with a look of stony indifference, and for a moment she had the slightly unsettling sensation of being looked at like a brick wall or an animal. But the sensation vanished as quickly as it had come, as the man offered no resistance and let himself be pulled over by her to the chemist's shop, where, quickly grasping her purpose, he hammered loudly on the panel of the door a few times with the butt of his weapon. The leonine head of the chemist, a man in his seventies, promptly appeared at a little glass window in the upper part of the door, anxiously peering out to see what all the noise was about. His face normally had a jovial, ruddy complexion, but now it looked grey and ashen.

Mrs. Doll nodded cheerily to the old man, and said to the Russian: 'It's fine, and thanks for your help. You can go now.'

The soldier's expression didn't change as he stepped back onto the street without so much as a backward glance. Now the key was turning in the lock, and Mrs. Doll was able to enter the chemist's shop, where the seventy-year-old was holed up with his much younger wife and her late-born child of two or three years. As soon as Mrs. Doll was inside, the door to the shop was locked again.

Though each individual memory of this first day of occupation was still fresh and vivid a long time after the events themselves, Mrs. Doll's recollection of what had been said inside the chemist's shop that day was unclear. Yes, she had her usual medication dispensed with the customary precision, and she knew, too, that when she went to pay for it her money was initially declined, and then accepted with a weary twinkle of the eye, like the playful antics of some silly child. After that, it was just casual talk; they told her, for instance, that she couldn't possibly set out on the long ride home with all those Russians about, and that she absolutely had to remain in the shop. And then, a few moments later, the same people who had urged her to stay were wondering if the house was still a safe place to be, or whether they would not have done better to go and hide in the forest after all. And they began to reproach themselves for not getting out much earlier and heading for the western part of Germany—in short, what Mrs. Doll heard here was the same wretched, pointless talk, the talk of people worn down by endless, anguished waiting, that could be heard in just about any German household around this time.

Here, however—given that Russian tanks were rolling past the windows of the chemist's shop—such talk was especially pointless. There were no more decisions to be made: everything had been decided, and the waiting was over! And anyway, Mrs. Doll had been outside, out in the sunny spring air, she had cycled in between the tanks, she had impulsively grabbed a Russian by the sleeve. The last vestige of that pervasive, unseen fear had left her—and she just couldn't bear to listen to any more of this talk. In the end, she asked the family rather abruptly to open the door for her again, and she stepped back out onto the street, into the bright daylight, mounted her bicycle, and rode off towards the town centre, weaving in and out between the growing number of tanks.

Mrs. Doll was presumably the last person to see the chemist and his wife and child alive that afternoon. A few hours later, he gave his wife and child poison, then took some himself, apparently in an act of senseless desperation; their nerves, stretched to breaking point, had finally snapped. They had endured so much over the years, and now, when it looked as if things were starting to get better, and nothing could be as bad as before, they refused to endure the uncertainty of even the briefest of waits.

But the same chemist's hand that had just now dispensed Mrs. Doll's medication for her bilious complaint with such practised precision proved less adroit in measuring out the poison for himself and his family. The very old man and the very young child, they both died. But the wife recovered after a protracted period of suffering, and although she was left alone in the world, she did not repeat the suicide attempt.

Alma Doll had not gone very far on her bicycle before a very different scene caught her attention and brought her to a halt again. Outside the small town's largest hotel, a group of about a dozen children had gathered, boys and girls aged around ten or twelve. They were watching the tanks rolling past, shouting and laughing, while the Russian soldiers seemed not to notice them at all.

The mood of wild abandon that had taken hold of these otherwise rather placid country children was explained by the wine bottles they had in their hands. Just as Mrs. Doll was getting off her bicycle, a boy slipped out of the front door of the hotel clutching an armful of new bottles. The children in the street greeted their companion with cries of joy that sounded almost like the howling of a pack of young wolves. They dropped the bottles they were holding, regardless of whether they were full, half-full, or empty, letting them smash on the pavement, while they grabbed the new bottles, knocked off the necks on the stone steps of the hotel, and raised the bottles to their childish mouths.

This spectacle immediately roused Mrs. Doll to fury. As a mother she had always abhorred the sight of a drunken child, but what made her even angrier now was that these children, not yet adolescents, were dishonouring the arrival of the Red Army by their drunkenness. She rushed forward and fell upon the children, snatching the wine bottles from their grasp, and handing out slaps and thumps with such gusto that the next minute the whole bunch had disappeared around the nearest corner.

Mrs. Doll stood quietly and breathed again. The fury of a moment ago had ebbed away, and her mood was almost sunny as she gazed upon the street, deserted by its residents, where apart from her there was nothing to be seen except tanks and a few Russian soldiers with submachine guns. Then she remembered that it was probably time to be heading home again, and with a soft sigh of contentment she turned to retrieve her bicycle. But before she could reach it, a Russian soldier stepped towards her, pointing to her hand, and pulled a little package from his pocket, which he tore open.

She looked at her hand, and only now realised that she had cut it when she was grabbing the bottles from the children. Blood was dripping from her fingers. With a smiling face she allowed the helpful Russian to bandage her hand, patted him on the shoulder by way of thanks—he looked through her blankly—got on her bicycle, and rode home without further incident. But at the very spot where the German army truck had been parked an hour earlier, Russian tanks were now rolling through. Had the truck got away in time? She didn't know, and would probably never know.

When Mrs. Doll reported back to her husband with this latest news, it only served to confirm his decision to await the victors and liberators at the door of his house. But as the Russians could turn up at any moment, even in this remote corner of the little town, Doll abruptly broke off his conversation with his wife and went back to his work on the shrub borders with a dogged determination that seemed almost beyond reason at such a momentous hour, intent on clearing the last tangles of wire and rolling them up neatly and removing the last of the ugly wooden stakes.

Neither the departure nor the return of the young woman had gone unnoticed on the neighbouring properties. It wasn't long before these neighbours came round looking for Doll—always on some plausible pretext, of course, such as wanting to borrow one of his tools—and, as they watched him work, they tried to find out in a roundabout way what Mrs. Doll had been doing in the town and what news she might have to report. If he'd been asked a direct question—which would have been entirely justified under the circumstances—Doll would have told them immediately what they wanted to know, but he hated this sort of mealy-mouthed beating about the bush, and he had no intention of satisfying their unspoken curiosity.

So the neighbours would have had to go away empty-handed, if Alma had not emerged from the house to join her husband. Like most young people, she couldn't wait to relate her adventures, all the more so as they had been highly enjoyable and reassuring.

And what the young woman had to tell them brought about a complete change of heart among the neighbours. There was no more talk of hiding in the forest. All of them now planned to follow the example of the Dolls and await their liberators in their homes. Indeed, some began to wonder quite openly whether it might not be better to retrieve items that had been hidden or buried, and put them back where they belonged, so as not to offend the victors by the appearance of mistrust. Such suggestions were greeted by other family members with much irritation and head-shaking: 'You wouldn't, Olga, surely!'—'What nonsense you talk, Elisabeth, better safe than sorry!' Or even: 'I don't think we've hidden anything away, Minnie, you must be imagining things!'

This neighbourly exchange reached its climax when two old men, who must have been in their seventies, got really fired up over the account of the scene in front of the hotel with the drunken children. At first, the fury of the two old men was indescribable. Had they not, for weeks and months past, been beating a path to the door of this self-same hotelier, whose regular customers they had been since time immemorial—and making that journey almost daily, despite their advanced years and the distance involved—and had not this villain, this criminal, this traitor to his own people, refused their requests for a bottle, or indeed just a glass, of wine, nearly always with the same refrain: that he just didn't have anything left, because the SS had drunk the lot?! And now it turned out that he still had wine after all, lots of wine most likely, a cellarful, whole cellarfuls, which had been unlawfully denied them, and which children were now emptying onto the street!

And the two old men stood there looking at each other — their faces, which had been grey and careworn just a few minutes earlier, now flushed red to the roots of their white hair, as if bathed in the reflection of the wine. They patted each other on their bellies, which had grown so slack over the past year that they no longer filled out their trousers, and recited the names of their favourite grape varieties to each other in fond reminiscence. One of them was short, invariably clad in a green huntsman's suit, and a passionate devotee of Moselle wines; the other was tall, always in shirtsleeves, and tended to favour French wines. As they danced around each other, shouting and patting each other on the belly, they seemed to be drunk already on the wine they had not yet imbibed. The uncertainty of the hour, the war that was barely over yet, the danger that might be lurking round the corner, all this was forgotten, and every memory of long-endured suffering was blotted out by the prospect of a drink. And as they now resolved, each egging the other on, to head into town immediately with a couple of handcarts, and fetch the wine that had been wrongfully denied them, Doll compared them in his mind to people getting ready to dance on an erupting volcano.

Thank heavens they both had wives, and these wives now made sure that the day's planned foray into town came to nothing, especially as the roar of heavy vehicles passing through the town, which could be heard very clearly across the lake, was getting steadily louder. Turning back to his loose wire ends, Doll said: 'But if things don't turn out quite as expected, we'll be the ones to blame because they didn't go and hide in the forest. Just as we'll be the ones to blame for everything that happens from now on ...'

19

'Well, I didn't say anything to persuade them one way or the other', said his young wife defensively.

'It's not about what you said', replied Doll, and yanked a staple out of the stake with his pincers. 'The point is that our dear neighbours have now found a scapegoat for everything that goes wrong.' He coiled up a length of wire. 'They won't show us any mercy, you can be sure of that! For the last few years they've always tried to put the blame on others for everything that's happened, and never on themselves. What makes you think they've changed?'

'We'll get through it', replied his young wife with a defiant smile. 'We've always been the most hated people in the town—a little bit more or less won't make a lot of difference, will it?'

And with that she nodded to him and went back indoors.

The rest of the afternoon passed agonizingly slowly. Once again they were back to this dreadful waiting, which they had hoped was finally behind them—and how often in the coming days and months they would find themselves waiting again, waiting and forever waiting! From time to time Doll stopped what he was doing and went down to the shore of the lake, either alone or with his wife; across the water from here, they could see a line of houses in the main street of the town. All they could see were the empty shells of buildings, with not a sign of human life anywhere, but their ears were filled with the endless roar of heavy vehicles and the blare of horns—a huge supply train rolling unseen, ghostlike, through the town and heading west.

Eventually—it was approaching dusk by now—the young woman shouted from the house that supper was nearly ready. Doll, who had spent most of the last hour fiddling about rather than working, packed up his tools, put them in the shed, and washed himself off in the scullery. They sat in the corner, around the circular supper table: the old grandmother, Doll, his wife, and the two children. The conversation went constantly back and forth between the old grandmother and her daughter. The old woman, who, virtually paralyzed, was confined to her armchair, was hungry for news, and this evening her daughter was very happy to oblige (which was not always the case, by any means). The grandmother wanted to know everything in exact detail, and would rather hear a thing three times than once. She bombarded her daughter with questions such as: 'And what did she say then?—And what did you say to that?—And what did she say after that?'

Normally, Doll was happy to listen to this steady burble of female chitchat, always wondering how the story would have changed inside the grandmother's old head the next time it was related. But this evening, when his good mood from the early part of the day had completely dissipated, it took a huge effort on his part to sit and listen to this idle chatter without becoming argumentative. He knew he was being unfair; but then he was in the mood to be unfair.

Suddenly the boy at the table called out under his breath: 'Russians!!' A noise at the door made them all stop talking and stare, the door opened, and three Russians entered the room.

'Everyone stay where they are!' commanded Doll under his breath, and stepped towards the visitors, his clenched left fist raised in greeting, and with his young wife at his side, who didn't think the order to stay seated applied to her. Now Doll was able to smile again, the tension, the angry impatience, had all gone, the time of waiting was finally over, and a new page had been turned in the book of destiny ... With a smile on his face, he said, '*Tovarich!*' and extended his right hand to welcome the three visitors.

Doll would never forget the manner and appearance of those first three Russians who entered his house that day. The one in front was a slim young man with a black bandage over his left eye. His movements were quick and nimble, there was an aura of brightness about him, and he wore a blue tunic and a sheepskin cap on his head.

The man behind him looked like a giant in comparison with this rather wiry and dainty figure, and seemed to tower all the way to the ceiling beams. He had a big, grey peasant's face with a huge drooping moustache, which was black but heavily streaked with grey. The most striking thing about this giant was the short, curved sabre in a black-leather scabbard that he wore at an angle across the front of his body, which was wrapped in a grey greatcoat. The third man, who was standing behind these two, was a simple, very young soldier, with a face that was only now starting to take on a character of its own. He was carrying a submachine gun with a curved, segmented ammunition clip under his arm.

Such were the three Russians, the long-awaited guests, whom Doll welcomed with his clenched left fist raised in greeting and right hand outstretched, the word '*Tovarich*!'—Comrade!—on his lips.

But as he did so, as he stood like this in front of the three men, something odd happened. The clenched left fist was lowered, Doll's right hand crept back into his pocket, and his mouth did not repeat the word that was meant to forge a bond between him and the three Russians. Nor was he smiling any more; instead, his face had taken on a dark, brooding expression. He suddenly dropped his gaze, which a moment earlier had been directed at the three, and looked at the ground.

How long they stayed like this—whether for two or three minutes, or just a few seconds—Doll was unable to say later. Suddenly the man in the blue tunic stepped forward between him and his wife and went on into the house, followed by the other two.

Neither Mr. nor Mrs. Doll followed them, but just stood there in silence, each avoiding the other's gaze. Then they heard the boy cry out: 'There they are again!'

Now they could see the three Russians at the back of the house. They had exited via the scullery; it had only taken them a moment to go through the entire house, which was basically a cabin with just four rooms. And now they were striding past the shed, without pausing or looking round, as if they knew exactly where they were going; they walked out on the jetty, climbed into the boat, cast off, and a few minutes later they had disappeared from sight behind the bushes that lined the shore.

'They've gone!' cried the boy again.

'There'll be more on their way!' said the young wife. 'That was probably just a first check to see who is living in each house.' She shot a glance at her husband, who was still standing there with his hands thrust into his pockets, brooding morosely. 'Come on!' she said. 'Let's go and eat before the soup goes completely cold. Then we'll put the children and grandmother to bed. We'll stay up for a bit longer; I've got a feeling that more of them will be coming this evening or during the night.'

'Fine', replied Doll, and went back to the supper table with her. As he did so he noted that even his wife's voice had changed completely: there was none of that bright, vivacious quality it had had when telling of her afternoon adventures. *She's noticed something, too*, he thought. *But she's like me—she doesn't want to talk about it. That's good.*

Later on, he preferred to tell himself that perhaps his wife had not noticed anything, that her voice had only sounded so different because a new time of waiting was then beginning, waiting for more Russian visitors to arrive. Waiting was now definitely the hardest part of life for every German, and they had to wait for many things, nearly everything, in fact—for days, months, and possibly even years to come ...

But thanks to the grandmother and the children, a lively conversation did now develop, to which the young wife also contributed. The main topic of interest, of course, was the three visitors, whose motley appearance was something they were not used to seeing in their own German troops (or else they were so used to seeing it, in fact, that they no longer noticed). Later on, they discussed at length whether they would get the boat back, whether the Russians would bring it back ...

Doll took no part in this conversation, and didn't want to talk at all for the rest of the evening. He was feeling far too worked up inside for that. He spoke just once to ask his wife quietly: 'Did you see the way they looked at me?'

Alma answered him just as quietly and very quickly: 'Yes! It was the same way the Russian looked at me this afternoon outside the chemist's shop—as if I was a brick wall or an animal.' Doll nodded briefly, and nothing more was said about this incident by either of them, either that day or subsequently.

But Doll pictured himself standing there in front of the three men, with a grin on his face, the greeting '*Tovarich*!' on his lips, his fist raised and his right hand extended in greeting—how false it had all been, and how embarrassing it had been for him! He'd got it all so wrong; right from the start, when he had woken early that morning feeling so cheerful, and then thrown himself into his work on the shrub borders so as to make the path 'safe' for their liberators, he had completely misread the situation!

And then he of all people had gone and boasted to the neighbours that he was going to meet the Russians at the door of his house and welcome them as liberators. Instead of reflecting on what his wife had said that afternoon and taking it as a warning, he had simply seen it as an affirmation of his own blind and foolish attitude. Truly he had not learned a single thing these last twelve years, however firmly he had believed otherwise in many a time of suffering!

The Russians had been right to look upon him as a vicious and contemptible little creature, this fellow with his clumsy attempts to ingratiate himself, who seriously imagined that a friendly grin and a barely comprehensible word of Russian would suffice to wipe out everything the Germans had done to the world in the last twelve years.

He, Doll, was a German, and he knew, at least in theory, that ever since the Nazi seizure of power and the persecutions of the Jews, the name 'German', already badly damaged by the First World War, had become progressively more reviled and despised from week to week and month to month. How often had he said to himself: 'We will never be forgiven for this!' Or: 'One day we'll all have to pay for this!'

And although he knew this perfectly well, knew that the word 'German' had become a term of abuse throughout the world, he had still put himself forward like that in the fatuous hope of showing them that there were 'still some decent Germans'.

All his long-cherished hopes for the post-war future lay in ruins, crushed under the withering gaze of the three Russian soldiers. He was a German, and so belonged to the most hated and despised nation on earth, a nation lower than the most primitive tribe of the African interior, which could never visit so much destruction, bloodshed, tears, and misery on the planet as the German people had done. Doll suddenly realised that he would probably not live long enough to see the day when the German name would be washed clean in the eyes of the world, and that perhaps his own children and grandchildren would still be bearing the burden of their fathers' guilt. And the illusion that they could persuade people of other nations by a simple word or look that not all Germans were complicit—that illusion, too, was now shattered.

This feeling of utterly helpless shame, which frequently gave way to extended periods of profound apathy, did not diminish with the passing months, but instead was intensified by a hundred little things that happened. Later on, when the war criminals were put on trial in Nuremberg, when thousands of shocking details gradually emerged to reveal the full extent of Germany's crimes, his heart wanted to rebel, unwilling to bear any more, and he refused to let himself be pushed down deeper into the mire. *No!* he said to himself—*I didn't know that! I had no idea it was* that *bad! I'm not to blame for any of that!*

But then came the moment—always—when he reflected more deeply. He was determined not to fall prey a second time to a craven delusion, not to end up standing—again—in his own parlour as a spurned host, rightly despised. *It's true!* he said to himself then. *I saw it coming with the persecution of the Jews. Later I often heard things about the way they treated Russian prisoners of war. I was appalled by all this, yes, but I never actually did anything about it. Had I known then what I know today about all these horrors, I probably still wouldn't have done anything—beyond feeling this powerless hatred …*

This was the other thing that Doll had to come to terms with entirely on his own: that he bore his share of guilt, had made himself complicit, and had no right, as a German, to feel that he should be treated like people from any other nation. A man despised, a figure of contempt—when he had always been proud of himself, and had children furthermore, four of them, all still unprovided for, all not yet able to think for themselves, but all expecting a great deal from this life — and now to be facing a life such as this!

Doll understood only too well whenever he heard or read that a large part of the German population had lapsed into a state of total apathy. There must have been many people who were feeling just like him. He hoped that they, and he, would find the strength to bear the burden that had been laid upon them.

CHAPTER THREE

The deserted house

Outwardly, the life of the Dolls changed dramatically in the first few days after the entry of the victorious Red Army. They had always kept themselves to themselves, living quietly at home and going about their business; but now, following a public proclamation, they were forced to report for work duty like everyone else in order to earn bread—a very small piece of bread initially. Shortly after seven in the morning, the two of them had to make their way to the designated assembly area in the town. On the way they were often joined by neighbours, but usually they managed to shake them off and be on their own, as they had been accustomed throughout their married life.

They walked side by side in the fresh May morning, Doll normally deep in thought and only half listening to the chatter of his wife, who was quite content with the occasional interjection of 'Yes, quite' or 'I see'. His wife's ability to carry on talking endlessly had prompted Doll to dub her his 'sea surf'. He said she reminded him of long walks he had taken earlier along the beach, accompanied by the constant rush and roar of the sea next to him.

When they reached the assembly area—the school yard—the togetherness they were used to, and the sea surf, came to an abrupt end: men and women were lined up separately, counted, registered, and assigned to all kinds of different work duties. If they were lucky, they could at least call out to each other as they were leaving and tell each other what kind of work they'd been given, so that each would know what the other was doing all the time they were apart. 'I'm going cleaning!' she might call to him. And he would reply: 'Stacking sacks!' Later on, both were given a fixed job: he was sent to mind the cows, while she was put to work carrying sacks.

They often didn't see each other again until the late evening, both of them exhausted by the unaccustomed physical labour, but both doing their best not to let the other know. Then he would talk derisively of his labours as a cowherd, where a herd of over a thousand cows, which were not from the same farm and therefore had no sense of solidarity, had to be kept together and prevented from getting into the cornfields. There were eight cowherds on the job, but his colleagues were inclined to stand around in the same place and pass the time chatting. It was the usual men's talk: how long would things go on like this, and the meagre ration of bread they got wasn't enough to feed a single man, let alone an entire family, and peacetime had not turned out quite how they had imagined, and the Nazis were up to their old tricks again, making sure they landed all the cushy jobs—it was all just hot air from start to finish, and it bored Doll stiff.

Meanwhile the herd of cows was scattering far and wide, straying from the fields of vetch into the barley crop, while Doll charged about like a madman, trying to herd a thousand cows on his own, throwing stones at them, beating them with his stick, and finally sitting down on a stone, utterly exhausted and out of breath, nursing feelings of despair, anger, and dejection. At that very moment, a Russian horseman would often turn up to check on the work of the cowherds. The other cowherds, who had wisely positioned themselves while they chatted so that they could see the rider approaching from afar, were now busy about their work, while the exhausted Doll was given a dressing-down for being lazy. But he could never bring himself to behave like the others. This whole way of carrying on — only working when the people in charge were looking, and in actual fact doing nothing at all — he found abhorrent, and typical of the hated soldiering life, where of course 'cushy numbers' are highly prized.

The only good thing about this cow-minding job was that when the cows had been driven in for the evening, cowherds and gasbags alike could stand in line with a jug — big or small, it could be any size — and they would get it filled to the brim with milk by the Ukrainian milkers. Thanks to this, the Doll family in those days could enjoy a bowl of soup for supper, which did them all good, young and old alike.

When it came to this kind of thing — getting hold of supplies — Alma Doll's efforts were a good deal more successful than her husband's, and she was more ingenious, too. Along with thirty or forty other women and girls, she had been given the job of clearing the remaining supplies from a hut camp formerly occupied by the SS, and transferring them to a large shed by the railway line. It was quite a distance, and the sacks that the women had to carry were often filled with heavy goods, so that the weight was sometimes too much for them.

What really made them angry, though, was the fact that all these preserved meats, these tins of butter, cheese, milk, and sardines, these cans of ground coffee, these packs of premium pressed leaf tea, these cartons filled with powdered chocolate (not to mention the racks of bottles containing wine and cognac and countless packs of tobacco goods) — what really made the women's blood boil as they lugged

31

all this stuff about was the thought that all this abundance had been withheld for years from starving women and children, including many children who had never tasted chocolate in their lives, only to be crammed into the greedy mouths of swaggering SS bully boys, who were directly responsible for much of Germany's misfortune.

Ever since the children, bottles of wine in hand, had got drunk outside the largest hotel in the town, most of the local population had taken a new line on property ownership: these were all goods to which they were actually entitled. The selfishness and greed of the merchants had kept these things from them—so it was only right that people should now take whatever they could get their hands on! It was a long way from the SS hut camp to the railway sheds, and the sacks were a heavy load to carry: every so often, a woman would disappear into the bushes that lined the path, and when she emerged again to join the tail end of the long, straggling column, having just now been at its head, her sack was only three-quarters full, and in the bushes was a nice little stash of supplies to be picked up that evening.

Alma Doll was no more scrupulous than the other women; like most of them, she had children at home who were not getting enough fats in their diet, and who would also like to find out what a cup of hot chocolate tasted like. Like the other women, she stockpiled supplies in the bushes, and when she discovered that these supplies were being plundered before the end of the working day, either by her fellow workers or by other people watching from a distance, she became even bolder. Hidden in the bushes, she waited until the tail end of the column had gone by. As soon as the last woman was out of sight, she hurried with her sack to a nearby house occupied by friends of hers, and left everything there, to be shared with them later. When it was time for the column to pass the spot again on its way back, she would get back into the bushes and then slip out, her empty sack over her arm, to rejoin the others.

Her absence had not gone unnoticed by the other women, of course, and they made free with their barbed remarks and innuendos; but as they were all doing more or less the same thing themselves, she had nothing worse to fear. As for the Russian sentries who marched at the head and tail end of the column, they either saw nothing of what was going on or chose not to see. More likely the latter: they doubtless all knew what real hunger felt like, and they behaved magnanimously, even towards a hated nation that had let the wives and children of those sentries starve to death without mercy.

In the evening, Alma would then sit with her husband, while their supper of milk soup heated up on the little makeshift stove, and the young wife would show him her latest acquisitions by candlelight—because the electricity had been cut off. They all ate tinned sardines on bread to start with, and then powdered chocolate was sprinkled into the milk soup. They didn't just eat the food—they devoured it, gorging themselves until they were fit to burst, all of them, from the five-year-old Petta to the old and virtually immobilised grandmother. They didn't care about overfilling their stomachs, or the effect this would have on their already disturbed night's sleep, nor did they ever think about keeping something back for the next day. They'd said goodbye to all such thoughts during the years of sustained aerial bombing. They had become children again, who live only for today, without a thought for the morrow; but they had nothing of the innocence of children any more. They were uprooted, the pair of them, this herder of cows and this carrier of sacks; the past had slipped away from them, and their future was too uncertain to be worth troubling their minds about it. They drifted along aimlessly on the tide of life—what was the point of living, really?

When Doll went to work with his young wife in the early morning, and when he hurried home on his own in the evening after tending the cows all day, his route took him past a large grey house with all its windows shut up, giving it a gloomy and forbidding air. On the door of the house was a very old brass plate, tarnished through neglect and stained with verdigris where the brass had been dented. Engraved on the plate were the words: 'Dr. Wilhelm — Veterinarian'.

When Doll and his wife walked past this gloomy house for the first time after the end of the war, she had said: 'He's topped himself, too — did you hear?'

'Yes …', Doll had replied, in a tone of voice intended to indicate to his wife that he did not wish to pursue the subject.

But Alma had ploughed on regardless, exclaiming angrily: 'Well, I'm glad the old boy's dead! If ever I hated anyone, it was him — in fact I hate him still …'

'Fine, fine', Doll had interrupted. 'He's dead, let's forget him. Don't let's talk about him again.'

And they didn't talk about him again. Whenever Dr. Doll approached the house, he fixed his gaze studiously on the other side of the street, while his wife kept on eyeing the house with a resentful or scornful look. Neither reaction suggested they had succeeded in forgetting, as Doll had wished, and they both knew — although they said nothing — that they neither could forget nor wanted to forget. The dead veterinarian Wilhelm had caused them too much heartache for that.

He called himself a veterinarian on his brass plate, but in truth he was such a coward that he had hardly ever dared to go near a sick horse or cow. The local farmers knew this so well that they only ever called him out to give injections to pigs with erysipelas, which is why he was known far and wide as 'Piglet Willem'. He was a big, heavily built man in his sixties, with a grey, sallow face that was twisted into a permanent grimace, as if he had the taste of bile in his mouth.

There was absolutely nothing about this vet to set him apart from the common run of men, except for one thing: he was a connoisseur of fine wine. He drank schnaps and beer as well, but only for its alcohol content, because he had been for a long time what one might term a 'moderate drinker'; he needed a certain amount of alcohol every day, but his intake could not be called excessive. Wine was his real passion, though, and the better the wine, the happier he was. At such times, the bilious wrinkles in his face would soften, and he was seen to smile. For a man of his means, it was a somewhat expensive passion, but he usually found a way to indulge it.

Shortly before five in the afternoon, nothing would keep him at home a moment longer, and not even the most urgent phone call could get him to attend a sick animal. He picked up his stick, put on his little Tyrolean hat with its badger-hair plume, and strolled sedately along the street, dressed invariably in knee breeches, and walking with his feet splayed out to the sides.

Dr. Wilhelm — Piglet Willem — was just a short walk away from his destination, a small hotel where at one time he had effectively had his own private supply of wine on tap. That was when the landlord was still alive, a man who dearly liked a drink himself. After his death, the establishment was run by his widow and then increasingly by their youngest daughter, a girl of mercurial temperament and fierce dislikes, one of which — and not the least of them — was the vet, Dr. Wilhelm.

To his profound dismay, the vet found that the daughter of the house now frequently refused to bring him the bottle of wine he had ordered, only bringing him a glass instead, though other tables were still getting their bottles often enough. If he then complained, speaking with his characteristic slow and measured delivery through that caustic, nutcracker mouth of his, she would cut him off as soon as he started with her quick, sharp tongue: 'You expect your wine every day. The others just come in occasionally—that's the difference! You'd drink us dry if I let you!'

Other times, she would not even deign to reply. Or else she would reach quickly for his glass and say: 'If you don't want the glass, I'll be happy to take it back again. You don't *have* to drink it!' In short, she took care to remind him every day that he was entirely dependent on her whims for the satisfaction of his drinking desires. He had to put up with her insults and her diminishing servings of wine with a grumpy sigh, but still he came back every day for more, without dignity or shame.

From the little hotel, the vet would then process sedately, with his curiously splay-footed gait, halfway across the town to the little railway station, where he generally entered the second-class waiting room shortly before six o'clock. Here he often had the good fortune to find the town's wealthy corn merchant sitting at the table reserved for regulars, where he himself had a seat, and this gentleman was always happy to share his wine with him. Sometimes the corn merchant would be sitting at a separate table with one or more of his customers, in which case the vet would go up to them, inquire gravely 'May I?', and was generally invited to join them. For here Dr. Wilhelm was able to trade on another side of his character: he had quite a repertoire of bawdy country jokes and stories, which he could recite in the authentic local dialect. His stories were frequently met with gales of laughter, their effect heightened by the fact that his sour expression didn't change at all—which put the corn merchant's customers in a sweeter mood.

Otherwise the vet generally did all right for himself in the station bar. He'd been a regular there for decades. For decades past, he had sat at the regulars' reserved table from around six to eight in the evening, accompanied by his wife in earlier years, but on his own since her death. The landlord, Kurz, kept him on a tight rein, but generally made sure that his old customer didn't go without.

Around suppertime, the waiting room emptied quickly, and Dr. Wilhelm also went on his way. What awaited him now in the little town's premier hotel was always an open question: it might be a lot, or it might be virtually nothing. The wine still flowed freely in this establishment, but the landlord was a man who liked to take his customers' money—and the more the better. Even when it made very little sense to take money off his customers, since there was hardly anything left to buy with money, the landlord kept on increasing the price of his wines sold by the bottle, so that the cost of even a single bottle was way beyond the means of a poor pig innoculator like him, whose daily earnings frequently amounted to less than five marks.

So here Dr. Wilhelm had to take potluck, and there were many times when he had to sit for hours over a glass of watered-down, wartime beer, while he morosely watched SS officers drinking one bottle after another. They never invited him over to their table: the SS always kept its distance from the ordinary German people. Or else there would be some Hitler Youth leader, not even twenty years old, knocking back dessert wines with his girlfriend—and no more interested than the others in the storytelling talents of the ageing vet.

So these were difficult times for an old alcoholic, for whom drinking was a necessity of life. As the hours went by and the night wore on, and the patrons became increasingly drunk and boisterous, and the white-haired landlord, ever smiling and full of bonhomie, called time on them ... as it became quite clear that there was nothing for him this evening, even though so many others were thoroughly well-oiled ... as he then, having paid for his beer, totted up the few miserable coins and notes in his pocket to see if he might have enough for a small schnaps at least, knowing full well that he didn't ... as he finally picked up his stick and his hat with a heavy, bitter sigh and stepped out into the night to walk back to his house ... and as he thought about the night ahead, in which he would have to summon up sleep with boring tablets instead of alcohol, which so divinely filled his sleep with sweet dreams ... then his leathery face became, if possible, even more jaundiced than before, he was racked with envy for everyone and everything, and he would have gladly let the whole world go to hell without a thought, in return for a single bottle of wine!

But the old vet had better days, too. All of a sudden, this premier hotel on the town square would be frequented by summer visitors or anglers on a fishing trip, who always loved to hear stories about this remote area that had scarcely been touched by the war. Or else a farmer would see the old man sitting there, which made him think how long it was since he had called him out to his farm, and his bad conscience would prompt him to invite Piglet Willem to join him at his table, chat to him, and give him a drink—for everybody knew about his weakness.

The best times, though, were when all the regulars came together around their table in this hotel. Unfortunately this only happened once or twice a month at most, whenever the circuit judge came over from the district town to hold the appointed court session in the little town. Then the hotelier would get straight on the telephone and notify a local landowner, the dentist, an agricultural-products wholesaler, and also Dr. Doll—but not the old vet, who turned up anyway.

How Doll had become a part of this motley company he was hardly able to say himself in later years. To begin with—and this was years earlier, at the time of his first marriage, when he was working a smallholding near the little town—he had probably been intrigued by such a mixed bag of drinking companions, and more especially by the stories they had to tell. The old judge in particular excelled in this regard, and told a far better story than the vet, whose jokes were often rather too broad, not to say downright vulgar. But Doll had quickly realised that even these people were utterly mediocre. By the second evening, the old circuit judge had to repeat the same stories; he only knew ten or a dozen, but he was more than happy to tell them a hundred times. It also became increasingly obvious that he liked to be given food for free, and to short-change the staff when it came to handing over his ration coupons. The dentist's head was filled with stories about women; his day job was just a pretext for him to grope his female patients while they were lying back in the dentist's chair. And as for the old vet, he was just an old soak who became more greedy and tiresome with every passing day.

It was the same story with the others: a dull, commonplace bunch, along with their sly landlord, who was only interested in making money. So Doll didn't always take up the invitation when he was summoned by telephone to join the other regulars. But he came often enough, maybe just because he fancied a few drinks or because he was fond of good wine himself, and because village life at home was even more dull than this crowd. He came and drank and played the generous host, being still fairly well fixed for money at that time, and any freeloaders, from the greedy vet to the cautious circuit judge, did well by him. On particularly good nights, the fat, white-haired hotelier would crawl into the furthest recesses of his cellar and emerge with bottles of Burgundy lagged with dust, or bottles of 'Mumm extra dry'. To go with the red wine he would serve fine cheeses — no mention of ration coupons! — which they ate in little wedges straight out of their hands. These were blissful times for the old vet, and his friendship with Doll seemed firmly established.

But that changed, and as is usually the case when male friends have a falling-out, it was all because of a woman. Quite how the old circuit judge came to meet this radiant young woman was a mystery; at all events, when Dr. Doll arrived a little late one evening to join the assembled company, he met there the wife of a Berlin factory-owner who had built himself a cabin on the shore of one of the many lakes in the area, so that he could come and enjoy some weekend fishing.

But on this particular evening the husband had stayed behind in Berlin, and his young wife was sitting alone among the all-male regulars gathered around the table. She tossed her strawberry-blonde locks, and gazed attentively at whoever was speaking, with her long, slender face and her lovely blood-red mouth — it was just as if this mouth was actually looking at you. Then she would throw her head back, her little white throat seeming to dance with laughter — heavens above, how she could laugh, my God, how young she was! Doll shoved the old vet aside and sat down next to this amazing youthful apparition, who was now sitting on the long corner sofa in between Doll and the old circuit judge.

How young she was, how full of life, and how alluringly she laughed at the judge's stories, however witless and inane! Doll began to tell stories himself, and if anyone could tell a good story, it was him. Unlike the circuit judge and the vet, he didn't just repeat the same old anecdotes he'd wheeled out a hundred times before; Doll's stories just popped into his head, from different times in his life, as if he had never thought of them before. He spoke more quickly — it all came tumbling out, his tales trumping everybody else's — and in between times he ordered wine, and more wine, and kept it flowing freely.

It turned into a great evening. It makes quite an impression on a man in his late forties when a beautiful young woman in her twenties lets him know that she finds him interesting. But the youthful interest being shown in him did not rob Doll of his powers of critical observation, and they alerted him to the fact that while he was talking intently with his neighbour on his left, the old vet on his right was looking after his own needs. The vet had long since lost any interest in stories or women; all he cared about was alcohol. There was plenty of alcohol around the table, but to Piglet Willem's way of thinking it was being drunk too slowly. When he saw that all eyes were fixed on the young woman, the vet reached out and felt for the bottle. He quickly filled his glass, drained it, and promptly filled it again …

'Whoa there!' cried Doll, who appeared to have his back to him, but had seen everything. 'That's not on! As long as I'm buying, I'll be the one to say when!' And with that, he took the bottle from Wilhelm's hand, though not ungently.

Needless to say, everyone promptly rounded on the old freeloader and soak, teasing him unmercifully. They made fun of him, dredged up the most embarrassing stories about him, and accused him to his face in the meanest fashion. But it didn't bother him very much; he felt no shame. He was long accustomed to having his human dignity insulted as the price for every cadged drink. This had been happening for so long, and so often, that by now all his human dignity was long gone. He despised them all, of course, and they could all have dropped down dead before his eyes—he wouldn't have cared, because alcohol was all he cared about now. So he let them mock and bait him, it all fell on deaf ears, and as his podgy, age-spotted hand gripped the stem of the wine glass, he thought to himself: *I've had two more glasses of wine than you have!* And: *If I get the chance, I'll try it again!*

Nor did he have to wait very long for an opportunity. Sitting at their table was a beautiful, blooming young woman, and a terrible flirt—they could have old Piglet Willem any time they wanted, but as long as *she* was in their midst, they were determined to make the most of her. So the vet sat there, ignored by everyone. This time, Doll really did turn his back on him completely. Three times he reached out and touched the wine bottle, and then drew his hand back. The fourth time he grabbed hold of the bottle and poured himself some more wine …

Immediately, Doll's head swivelled round over his shoulder, and this time he said, without any attempt at gentleness: 'If we're drinking too slowly for you on this table, maybe you'd like to go and sit somewhere else? There are plenty of tables free …' And as the vet looked at him with a hesitant, incredulous, almost beseeching expression, he made his meaning even clearer: 'Did you not understand? I want you to leave the table, now! I've had enough of your cheek!!'

Slowly, the old man got to his feet. Slowly, he walked across the room to a table in the far corner. (As it was very late, long after closing time, the room was empty except for the regulars around their table.) For a moment he had hesitated, but then he had picked up the glass that had cost him so dear and bore it before him with infinite care, like some holy relic. It was, after all, the last glass of wine that he was likely to drink on this ill-fated evening that had started so well. Behind his back, these fat, well-oiled burghers were mocking him in the cruellest fashion, utterly beside themselves with glee and *schadenfreude*. Doll himself, of course, took no part in this further humiliation of a man who was already down, and perhaps he was even regretting his angry outburst—Wilhelm was an old man, after all. But if he did regret it, his regret didn't last, because the young woman suddenly said: 'Quite right, Mr. Doll, I've never been able to stand the old sneak either!'

The drinking and the lively talk around the table continued—talk that became increasingly drunken. The old vet was forgotten. But he was still sitting there at his little table, his hand still wrapped around the stem of his wine glass, which had been empty for a long time. He sat, he watched, he listened, he counted. He counted the bottles as they were brought to the table, he counted the glasses that each person drank, and with every glass that was drunk around the table, he thought to himself: *I should have been included in that round!*

Dr. Wilhelm waited until they had all finally had enough, and made to pay the bill. Then the vet slipped quietly out of the bar and took up his position on a dark street corner across from the hotel.

He had a long wait before the two of them appeared, both wheeling their bicycles. He saw the woman's white dress; she was wheeling her bike in a perfectly straight line, while the man kept veering off to the side, and frequently had to stop. Then he started off again, bumped into his companion's bicycle, and dropped his own. He broke into drunken laughter, and held onto the woman. Dr. Wilhelm also noted that they did not part company at the street corner where they should have gone their separate ways. Doll accompanied the young woman on her way home, stumbling, falling, cursing, and laughing. Nodding his head, and with his leathery face twisted into a grimace, as if he was eating pure bile, the vet set off for home, walking slowly and sedately, with his feet splayed out to the sides.

Next morning, rumours of the 'orgy' that had taken place at the town's premier hotel were flying through the streets and alleys, and were soon getting out into the surrounding countryside on the milk carts. Doll was summoned into town by a distraught phone call from the young woman, who told him that the hotelier's extremely straight-laced wife had banned her from the bar permanently 'because of her immoral behaviour'. The young woman was upset and angry; for the first time in her life, she had come up against small-town prejudice, which condemns the accused without a hearing, and against which there is no appeal or defence.

'But we've done nothing wrong! Nothing happened, not even a kiss! And this swine of a vet has been telling people I was sitting on your lap the whole evening, and that I took you home with me in the night! When the whole hotel knows full well that you stayed there overnight!'

This was true. When it became clear that Doll was in no condition to walk or ride a bicycle, his companion had brought him back to the hotel, where he had then taken a room.

'Mr. Doll, you've got to talk to the landlord! The ban on me must be lifted, and someone needs to put a stop to these vile rumours! You've got to help me, Doll. I'm very upset! How horrid it all is! People round here hate a woman just because she's good-looking and laughs a lot. For two pins, I'd sell our weekend house right now and never come back!'

Tears welled up in the young woman's eyes, and Doll promised to do everything she asked. He would have done it anyway without the tears, for he too was full of anger and hatred. But he was soon to find that rumours of this kind are easier to start than they are to stop.

The hotelier, whose straight-laced wife had him completely under her thumb, twisted and wriggled like a worm; in the end, when the argument grew more heated, he slipped quietly out of the room and was not seen again for the rest of the day. The circuit judge, called in as a witness for the defence, and obviously madly jealous of the younger, more successful Doll, gave an inconclusive account of events: in the bar itself he had not observed any lewd behaviour, but as to what happened in the night out on the street, well, he simply couldn't say. And he really preferred not to get involved in this sort of thing …!

Doll responded furiously: 'What could possibly have happened out on the street? Everyone in the hotel knows that I spent the night here!'

The hotelier's wife bowed her head and quietly pointed out that between the time the two of them left together and the time that he, Mr. Doll, returned to the hotel, more than an hour had elapsed.

'That's a wild exaggeration!' cried Doll. 'A quarter of an hour, maybe—it can't have been more than half an hour at the absolute outside!'

The hotelier's wife and the circuit judge smiled, and then Mrs. Holier-than-thou opined that even half an hour was quite a long time, and a lot could happen in half an hour …

At this point the circuit judge, too, edged his way out of the room, and he only heard Doll's angry response—where did she get the nerve to insinuate, without a shred of evidence, that two persons of blameless character could not spend half an hour together without getting up to something?—as he was retreating down the passageway. He didn't wait to hear more. It was already looking as if this might end up in court, and he had no desire to be called as a witness in a case of this sort.

After that, Doll began to run out of steam in this battle against a sanctimonious woman who responded to all his arguments and challenges with a weak smile and evasive, equivocal replies. She wouldn't even give a clear 'Yes' or 'No' answer when he asked her directly if she planned to enforce the ban on the young woman.

Then Doll abruptly broke into laughter and walked out on the hotelier's wife. What was he fighting against here? Arguing with this woman, who for certain had voted every time for her adored Führer, was about as pointless as Don Quixote tilting at windmills. No: if he was going to get anywhere in this matter, he had to tackle the man who had started all these rumours—that old gossip and scandalmonger in trousers, the freeloading, free-drinking vet. He'd soon give him what for! And so, swept along on a fresh wave of anger, he set out to find Dr. Wilhelm. But it was a fool's errand, because the vet wasn't to be found anywhere—not at home, not in the town, not in any saloon bar. It was as if the old man, suspecting what was in store for him, had gone into hiding—and perhaps he had done exactly that.

So Doll had no option but to go to a lawyer and have him write formal letters to the vet and the hotelier's wife. Doll learned from the lawyer that private actions for defamation could not be brought, now that there was a war on. But the others didn't need to know this, and so letters threatening them with such an action were duly despatched. Maybe they had lawyers, too, or else they knew the score; at all events, they didn't respond. The rumours continued.

All this only made him more bitter, just as the departure of the young woman only served to increase his anger. She had been forced to flee in the face of the jealous, rancorous talk of these small-town bigots. He felt like someone trying to fight his way through a wall of feathers and cotton wool: he could hit it as hard as he liked, but it made no difference. In his present state of mind, the letters written by his lawyer seemed to him far too mild and diplomatic, so he sat down and wrote a letter of his own to Dr. Wilhelm, in which he announced his intention of publicly slapping him in the face as a slanderer the next time their paths crossed ...

Having sent the letter, he was overcome with regret. This was unworthy of him; he had sunk to the level of his enemies, instead of just quietly despising them, which had been his stance up until now. But the time would come when he would regret this letter even more. One morning, he walked into the waiting room at the station—and there was Piglet Willem, sitting on the sofa, with a bottle of wine in front of him!

Doll wished he could have turned around in the doorway and left, and it would certainly have been better for his peace of mind if he had. But as well as many strangers, there were also quite a few locals in the room, who were now looking back and forth expectantly from him to the vet. Doll knew that Wilhelm, like all old gossips, had shown the letter to the bar-room regulars and half the town, and his enemy's threat—to slap him in the face when he saw him—was common knowledge. If Doll retreated now, the vet would have won, and the whole rumour mill would start up again.

So Doll entered the room and sat down opposite the other man. The landlord, normally so talkative, said nothing as he brought him the bottle he had ordered. All the locals were waiting for the strangers to leave the waiting room—their train was due to depart in a quarter of an hour. Meanwhile Doll sat clutching the stem of his wine glass, battling inwardly with himself. *He's not worth it*, a little voice said inside him. *He's just an old man, a gossip, and a scandalmonger. What's he got to do with your honour?* And with a quick glance at the other man, who was sitting there in silence, like him, clutching his wine glass: *But they'll think me a coward, all of them, and him especially, if I do nothing. I've got to show these people that I won't just take this lying down! I can't back out now!*

The strangers filed out of the waiting room, and only five or six locals were left. The room was completely silent. Then the landlord Kurz, who was polishing his glasses behind the counter and watching like a hawk, began to pass the time of day with a painter and decorator. 'They're in for another bad day in Berlin', Doll heard him say, as the drone of enemy bomber formations passing overhead came to their ears ...

Now he got to his feet directly in front of his own enemy. Leaning on the edge of the table with both hands, he thrust his face into the odious, yellow, liverish visage of the other man, and asked in a whisper: 'So are you going to take back your vicious lies right now, in front of these people?'

The landlord was at his side now, and said in a tone that was half-plea, half-reprimand: 'Don't do that, Dr. Doll! I won't have any fighting in my establishment! Go outside, if you want to ...'

Doll carried on regardless, speaking softly as before: 'Or do you want me to slap you in the face, right here in public? Punish you like a child who has been telling lies?'

The elderly, heavily built man had stayed sitting still in his seat on the sofa. Under Doll's menacing gaze, the yellowish colour of his face changed slowly to an ashen grey, while his fishy eye stared at his oppressor without blinking and without visible expression. When Doll finished speaking, it was as if he wanted to say something in reply: his lips moved, and the tip of his tongue came out as if to moisten them, but no sound emerged.

'Look, I think you should leave, Dr. Doll!' said the landlord with urgent insistence. 'You can see that Dr. Wilhelm is sorry ...'

At this point, the old vet suddenly began to shake his head with a weirdly mechanical persistence, like some nodding Buddha.

'Pssst! Pssst!' said the landlord, as if he was shooing some hens away. 'Don't do it, Willem!'

For a moment Doll had stared fixedly at this Buddha-like figure shaking his head, but now he raised his hand and slapped the slanderer lightly in the face with his open palm.

At this, the witnesses to this scene vented their collective relief with a long-suppressed 'Ah!'

'That's it!' said the landlord, plainly relieved that the slap had not been harder—and that Wilhelm had not hit back.

For a moment Doll had gazed into the face of his enemy, with a look that was both menacing and relieved. The violent urges that fought within him had calmed down; he was finally free again, free from hatred and free from anger. But then something awful happened, something utterly unexpected: two large, clear tears welled up from the expressionless eyes of the old man. For a moment, they hung on the edge of his eyelids, then rolled slowly down his cheeks. More tears followed, more and more, until they were streaming down his leathery nutcracker face, making it all shiny. His throat began to heave and sob: 'Oh! Oh! Oh!' sobbed the old vet. 'Oh, my God, he hit me, he hit me in the face with his hand! What am I to do?! Oh! Oh! Oh! I can't look anyone in the face any more, I shall have to kill myself! Oh! Oh! Oh!'

When Doll struck him, the sympathies of everyone in the room were undoubtedly on his side, as attested by the deep sigh of relief that came from their throats. But the old vet's tears changed all that. Doll was convinced from the outset that they were only crocodile tears, carefully calculated to negate the effect of his chastisement and get the townsfolk on the victim's side.

'Oh! Oh! Oh!' sobbed Dr. Wilhelm, as the tears continued to flow. 'He hit me—today of all days, on my sixty-third birthday! And I've never done anything to him. I've always stood up for him when other people were speaking ill of him. I was so grateful to him for all the wine he gave me!'

At these last words, Doll felt all his anger and hatred flare up again. He vividly recalled the whole episode where he had forced the vet to leave the table because he was helping himself too freely to the wine. The slanderous rumours had begun, not because he had given him so much wine on so many occasions, but because he had once refused him wine. 'That's enough!' he cried angrily. 'You're just an old scandalmonger and gossip, and that's why I slapped you. And if you carry on with your lies here, I'll slap you again—never mind your fake tears!' And he raised his hand as if to strike.

But Doll had reckoned without the other people in the room. They should have known what kind of a man old Piglet Willem was, and indeed they knew him of old, and thought very little of him. But in the face of these tears and laments, they promptly cast experience aside and abandoned their reason. The sight of an old man breaking down in sobs always touches the emotions, and so they all now ganged up on Doll, led by the landlord of the station bar: 'Look here, that's enough now! Surely you're not going to hit the old man again! I think it's best if you leave now—you can take your open bottle of wine with you!'

And in an instant, Doll was hustled away from his enemy, he was handed his hat, the landlord quickly put a stopper in the wine bottle and placed it in his briefcase, and the next moment Doll found himself standing outside on the station forecourt. Looking troubled as he gazed at him through bloodshot eyes, the landlord said: 'You never should have done that, Mr. Doll. You'll turn the whole town against you now! A gentleman doesn't do that kind of thing—hitting people! Well, maybe it'll all come right in the end …'

But unfortunately it didn't all come right. Instead it was the landlord who was right: Doll forfeited all remaining sympathy in the town, and he became what he would forever remain: the most hated man far and wide.

Dr. Wilhelm exploited the situation with devilish cunning; on this occasion, his bilious brain counselled him most wisely. After Doll's departure he had carried on weeping, and averred in a sobbing voice that he could not live with this dishonour. He would have to take his own life, and on his birthday, of all days …

They gave him wine to drink to calm him down—a great deal of wine—and then they took him home. But the news of his public humiliation soon went round the whole town, and aroused sympathy even in places where he had never attracted any before. His reiterated lament—that it was all so much worse because it had happened on his birthday—was not without effect: days later, he was still getting presents, in the form of food, wine, and schnaps, from people who would never have dreamed of marking the old sponger's birthday, were it not for this incident.

Meanwhile the war dragged on—another year, another two years. People had more important things to worry about now than Doll and his despicable conduct.

Doll himself had other things to think about, too. This was the year in which his marriage was dissolved. He had many cares and worries, and so it was all the more painful to feel the old hatred, which he thought he had put behind him, welling up within him again at the sight of the vet, still as strong as ever, undiminished by the passage of time, still the same old feelings of humiliation …

And then the young woman turned up in the town again after a long absence. This time, she was dressed in black. Doll learned that she had been a widow for quite some time. When people heard this news, they studied his face with eager curiosity, but failed to detect anything but indifference. And indifference was exactly what Doll felt. If he had felt something more for this woman two years previously, in a moment of passion, all that was long since forgotten, and he no longer remembered …

But life in a small town is lived according to different rules. In a city, people's paths cross and they never meet again. But here was this outsider, Doll, a man who, despite his money, only aroused suspicion with his high-handed ways. And now there was this young woman, clearly widowed, twenty-three years old, no more, though she was already the mother of a five-year-old child, wearing her widow's weeds with painted fingernails and dark-red lipstick. The small town knew what to make of such a woman, just as it knew all about Doll!

Faced with a united front against them, excluded from the life of the community, spied upon, suspected, maligned, they were bound to meet and find common cause sooner or later.

'Hello!' said Doll nervously. 'It's a long time since we last saw each other …'

'Yes', she replied. 'And a lot has happened since then.'

'Of course!' he remembered, and looked at the young woman. He thought her even more beautiful in her widow's weeds. 'You lost your husband …'

'Yes', she said. 'It's been very difficult at times. My husband was ill for more than a year, and I nursed him myself throughout. Every time the siren went, I had to get myself and him down to the basement, and him a sick man, the apartment half-gutted by fire …'

'Difficult times!' he agreed, and then laughed scornfully at the inquisitive look they got from a passing local, the wife of a naval lieutenant. 'But this place hasn't changed—by this evening, we'll be the talk of the town again.'

'Yes, I'm sure!' she agreed. 'Will you walk with me a little? If they're going to gossip, let's give them something to gossip about! Would you like to have lunch with me today? I've just got a chicken from a farmer—that way', she smiled, 'you won't need ration coupons.'

'All right!' he replied. 'Gladly. I don't have to answer to anyone any more.'

'I know', she said.

That was how it all began, and everything else followed on from that. They were drawn to each other out of defiance, protest, a sense of isolation within the community. *At last*, they thought, *someone I can really talk to, who won't betray me.* Over time, this became something more—genuine affection, love even. They had long since ceased to care about the small-town gossip. They moved in together, living in the little chalet that belonged to the young woman, putting two fingers up to the scandalised locals. Nor did Doll care any more that Wilhelm the vet—so everyone was saying—was now telling all and sundry 'I told you so', claiming that every word of what he'd said before had been 'right on the money'. Let his enemy crow: Doll couldn't care less.

But later on, after they had married, not in the little country town but in the big city of Berlin, and were sitting together in the kitchen of their badly fire-damaged apartment, writing out addresses for the wedding announcements—then the old hatred rose up again in both of them, and they did not forget a single one of their enemies. Every one of them received their wedding announcement, and Piglet Willem and the hotelier's sanctimonious wife were top of the list!

What effect they thought these announcements would have, they wouldn't have been able to say exactly. But to them it was something of a triumph just to have married—in defiance of them all, a poke in the eye for prudery!

From Berlin, they went back to the small town only on the odd occasion. They often forgot about the place for days on end in the chaos of the big city, in its gathering gloom, relieved only by the ghastly flickering firelight of whole streets in flames. They sat with each other in air-raid shelters that afforded little protection, heard the drone of the approaching bombers and the impacts of the bombs getting closer and closer ... They held each other tightly, and the young woman spoke words of reassurance: 'They've gone on!' Then there was a deafening cracking and crashing sound, the light flashed bright yellow and died ... They could taste plaster dust in their mouths, as if they were eating their own death.

But when they had fought their way out of Berlin again, passing railway tracks and stations destroyed by the bombing, when the train took them deeper and deeper into forests that appeared completely untouched by the war, and when in the evening, before embarking on the last homeward stretch, they entered the station bar again to have a quick beer, they found everything just as it had always been. The landlord had become a little more mean with his provisions and a little more insolent towards his patrons, but the leathery old vet was still sitting in his usual place on the sofa.

But the moment Doll saw this man again, the old hatred suddenly flared up within him once more. It erupted with elemental force, and it was only later that the memories of all the trouble this man had caused them came back to him, as if to rationalise the feeling after the event—for all the good that did him. This hatred seemed senseless to Doll, when there was so much hardship to be borne in these times, and when life itself felt like a new gift after every air raid. This mean-spirited hatred seemed senseless to him, and yet he had to deal with it somehow. He had made room for this hatred in his heart, had allowed it to lodge itself there—and now he had to live with it, probably for the rest of time.

For the rest of time—but, as it turned out, only for the rest of the other man's time. When he walked past the old vet's closed-up house now on his way to work with his young wife, the place looking so gloomy and forbidding, or when he passed the battered old brass plate, flecked with verdigris, on his way home by himself, he averted his gaze from the house—but not because he still hated the dead man. No: the hatred had gone when he died, and in its place was a kind of emptiness, a vague memory of a feeling that he had felt ashamed of. In this time of the country's collapse and defeat, no feelings lasted for long; the hatred passed away, leaving only emptiness, deadness, and indifference behind, and people seemed remote, out of reach. Never had he felt so alone. No man had ever felt so alone. Only the young woman was still with him. But he let her know, too: 'Let's leave it there. We won't talk about it again. The subject is closed.'

No: there was another reason why Doll averted his gaze from this house of the dead. There was one thing that he kept on turning over in his mind: *I saw him sitting there in the station bar, with tears streaming down his face, and telling everyone he would have to take his own life because of the humiliation he had suffered. But the old whinger hadn't taken his life: instead he had turned his humiliation into a business opportunity, without dignity or shame! He'd been a coward all his life, this Dr. Wilhelm, scared of being kicked by a horse, gored by a cow, or bitten by a dog, and reduced to giving injections to pigs when they were too young to be dangerous: Piglet Willem! The nickname was well-deserved, and he had never protested when they called him that and ribbed him mercilessly for filling his glass at somebody else's expense … he'd always been a man without dignity or courage.*

And yet, Doll brooded, this same Dr. Wilhelm *had the courage to do what I lack the courage to do — even though my own dignity and self-respect, shame, faith, and hope are ebbing away with every passing day. I can't do it, and yet I have always imagined myself to be a moderately courageous man. But he was able to do it, coward though he was. The coward whose face I slapped, he had the courage — and I don't.*

Such were Doll's thoughts as he walked past this house, painful thoughts that tormented him every time; he would have given anything to be free of them, but they wouldn't let him go, whether he averted his gaze or not. Then he would try to picture the room where this man had spent the last hour of his life, the room where he had done 'it'. Doll knew that at the end the old vet had owned virtually nothing apart from a bed, a table, and a chair. Everything else had gone to pay for alcohol. He tried to picture the man sitting on this solitary chair, the pistol lying on the table in front of him. Perhaps the tears had been streaming down his face again, and perhaps he had sat there sobbing 'Oh! Oh! Oh!' again …

Doll shook his head. He didn't want to picture the scene; it was just too painful.

But one thing was certain: the old man with the leathery skin had gone, and Doll was left behind, empty inside, filled with self-reproach and doubt. So many certainties had been thrown into doubt at this time, and because of the old vet, Doll now lost both his inveterate hatred and his belief in himself as a man of courage. In all probability he was nothing at all, an empty husk; he had nourished himself with self-delusions, and now it had all vanished into thin air! There was no Doll any more.

56

How gladly he would have taken a different route, avoiding this closed-up house altogether. But the position of the town, sitting as it did on a peninsula, forced him to walk past it every time. Forced him to revisit these painful thoughts. Forced from him the admission that he was nothing, had never amounted to anything, and for the rest of his life, however long or short that might be, would never be anything other than a nobody. A nobody, for all time!

So it really was best just to say to his young wife: 'Fine, he's dead. Let's forget him. Let's not talk about him ever again!'

It was a lie. Nothing was 'fine'; nothing could be forgotten. But what did a lie matter these days? Let the woman go on thinking that he hated the old boy as much as ever. He couldn't hate anybody any more, but lying—he could manage that. And anyway, lying was somehow more in keeping with his own mediocrity.

CHAPTER FOUR

What the Nazis did next

Doll's career as a cowherd was short-lived, because a sequence of chance events resulted in his being appointed mayor of the town, and of the whole surrounding district, by the Russian town commandant. This was the kind of thing that happened in these turbulent times: the most hated man in the town was put in charge of his fellow citizens.

The string of chance events began when a rucksack was tossed over the fence into the Dolls' garden one night. It was a Wehrmacht-issue rucksack, and it contained the uniform of a senior SS officer. No doubt the dear neighbours who had laid this cuckoo's egg in the Doll nest felt it was getting too dangerous to have these items of uniform in their possession, now that increasingly thorough house searches were being conducted. Why they didn't put a few stones in the rucksack along with the uniform, and drop it into the lake that was right on their doorstep, is another story, which says as much about the neighbours' decency as it does about Doll's popularity.

He, of course, had no idea about this morning gift that lay in his garden. He lay awake and eventually fell into the brief, troubled sleep that was now almost normal for him. On this occasion, he was roused from this brief sleep at the crack of dawn by a Russian patrol, which gave him a very hard time. At first he couldn't understand what they wanted from him, and he went through a very unpleasant quarter of an hour before he realised what the implications of this rucksack and SS uniform were: the Dolls were suspected of secretly harbouring an SS officer! The entire house, attic, and outbuildings were searched from top to bottom, and even though no trace of the fugitive (who didn't exist, of course) was found, Doll was put into a two-horse hunting carriage and driven off into town to the commandant's office. Soldiers with submachine guns sat on either side of him. Such was the sight that greeted his fellow citizens, who assuredly felt no sympathy for him—partly because they all had enough worries of their own, and partly because this was Dr. Doll, after all. And whatever kind of trouble he was in, it was fine by them!

But at the commandant's office his troubles were quickly ended. There was an officer who conducted the interrogation, and an interpreter in civilian dress who translated Doll's answers. Having by now fathomed the mystery of the rucksack so treacherously left in their garden, Doll had no qualms about directing the attention of the Russians to the house next door, where the wife of the SS officer lived—a woman who was as stupid as she was malicious, since the provenance of this uniform was always bound to come to light.

A quarter of an hour later, Doll was allowed to return home, into the arms of his anxiously waiting family.

The following day was the 'Day of Victory', and everyone was given the day off work. The entire population was ordered to assemble on the square in front of the town commandant's office and told that the Russian commandant was going to give a speech. When Doll entered the square with his wife, there stood the officer who had interrogated him the day before, accompanied by his interpreter. Doll greeted them politely, and the two of them, after returning his greeting, looked at him earnestly and had a whispered conversation with each other. Then Doll was beckoned over, and the interpreter asked him on behalf of the officer if he felt up to addressing the local German population on the significance of this Day of Victory.

Doll said that he didn't think he had addressed a public gathering like this before, but he felt sure that he would make as good a job of it as anyone else. Whereupon he was led into the town commandant's office—his wife had to remain outside, with the waiting crowd—and put in a room on the top floor. Through a glass door, he could see the commandant addressing the crowd from the balcony, and the interpreter whispered into Doll's ear, giving him a few pointers as to what sort of things he should say. Then it grew very quiet in the room, while outside the town commandant was still speaking. He was a short man with a pale, brownish, handsome face, the archetypal cavalryman. He had taken off the white gloves that he normally wore, and was holding them in one hand, occasionally gesturing with them to underline something he had said. The commandant would speak for two or three minutes at a time, then pause to allow the interpreter to translate. But the translation barely took a minute to say, which is usually the case with poor interpreters. An occasional 'Bravo!' could be heard from the invisible crowd below.

Just you wait! thought Doll angrily. *Barely three weeks ago you were still shouting 'Heil Hitler!' and kowtowing to the SS, and jockeying for rank and position in the* Volkssturm. *I'll be sure to tell you what I think of all your 'Bravos' now!*

All the same, he was finding the day plenty warm enough. It was a fine spring day in May, certainly, but it was only ten o'clock in the morning, and already his brow was beaded with sweat. The interpreter bent down to him again, and asked if Doll was feeling agitated. Would he like a glass of water, perhaps?

Doll opined, with a smile, that he would prefer a glass of schnaps. Whereupon he was whisked off to the officers' mess and given a whole tumbler of very strong vodka.

Five minutes later, he was standing at the balustrade of the balcony, the town commandant a couple of steps behind him with his interpreter, whose job it was to translate what Doll said. There were other officers besides on the balcony, officers whom Doll would get to know very well indeed in the coming weeks. But today he didn't even notice them; all he could see was the mass of people below him, a great crowd of his fellow citizens who were all gazing expectantly at him with upturned faces.

At first, all these faces merged into a single, pale-grey line above the darker, broader band of colour that was their clothing. Then, as he was speaking the opening sentences of his address, he could suddenly make out individual faces. While he was listening a little anxiously still to his own voice, which had never been very powerful, yet now seemed to fill the square beneath him quite easily, he suddenly caught sight of his wife, almost directly below him. There she stood, calmly smoking a cigarette with her accustomed nonchalance; the people around her kept their distance, while everywhere else in the square the crowd was packed tightly. Consciously or not, their demeanour reflected the isolation in which the Dolls had always lived in this small town, and in which Doll now found himself, plainly visible to all eyes, up on the balcony of the town commandant's office.

He gave her a slight nod, imperceptible to anyone except her, without interrupting the flow of his speech, and she smiled back and raised the hand that held the cigarette in greeting. His gaze moved on, and came to rest on the grey-bearded face of a National Socialist town elder, a building contractor by trade and a quiet man by nature, who had nevertheless cunningly abused his position in the Party to put all his competitors for miles around out of business. Not far from him stood another short man, with a face as sly as it was brutal: he had collected the Party subscriptions, and used the opportunity to spy for his masters, the Party bigwigs who had all fled to the Western zone ...

But there were enough of the smaller fry left in the town: over here, the mail clerk who had been a sergeant in the local *Volkssturm*; over there, a schoolmaster, a feared informer; Kurz, the landlord of the station bar, a bully and, as it now turned out, another Nazi spy; and then — Doll's eyes lit up — standing close together with a look almost of derision on their faces, as if they were watching some trashy theatre show, two women, the wife and daughter of that SS officer whose uniform had nearly been his undoing on the morning of the day before.

Doll leaned forward, speaking more quickly, more loudly, talking now about the times just past, the people who had profited from them, the guilty ones and the ones who had just gone along with it all. And as he continued to speak, and as they persisted in shouting 'Bravo!' and 'Quite right!' (as though he couldn't possibly be talking about any of them), it struck him how different these fellow citizens of his now looked. It was not just their pale faces, which were scarred by fear, worry, grief, and sleepless nights, and it was not just the ones who, in order to avoid the initial confrontation, had spent days lying in the forest, so that their clothes were now torn and faded — no, all of them suddenly had a tattered and beggarly air about them, all of them seemed to have slipped several rungs down the social ladder, had given up, for whatever reason, a position they had occupied all their lives, and now stood without shame among their equally shameless brethren. That's exactly how they looked now, plain for anyone to see, and that's how they had always looked when they were alone with themselves. For these people from a nation that bore its defeat without dignity of any kind, without a trace of greatness, there was nothing left worth hiding. There was the fat hotelier, whose plump, smiling face was normally flushed from drinking wine, but now was pale and ashen, darkened by a beard that had not been shaved in days. And there was his pious and parsimonious wife, who ran the hotel with him, who had wrung the last penny out of the poorest customer, and if she had had her way would have weighed every bag twice, a woman who had always gone around in shapeless black or grey frocks, and now had a dirty white cloth wrapped round her face, like the cloths worn by toothache sufferers in the cartoons of Wilhelm Busch. Her scrawny body was now covered by a blue apron, like the ones worn by washerwomen, and her hands were wrapped in grubby gauze bandages.

It's finished, this nation, thought Doll. *It's given up on itself.* But in the fervour of his speech, he had no time to think about himself, who privately was in a very similar situation, after all. He called for three cheers for the 7th of May, the Red Army and its supreme commander Stalin, and watched them shouting and cheering (for, as well as justice and freedom, they had also been promised bread and meat) and raising their arms — the right arm still, in many cases, raised in the salute that had been drilled into them over many years.

The speech seemed to have gone down well with the commandant and his officers, too. Doll was invited to come along to the officers' mess with his wife and have a drink with them. The vodka glasses now seemed to be even larger, the schnaps even stronger — and they didn't stop at one glass. As Doll and his wife made their way home along the sun-drenched streets, both of them were swaying a little, but Doll more so. Thank goodness the local residents were still eating their lunch, and all of them were condemning the man then walking past their windows as a traitor and defector on account of the speech he had made, yet there wasn't one of them who wouldn't gladly have swapped places with him!

By the time they reached the outskirts of town, where there were hardly any houses, along the stretch of road officially known only as the 'Cow Causeway' that ran through sparse, deciduous woodland, Doll began to stumble about. The vodka saw to it that a stumble quickly turned into a fall, and he lay where he landed. He fell asleep. Mrs. Doll did her best to coax him back up, but he just went on sleeping, and she didn't feel strong enough herself to bend down and try and get him back on his feet. She was feeling pretty unsteady on her own feet by now. So she tried kicking him in the side, but the kick she gave him, which nearly made her fall over herself, failed to rouse her sleeping husband.

It was a difficult situation. They were still a good ten minutes' walk from their house, and even though she thought she could make it on her own, she really didn't like the idea of leaving her husband lying in the road, which would give the small-town locals the perfect excuse for more gossip. Luckily for the Dolls, two Russian soldiers now came down the road. Alma beckoned them over and conveyed to them through a combination of words and gestures what had happened, and what now had to be done. Whether the two Russians understood her or not, they clearly understood the plight of the man lying in a drunken stupor. So they picked him up and carried him home. With much laughter, they took their leave of the young woman ...

But if she thought they had successfully escaped the attentions of the local gossips, she was very much mistaken — again. In a small town like this, there are eyes everywhere, even on the 'Cow

Causeway', where 'there aren't really any houses', and whatever wasn't seen was just invented. A rumour now went from house to house, and was retold every time with mockery and relish: 'You know Doll, the fellow who tried to cosy up to the Russians with that speech of his? Well, he's come a real cropper! Have you heard? You don't know the story? Well, the thing is, the Russians were so upset by his speech that they gave him a right royal beating! They worked him over so thoroughly that he couldn't even walk, and two Russian soldiers had to carry him home! He won't be up and about in a hurry—and serve him right!'

This was the story that got around, and as is the way with small-town gossip, it was generally believed, even by those who had seen Mr. and Mrs. Doll staggering past their window at lunchtime that day. Great was the general rejoicing, and so it was all the more gutting when, less than a week later, they learned that the same Doll who had been so royally beaten up had now been appointed mayor by the Russian town commandant.

Of course, from this moment onwards it was hard to find anyone who didn't change his tune and discover that in actual fact he had always thought a great deal of Doll, and had always wished only the best for him. When they had said as much to their friends and neighbours half a dozen times, they really believed it themselves, and would have called anyone a liar and a slanderer who reminded them of what they had said earlier about this self-same Doll.

For his part, Doll had not wanted to take on the job of mayor, but he was given no choice in the matter. He'd never been someone who took part in public life, and he was certainly not cut out for officialdom; and just because he had given one speech, fired up by vodka, that did not mean he had any desire to pursue a career in public speaking. Moreover, as already noted, he was in a state of deep personal crisis at the time. He was tormented by doubt and lack of faith in himself and in the world around him; a profound despondency robbed him of all strength, and a wretched apathy prevented him from taking an interest in anything that was happening in the world. Furthermore, his instinct told him that this office, by virtue of which the fortunes of his fellow citizens were placed in his hands, would probably bring him nothing but worries and cares, and a lot of extra work. His wife said: 'If you become mayor, I'm going to jump in the lake!' When he took the job because he was ordered to, she didn't do it, of course; she stayed with him, lived only for him, and did her best to make the few hours he spent at home as comfortable as possible. But it was effectively the end of their normal family life together.

For Doll had been absolutely right in his prediction — his position as mayor would bring him little joy, but a whole load of trouble and care. He was inundated with work, more than he could really cope with, and while his area of jurisdiction was not that large, with the small town and some thirty or so rural parishes, he still had to work from the early morning until late at night — and even the mayor of the biggest city on earth can't put in more hours than that. There were an endless number of things that needed rebuilding, organizing, setting up and sorting out, and there were virtually no resources available: everything had been plundered and destroyed by the Nazis and the SS, including the spirit of cooperation among the local population. They were so mean-minded, petty, and self-centred that they had to be ordered, pushed around, and often threatened with punishment. Behind his back, they did everything they could to undermine the common cause and feather their own nests. In fact, they often wrecked things out of pure *schadenfreude*, without any benefit to themselves.

But Doll had more or less foreseen all this, and when they were obstructive and malicious it just made him more determined to get his way; and he could always rely on the support of the Red Army officers. They were planning and working for the long term, and not just thinking from one day to the next. But what Doll had not foreseen was a new loss of self-esteem, and even though he was doing this job, he felt somehow diminished in his inner being. That's what it felt like, and the longer this feeling persisted, the stronger it grew, even now when he was leading such a busy life, as if Doll—and no doubt many other Germans like him—was now to be stripped of his last remaining inner resources. They would be left naked and empty, and in letting go of the lies that had been drip-fed to them all their lives as the most profound truth and wisdom, they would be stripped of their inner resources of love and hate, memory, self-esteem, and dignity. In those days, Doll often doubted whether the empty space inside him would ever be filled up again.

For twelve years he had been bullied and persecuted by the Nazis: they had interrogated him, arrested him, banned his books some of the time, allowed them at other times, spied on his family life; in short, they had made his life a misery. But as a result of all these hurts, great and small, inflicted upon him, and as a result of all the vile, disgusting, and horrendous things he had seen and heard in those twelve years, and read between the lines of all the vainglorious news bulletins and swaggering editorials, a lasting feeling had grown up within him: an utter hatred of these people who had destroyed the German nation, a hatred so profound that he could no longer stomach the colour brown, or indeed any mention of the very word. If he saw anything brown around him, he had to paint it over, paint it out: it was an obsession with him.

How often he had said to his wife: 'Just be patient! Our turn will come again! But when that day comes, I won't have forgotten anything, and I won't be forgiving anyone. There is no way I'm going to be "magnanimous"—who is ever "magnanimous" to a poisonous snake?'

And he had described how he would haul the schoolmaster and his wife out of their house, how he would interrogate them, harass them, and finally punish them, this pair who had not scrupled to make children of seven or eight spy on their own parents! 'Where has your father hung his picture of the Führer? What does your mother say to your father when the man comes round collecting for the Winter Relief Organisation? What does your father say in the morning—does he say "Good morning" or does he say "Heil Hitler!"? Do you sometimes hear people speaking on the radio in a language that you don't understand?'

Oh yes, the hatred he felt for this educator of our youth, who had shown photos of horribly mutilated corpses to seven-year-old children, that hatred seemed to have taken permanent root.

And now this same Doll had become mayor, and a portion of that retribution of which he had so often spoken, feeding his hatred by imagining how it would be, had now become a duty laid upon him. It was his job—among his many other responsibilities—to classify these Nazis as harmless fellow travellers or guilty activists, to root them out from the bolt holes where they had been quick to hide themselves, to kick them out of the cushy jobs they had cleverly and shamelessly landed for themselves once again, to strip them of the possessions they had acquired by fraud, theft, or blackmail, to confiscate the stocks of food they had been hoarding, to quarter the homeless in their big houses—all of this had now become his bounden duty. The local Party bigwigs and principal culprits had, of course, fled west a long time ago, but the National Socialist small fry were just as disgusting in their way. All of them claimed—either with righteous indignation or with tears in their eyes—that they had only joined the Party under duress, or at most for economic reasons. All of them were willing to sign a statement under oath to that effect, and if they'd had their way they would have sworn it right there and then, before God and the whole world, with the most sacred of oaths. Among these two or three hundred National Socialists there was not a single one who claimed to have joined the Party out of 'personal conviction'. 'Just sign the statement', Doll would frequently snap impatiently. 'It doesn't alter anything, but if it makes you happy …! Here in the office we've known for a long time that there were only ever three National Socialists in the world: Hitler, Göring, and Goebbels! Off you go—next, please!'

Mayor Doll would subsequently visit the houses and apartments of these National Socialists with a few policemen (some of whom, in those early days, were pretty dubious characters themselves) and a clerk to take notes. He found cupboards piled high with linen, some of it hardly used, while up in the attic a mother evacuated from her bombed-out home in Berlin didn't know how she was going to put clothes on her children's backs. Their sheds were stacked to the ceiling with dry logs and coal, but the door was securely padlocked, and none of it was shared with those who lacked the wherewithal to warm a pot of soup. In the cellars of these brown hoarders they found sacks of grain ('It's just feed for the chickens!'), meal ('For my pig! Got it on a ration coupon from the Food Office!'), and flour ('It's not proper flour, just the sweepings from the mill floor!'). In their pantries the shelves were packed with supplies, but for every item they had a lie ready to hand. They feared for their precious lives—it was clearly written in their faces—but even now that fear could not stop them fighting to the bitter end for these supplies, claiming that everything had been acquired by legal means. They would still be standing there, next to the cart, when their hoarded treasures were taken away. They didn't dare cut up rough, but their faces wore an expression of righteous indignation at the injustice visited upon them.

Doll's own expression when carrying out these confiscations was invariably one of anger and contempt, but inside all he felt was disgust and weariness. As someone who had always preferred to live quietly on his own, and who even within his marriage had defended his right to solitude as something sacrosanct, he now had to spend nearly the whole day with other people, talking to them, trying to wring something out of them, seeing tears, listening to sobs, protests, objections, pleas; his head often felt like an echoing abyss filled with noise.

Sometimes he thought fleetingly: *What happened to my hatred? These are the Nazis I swore to be revenged on, after all, whose vile deeds I said I would never forget and never forgive. And now I'm standing here, and the only thing I feel is disgust, and all I want is my bed, and the chance just to sleep and sleep and forget about all this—just so that I don't have to look at all this filth any more!*

But in these days and weeks when he was constantly overworked, he never had time for himself. He could never think his own thoughts through to the end, because his mind was constantly taken up with other things. Sometimes he had the unsettling feeling that his insides were leaking away, and that one day he would just be a hollow skeleton with a covering of skin and nothing else. But he had no time to dwell on this thought, and he couldn't decide whether he really had stopped hating the Nazis, or whether he was just too tired to feel any kind of strong emotion. He wasn't a human being any more; he was just a mayor, a machine for doing work.

There was only one case where the feelings of hatred seemed to come alive again in Doll. A certain Mr. Zaches had lived in the little town for as long as anyone could remember, like his parents and grandparents before him—a genuine local, therefore, and the only kind recognised as such by the natives. Now up until the time when the Nazis seized power, this Mr. Zaches had run a small, struggling beer wholesaling business, and also used to make fizzy drinks for children from spring water, carbon dioxide, and coloured flavourings; latterly he had also supplied wholesale tobacco goods to the hospitality trade. But all of this combined had not been enough to support Zaches and his family. So the two nags he kept to transport beer were also pressed into service for all kinds of other haulage jobs—fetching suitcases and crates from the station, hauling timber out of the forests, ploughing and working the fields of local smallholders. Yet even with all this, the family could barely make ends meet; Zaches was constantly on the brink of ruin, the loss of a customer was enough to put the whole business at risk, and the days when payments to the brewery became due were days of fear and trepidation for the Zaches household.

But when the Nazis came to power, all that changed completely. Like many businessmen threatened with ruin prior to 1933, Zaches had joined the Party, bedazzled by all the talk of 'smashing the tyranny of usury' and of the universal prosperity that would surely follow. He wasn't a bit interested in politics, of course, but only in doing well for himself—and in that he succeeded after 1933. Quietly at first, but then more and more brazenly, he set about stealing business from his competitors, who had not been smart enough to join the Party in good time. He put pressure on landlords to order goods only from him, and those who complied were rewarded with little favours. He made minor political difficulties disappear, secured advantages for them by having a word with the local mayor, and generally used his position on all manner of committees, boards, and councils to ruthlessly advance his own interests. If anyone opposed him, he secretly gathered evidence against that person, set his spies to work to listen and watch, and then either issued threats or drew the net closed, whichever best suited his own needs.

As a result, his business flourished. As well as the cart horses, he now kept a separate team that only hauled crates of beer and barrels. And Zaches, the obsequious, ever-courteous pauper had now turned into Mr. Zaches, the National Socialist Party member, a man with a finger in every pie and a sharp tongue in his head, who knew that he had a lot of money behind him, as well as a Party that could make or break its fellow citizens, and held the power of life and death over them. On the back of all this, Zaches had become big and fat, and only his unhealthy, sallow complexion and his dark, piercing eyes, which avoided the direct gaze of others, recalled the lean years of the past. When the war broke out and merchandise in his line of business became particularly scarce and sought-after, his substantial earnings were unaffected; on the contrary, he made more money from a limited supply of inferior merchandise than he had been making from the good stuff. On top of that, the departure of so many men to go and fight in the war brought him a number of new posts, and like all National Socialists he did not feel bound by the rules governing the rationing of food. He took whatever he needed from the land—bacon, eggs, poultry, butter, and flour—and what he couldn't eat himself he sold on at extortionate prices, secure in the knowledge that an old Party member was effectively untouchable.

And so he remained—until the Red Army arrived on the scene. Zaches was one of the first to be arrested. His sworn statement that he had only joined the Party for economic reasons was surely no less than the truth in his case, but for many years now he had been such a selfish parasite and enemy of the people that economic reasons were no mitigation whatsoever. Yet once again he had more luck than he deserved. The authorities soon had to grant him a measure of freedom again, because he was needed for work in the town's dairy. In his youth, Zaches had learned the dairy trade, and when times were tough he had helped out there from time to time — so now he was just the man to step in and lend a hand. For better or worse, it was necessary to employ him there, though nobody liked the idea — least of all Doll. But the pressing need to feed the mothers and children of the town meant that political interests had to take a back seat for now.

Things went on in this way for a while, until certain rumours began to reach the ears of the mayor, and he summoned the onetime beer wholesaler and now dairy manager Zaches to his office. 'Look here, Zaches!' he said to the sallow-faced and still portly man, who couldn't bring himself to look Doll in the eye, 'I'm hearing all kinds of stories about a big stockpile of goods you're supposed to have hidden somewhere. What's that all about?'

Not surprisingly, Zaches assured him that he had no such hidden stock of supplies. He freely admitted that he had had cases of wine and schnaps buried in his garden in seven different places. But these hiding places had all been discovered, he said, and now he had nothing more hidden away.

While Zaches was speaking thus, in all apparent honesty, Doll had been observing him closely, and now he said: 'Everyone in the town knows about the seven hiding places. But there's a persistent rumour going around that what they found was just a trifle compared with the big hoard that hasn't been found yet …'

'There is no big hoard any more, Mr. Mayor', insisted Zaches.

'It's all been found. I don't have anything more.'

'Repeat what you just said, Zaches, and look me in the eye while you're talking!'

'Eh?' Zaches was thrown into confusion by such an unusual request. 'How do you mean— ?'

'Forget that I'm the mayor. I want you to look me in the eye and tell me again, man to man, that there is no big hoard anywhere!'

But Zaches couldn't do it. Before he'd said more than three or four words, his gaze slid away, and though he tried again, his eyes promptly wandered off once more. Zaches became confused, started stammering, then tailed off into silence ...

'So', said the mayor slowly after a lengthy pause, 'now I *know* you're lying. There's some truth in the rumour.'

'Not at all, Mr. Mayor! On my mother's life ...'

'Don't give me that, Zaches!' said Doll in disgust. 'Just think for a moment, use your brain ... You've always been a Nazi—'

'I was never a real Nazi, Mr. Mayor! I only joined the stinking Party because I had a knife at my throat. I'd have had to file for bankruptcy otherwise, and that's the honest truth, Mr. Mayor!'

'You have absolutely no chance of getting your property back again, and as for enjoying the stuff you have hidden, you can forget it! But the fact of the matter is', Doll went on, appealing to his better nature, 'that any hidden goods I find as mayor are for distribution to us Germans, Zaches. You know as well as I do that there are hundreds of people in this town, Zaches, who lack the basic necessities of life. And then there's the newly established hospital—they've got eighty patients there already—just think how much good a glass of wine would do them, and how quickly their spirits would be lifted if we could hand out a few cigarettes! Be a man, Zaches, and don't think about yourself for once: think about all the people who are having a hard time, and do something to help them! Just think of it like this: you are making a generous donation. So tell me where you have hidden the stuff!'

'I'd love to help all those people', replied the fat man, and there were tears of emotion in his eyes. 'But I haven't got anything else, I really haven't, Mr. Mayor! May I be struck down dead if I have hidden anything else away ...'

'You've lived a life of plenty for twelve years now, Zaches', continued Doll, appearing not to have heard the other man's impassioned assurances, 'and you've never thought about anyone else. Now you've found out for yourself—but only in the last six weeks, mind, only in the last six weeks!—what it's like to do heavy work you're not used to, and to feel the pangs of hunger. Just think about other people for once, who are having to go without everything. Prove to the town that you've been unjustly maligned, that you can do the decent thing! Tell me where you've hidden the stuff!'

For a moment, Zaches appeared to hesitate, but then he came out with all his protestations and beastly oaths again. The mayor kept on at the former beer wholesaler for another hour. The longer it went on, the more convinced he became that the man had hidden something else away, and possibly a great deal; but he couldn't get it out of him. He was rotten and corrupt to the core. And it made no difference when Doll told him how much trouble he'd be in if they did find something. Then the dairy would just have to manage without him; he would be thrown into a black hole and kept on bread and water, and they'd make him work all day long, lugging heavy sacks of grain. 'You wouldn't survive that for long, Zaches, all bloated with alcohol as you are! And I gather you have diabetes, too! You'll probably end up paying for this futile lie with your life!'

But it was no use: no amount of persuasion could get the man to reveal his hiding place. He sat on his hoard like a malevolent little hamster, and would rather be beaten to death than give it up. A wasted hour behind him, Doll shrugged his shoulders and had the man escorted back to the dairy. He didn't doubt for a moment that this hiding place existed, quite possibly stuffed with very valuable goods. And then, with a hundred other matters to attend to, the mayor gave no more thought to the beer wholesaler.

Just how large and well stocked the hoard in question was, Doll learned only a few days later from his police constable. 'You should get along to Seestrasse, Mr. Mayor, and see for yourself what the Russians are loading up from the cellar of Zaches' place!'

'Is that right?' replied Doll, acting all indifferent, although his heart was already aching with grief and anger. 'So they've found his hiding place, have they? I always knew there was one, as soon as I started questioning the man. I thought I might go and poke around over there myself, but I never got round to it ...'

'You wouldn't have found it anyway', said the police constable by way of consolation. 'Zaches bricked up an entire coal cellar over a year ago—those Nazis, it just goes to show you again how deeply they believed in their precious Führer's victory! But nobody would have found this hiding place—someone spilled the beans, of course.'

'Who was that?' asked Doll.

'A servant girl who used to work for Zaches. She thought the Russians would let her have some of it, of course. But they told her to get lost—they've got their own views about informers like her!'

But when Doll learned in the course of the day how large had been the stockpile of goods stashed away by this lowly, rank-and-file member of the National Socialist German Workers' Party, he was overcome with anger again, and he gave orders for Zaches to be

77

fetched from the dairy there and then.

'Well, Zaches!' he said to the fellow, who knew everything by now, of course, since news like that travels fast in a small town. 'Your storehouse has been busted, and how many days ago is it since you were standing right there and swearing on your mother's life that you hadn't hidden anything away?! You've been lying through your teeth!'

Zaches said nothing; he stood there with bowed head, his gaze wandering back and forth, but never looking the mayor in the face. 'Do you realise how much damage you've done to the town and to all Germans everywhere?!' And the mayor began to list the haul: 'One van packed with tobacco, cigars, and cigarettes. Two vans filled with wine and schnaps—and those are all goods that have been stolen from the German people, because they were supplied to you for distribution to the trade. But you just lied about it, of course, and claimed you hadn't received any deliveries, and kept it all for yourself instead, true to the good old Party principle: private greed before public need!'

Looking even more sallow and ashen than usual, the man just stood there and let the tide of anger wash over him, saying nothing in reply. 'But that's not even all of it', said Doll, and went on with his list. 'One van full of linen—and I don't have a single sheet, a single towel, left for the hospital. Five large wireless sets, three typewriters, two sewing machines, one sun lamp—and a whole van full of clothing and other stuff. Shame on you, you degenerate, for betraying your own people like that. I can't believe all the stuff you've stolen and hoarded!'

Doll was getting more and more angry as he looked at the man, his impassive silence driving him to distraction. The time before, he had not succeeded in getting any reaction out of him, any sign of human feeling, and it was just the same this time.

'And another thing', Doll went on, collecting himself again, 'hasn't it occurred to you how much damage you have done to whatever might be left of Germany's reputation! If I have to go cap in hand to the town commandant because I've run out of food again for the babies, the tuberculosis patients and the seriously ill, or because I can't allocate any beds for the hospital, do you know what they'll say to me? "Mayor must go find himself! Germans still have everything, only hidden! All Germans lie and deceive. Mayor, go find!" And do you know what? The Russians are right! How are they supposed *not* to think that, when they find something like they did at your place, you scumbag?! And now hundreds of people will carry on freezing, because you didn't speak up at the right time, you scumbag!'

It was at this point that the man who had been hauled before him and berated opened his mouth for the first and only time, and what came out was a classic piece of National Socialist thinking, which perfectly exemplified the mindset of Party members: 'I *would* have told the mayor about my hiding place if he had let me keep a share of the stuff, however small ...'

Mayor Doll stood there motionless for a while, shocked by this shameless display of heartless egoism, which was not in the least bit troubled by the sufferings of others, just as long as it didn't have to suffer itself. And he was reminded of a conversation he had had recently with an adjutant in the town commandant's office. The adjutant had told him how the ordinary rank-and-file soldiers in the Red Army had pictured the German people living much like their own people: frequently enduring abject misery because of the war, facing starvation ... That was the only way they could explain the way the Germans had so ruthlessly despoiled the Russian homeland. But then, as their armies advanced, they had entered German territory and seen with their own eyes farming villages amply supplied and provisioned, the like of which simply didn't exist any more back home, cowsheds bursting with well-fed cattle, and a rural population that was healthy and well nourished. And in the solid stone-built houses of these farming families they had found not only huge wireless sets, refrigerators, all the comforts of life, but also, in among these things, cheap, basic sewing machines from Moscow, brightly coloured scarves from the Ukraine, icons from Russian churches, all of it stolen and plundered: the rich man, who had plenty, had robbed the poor, who had nothing. And the soldiers of the Red Army were consumed with rage at these Germans, and felt utter contempt for a nation that had no shame, that could not control its greed, that wanted to grab up everything, possess everything for itself, without caring whether others perished in consequence.

Here was a perfect example of that nation, standing before his mayor. And they were exactly as described — in the end, it was all the same to them whether Russians or Germans perished. The very people whose Party principles put the good of the nation first did not have an ounce of fellow feeling in their bodies. They had an eye to the main chance in everything, and didn't care if thousands perished as long as they got what they wanted. The man who was standing there now was just one of many. Doll told the police constable to take him away and bang him up in jail on bread and water; they'd find someone else to take his place at the dairy. He gave orders for him to be put to work carrying sacks all day long under strict supervision, and with any luck this creature who had betrayed his own people would soon be done for!

With that, the former beer wholesaler Zaches was led away. Doll never saw him again, and never found out what became of him.

Shortly afterwards, Doll became seriously ill, the outbreak of his illness brought on, or at least hastened, by this whole episode.

The man had been led away, and the mayor was sitting alone in his office. He was sitting at his desk, his head resting on his hand. He could feel that the anger inside him had completely subsided, and he was filled with a deep, nameless despair. The anger had been easier to bear than this despair, which was devoid of any hope. He suddenly realised that in this despair his hatred, too, had gone. He struggled to recall all the things the Nazis had done to him: years of persecution, arrest, surveillance, threats, countless prohibitions. But it made no difference; he felt no more hatred for them. And he also realised that he hadn't hated them for quite some time now. If he had come across as harsh and abrasive when carrying out these confiscations at the homes of Party members, it was only because he felt duty-bound to act like that. He was slightly shocked to realise that he wouldn't have behaved any differently in the homes of non-Party members. He found them all equally contemptible. He couldn't hate them any more, they were all just vicious little animals — which was exactly how the first Russian soldiers had looked upon him and his wife, and exactly how he now saw the Germans himself — all Germans.

But he was one of those Germans, he was born a German — a word that had now become a term of abuse throughout the world. He was one of them, and there was nothing that made him any better than all the others. It was an old saying, but no less true for that: if you fly with the crows, you'll get shot with the crows. He too had eaten of the bread stolen from nations they had plundered and looted: now it had come back to haunt him! Oh yes, it all made perfect sense: he couldn't hate them any more, for the very good reason that he was one of them. All that was left to him was a feeling of helpless contempt—contempt for himself as much as for anyone else.

What was it they had said to him in the town commandant's office? All Germans lie and deceive. A sequence of chance events had led to his appointment as mayor of this small town, and as mayor the truth of the remark about lying and deceiving was borne in upon him every day. The memories came flooding back: once again he saw that woman, mother of two small children, who'd come to see him during his consultation hour. Her face was streaming with tears, she'd lost everything in the bombing of Berlin, and she didn't have a bed, a cooking pot, or clothes to put on her children's backs: 'Have pity on me, Mr. Mayor, you can't send me away again like this! I can't go back to my children with nothing!'

The mayor had nothing either, but he went to see what he could find. He sought out Party comrades who had plenty and to spare, and he took from them to give to their 'fellow German citizen'—not an abundance, but a sufficiency. But the following day another woman stood before him in tears, the neighbour of the woman he had just provided for, likewise a mother of children, likewise living in abject poverty; and the woman who had just been given gifts and furnished with what she needed had stolen her neighbour's few pieces of tattered laundry from the washing line during the night! Germans against Germans, every man for himself, and every woman, too, keeping up the fight against the whole world and everyone else.

The mayor also recalled the carter who was given the job of taking the belongings of a paralyzed old man to the old people's home. But when he got there, anything worth keeping had been stolen from the cart, either by the carter himself or by passers-by, as he maintained. Germans against Germans …!

He also thought about the despicable doctor who, in order to settle some wretched private score from earlier times, certified a sick woman as healthy, and indeed fit for heavy work — the same doctor who, when medicines were in short supply, always had plenty for his friends, but never any for his enemies or strangers. He was happy to let them suffer — serve them right, the more the better! Germans against Germans!

He remembered how they stole horses from each others' stables, and poultry, and the rabbits they had so painstakingly fattened up, how they broke into each others' gardens and tore the vegetables out of the ground and the under-ripe fruit from the trees, breaking off the fruit-bearing branches in the process, which caused a lot of damage and did nobody any good. It was as if a herd of madmen had been let loose and were now just behaving as their crazy instincts directed them. He also knew about their denunciations — often completely absurd accusations, so obviously false that they wouldn't bear any kind of scrutiny, made out of pure malice, just to scare their neighbour and put the fear of God into him. Germans against Germans … !

So Doll sat there at his mayor's desk, his head in his hands, feeling completely drained. It had been an illusion, the idea that the world was just waiting to help the German people out of the mire, out of this huge bomb crater into which the war had flung them all. And it had also been an illusion that he, Mayor Doll, should be seen as any different from his fellow Germans: just like all the rest of them, he was nothing but a vicious little animal. Someone you didn't shake hands with, someone you looked straight through, like staring at a brick wall.

And they were right to hate and despise the German people, every last one of them. Doll had hated, too, after all — in private the old vet, Piglet Willem, and a good few others, but then more generally all the Nazis, every one of them. But his hatred, the small private one and the big general one, they had gone away, because he himself was just as hateful as the people he hated.

There was nothing left, Doll was drained and empty—and a profound apathy descended upon him. This apathy, which had been constantly lurking in the background in recent months, held at bay only temporarily because his duties as mayor had kept him so busy, now engulfed him completely. He looked over his desk, strewn with dozens of things that had to be dealt with as quickly as possible—but what did any of it matter any more? He was doomed, finished, he and all the rest of them! All effort was futile!

His secretary opened the door: 'There's someone from the town commandant's office here—they want you to go and see the commandant straightaway, Mr. Mayor!'

'All right', he replied. 'I'll go straight there …'

But he didn't go straight there. He stayed sitting at his desk for a good while yet; his secretary had to remind him about the commandant a couple of times. Not that he was thinking any definite thoughts, or that he decided, in his state of apathy, that this too was a pointless errand, just as all errands were pointless, since all errands, for a German, just led nowhere …

No, he simply sat there, thinking about nothing in particular. Had he wanted to describe what he felt like inside, he might have said that his head was filled with fog, a grey, opaque fog that nothing could penetrate—no gaze, no sound. And otherwise nothing …

Eventually—when his secretary reminded him again with some urgency—he stood up and went to the commandant's office, just because he had been there a hundred times before. It was no worse, and no better, than anything else he could have done. It didn't matter. Nothing mattered any more—including Dr. Doll himself. He was wounded in his vital core, and had lost his instinct for survival.

Shortly after this, Mayor Doll fell seriously ill; now he was no longer mayor. His wife, who was also ill, went with him to the local district hospital.

CHAPTER FIVE

Arrival in Berlin

On 1 September of this pitiless year, 1945, Mr. and Mrs. Doll travelled to Berlin. They had lain in the local district hospital for nearly two months, and they were still far from well. But the worry that they might lose their apartment in Berlin altogether if they waited any longer had driven them from their hospital beds.

The train was supposed to leave at noon, but it had not been released until after dark; it was completely overcrowded, with its broken windows and dirty compartments. As they boarded the train and made a dash for the pitch-black compartments, all the passengers were in a foul mood, flying off the handle at the slightest provocation and viewing every rival for a seat as their personal enemy.

The Dolls had managed to bag two seats, where they sat squashed up by their seated neighbours and people standing in front of them. Boxes were shoved up against their legs, and rucksacks were dragged painfully across their faces. It was so dark that you couldn't see a thing, but the hatred that everyone felt for everyone else seemed to manifest itself in the stench that hung about the compartment, despite the shattered windows. It smelled to high heaven in there, and it just got worse as more people boarded the train during the journey, squeezing into the already packed compartment and cursing anyone who already had a seat.

These later arrivals were mostly Berliners who had been foraging for mushrooms, who simply parked their baskets of mushrooms on the laps of the people in the seats, sullenly muttering something about taking them away later. But since the compartment was already overfull to start with, the baskets stayed where they were: Mrs. Doll had four on her lap; Doll had three.

But they made no protest, spoke not a word to their fellow passengers, and kept themselves to themselves. They still felt far too weak and ill to get involved in these sorts of arguments. It was only the thought of at least hanging on to their apartment that kept them going, and especially the husband: to him it seemed the last opportunity they had to begin a new life again.

Doll knew, of course, that he was clutching at straws with his hopes for the apartment, but he wanted to give fate this opportunity at least of saving them — as he sometimes said ironically to his wife, whose constant gallbladder attacks had made her quite despondent and easily influenced by her husband's depressive moods. 'We're probably going to die soon anyway, but you can do it more discreetly and comfortably in the big city. They have gas, for one thing!'

If the others had too much luggage with them, perhaps the Dolls did not have quite enough. All they were carrying was a small weekend case, which contained a little bit of bread, a can of meat, and a quarter-pound of coffee beans wrapped in a twist of paper, plus two books and a few basic toiletries. Doll was wearing a lightweight summer suit, while Mrs. Doll had at least managed to borrow a pale summer coat from a friend before leaving. In his pocket, Doll had barely three hundred marks, which he had borrowed from an acquaintance; the only precious item they had with them was the young wife's diamond ring.

The train halted for ages at every station, and when it was

moving its progress was very slow. The Dolls could dimly see the fiery lines and dots shooting into the night sky from the chimney of the locomotive, which was burning brown coal. They had seen rather too much in the way of fireworks during the war to take any pleasure in the sight. The memories were still painful. But in the light of these dancing glow-worms, they could make out figures standing on the running boards, ducking down with their backs turned towards the dense shower of sparks. The contents of their rucksacks must have been very precious to justify burning and singeing their precious clothing, and hanging on precariously by one hand to the cold brass rail, at constant risk of falling off.

Most of the rucksacks probably held nothing more than a few potatoes, or a little bag of flour, or a few pounds of peas—enough food for a week, at most. But there they were, hanging on for dear life in the sparks and the cold, letting their clothes get singed with a kind of brutish resignation. They were doubtless all poor folk who used this mode of transport; there would be a wife and numerous children waiting somewhere for what these men were carrying. The black marketeers, who bartered items for more valuable commodities—butter, bacon, eggs—and who picked up potatoes and flour by the sackful, they didn't risk their lives when they travelled; they recruited truck drivers in return for a share of the goods, and they didn't have any starving children waiting at home …

But who was a black marketeer and who wasn't? When the Dolls ate some of their bread and tinned meat in the total darkness of their compartment, some of the others smelled it through all the stench and began to pass pointed remarks about the sort of people who could still get hold of meat to eat. There was definitely something funny going on, and it needed to be looked into, in the cold light of day!

The Dolls said nothing, but quickly ate up what they had in their hands, and put the rest back in the little case before snuggling up more closely together. Mrs. Doll draped her thin, borrowed coat around them both, as the temperature was dropping fast. They put their arms around each other and held each other tightly. Doll rolled himself a cigarette from the last of his tobacco, and immediately someone piped up in a shrill voice: 'That's the third one he's smoked! It's like I always say: some people have it all, and the rest never get a thing, no matter what happens!'

The conversation ranged more widely over the racketeering and petty officialdom that were just a fact of life, and for the moment the Dolls were forgotten. They had a whispered conversation about their Berlin apartment; now that they were getting closer to their goal, and indeed had a goal to aim for again, the fact that they had heard nothing more about the apartment since March weighed heavily on their minds. There had been fierce fighting in the city since then, which had caused a whole lot more destruction, apparently—maybe their apartment didn't even exist any more?

'Wouldn't that be just like it? All this travelling, half frozen to death, and when we get there, the apartment's gone! I'd die laughing ...!'

'I have a feeling it's all still there, just as we left it. And it won't take much to get Petta's room sorted out—there wasn't a lot of damage.'

'I can always count on you to look on the bright side!'

'I've got lots of good friends in Berlin, you know! When my first husband was alive, we helped so many people—now they can do something for us in return! I'm pinning my hopes on Ben, in particular. Ben had an English mother, so he's bound to be doing very well now. Ernst'—the young woman's first husband—'got him out of the concentration camp, so he'll always owe me for that!'

'Let's hope so, Alma! Let's hope for all kinds of good things—but not take anything for granted. The only thing we can be sure of is that we have each other, and that we will always be together! And that nothing can ever separate us. Nothing!'

'That's right!' she said. Shivering, she snuggled up more closely to him. 'It's cold!' she whispered.

'Yes, it's cold', he agreed, and hugged her more tightly.

Berlin! Back in Berlin again, this beloved city where they had both grown up—he thirty years earlier than she, it's true—this bustling, restless place glittering with lights! Seemingly caught up in an endless frenzy of pleasures and delights—but only if you ignored the grim, sprawling suburbs where the workers lived. Berlin, the city of work! They were going back there again to start a new life: if there was anywhere on earth where there was a chance for them to start again, it was right here in Berlin, a city reduced to rubble, burnt out and bled to death.

It was half-past two in the morning when the Dolls left the train at the Gesundbrunnen underground station, with the curfew still in place until six o'clock. An icy wind whistled through the station; every pane of glass seemed to be broken, so there was nowhere to shelter from the cold and the wind. They tried various places, but everywhere they were frozen to the bone. Even the little waiting room on the platform, which had somehow survived, was no warmer. The wind rushed in through the broken windows; people were sitting bunched up together on the floor, waiting disconsolately or grimly for the morning.

Mrs. Doll squeezed in between them, seeking shelter from the icy gusts. But scarcely had she stood her little suitcase on the ground and sat down on it before she had to get up again: she was told she was blocking the passageway! And this woman who always had an answer for everything, who was normally so breezy and spoiling for a fight, now sat down without a word at the outer edge of the clump of people. She pulled her thin coat more tightly around her, trying to shelter from the icy wind that now struck her with full force.

Doll scraped together the last few strands of tobacco in his pockets, rolled a droopy little cigarette with hands that were trembling from the cold, and ran up and down. He stood for a moment in the ruins of the former station building and looked out at the darkened city, over which a half-moon cast a pale light. All he could make out were ruins.

'Don't go outside!' a voice warned him out of the darkness. 'The curfew hasn't ended yet. The patrols sometimes shoot without warning.'

'Don't worry, I'm not going out there!' replied Doll, and flicked the butt of his very last cigarette into the rubble.

And he thought to himself: *What a start! Things always turn out differently from what you expect. What you think is going to be hard is often easy, and something you don't even think about turns out to be difficult. Standing here for two freezing hours in a completely bombed-out station, with nothing more to smoke—and Alma is ill! Her face looked so yellow ...*

He turned round and went back to her.

'I can't stand it any more', she said. 'There must be a first-aid station or a doctor somewhere who can help me. Let's go and ask someone. I'm frozen stiff, and it hurts so much!'

'But we can't go into the city. The curfew's still in place! They say the patrols sometimes shoot without warning.'

'Let them shoot!' she replied in desperation. 'If they hit one of us, at least they'll take us somewhere warm where a doctor can help us.'

'Come on then, Alma', he replied gently. 'Let's see if we can find a first-aid station of some kind, or a doctor. You're quite right: anything is better than sitting here in the icy cold and freezing half to death.'

They walked out of the station and picked their way through the rubble. The pale moonlight was more of a hindrance than a help in lighting their path. Doll could see hardly anything with his poor eyes.

'Come on!' she said as she walked on ahead. 'That looks like a street turning over there! According to the description, that must be the one where there might be a first-aid station.'

He followed her, feeling unsure. Suddenly he tripped over an obstacle and fell forward into a dark cavity.

'Look out!' said his young wife. 'Have you hurt yourself?'

'Well, there's a thing!' an indignant voice called out of the total darkness, speaking in a strong Berlin accent. 'The wife just lets her husband fall in, and doesn't even fall in with him. Scandalous, is what I call it!'

'What good would it have done me', asked Doll, and found himself laughing despite the pain, 'if my wife had fallen in with me? Where are we, anyway?'

'Gesundbrunnen underground station', another voice piped up. 'But the first train isn't due until half-past six.'

'Thanks!' he replied, and they went on their way, arms linked now. 'That was a proper Berlin welcome, a bit painful, but the real deal. I've kissed the ground of this city like a conqueror and taken possession of it, and what Berlin had to say about it was pretty good, too.'

'Did you hurt yourself?'

'Not really—just took the skin off my hands a bit and bruised my legs.'

They dived into the dark sea of ruins, where the moonlight was unable to penetrate all the way down to the bottom of the street canyons. They picked their way slowly forward. The street was deserted; all was deathly silence, apart from their echoing footsteps.

'We'll hear any patrols coming from a long way off', said Doll. 'So we'll have plenty of time to hide.'

'Hang on', she replied. 'This looks like the first-aid station. Strike a match.'

It really was the first-aid station, but everything was in darkness, and although they rang the bell and knocked on the door, nothing stirred in the dark ground floor of the building.

'I expect the bell isn't working', said Doll eventually. 'What now? Shall we go back to the station?'

'No, no, anything but that! Maybe we can find a doctor, or a police station. A police station would be best. They'd surely let us sit inside so that we could warm up a bit.'

So they wandered on through the silent city, with not a single light to be seen at any of the windows, and eventually they did find a police station. After they had been ringing the doorbell for some time, a police officer came out.

'What do you want?' he asked brusquely.

'We travelled into town on the train a while ago, and my wife is ill. The first-aid station is shut. Could we come in and sit down until six o'clock, so we can warm up a bit?'

'I can't let you do that—that's not allowed', replied the policeman.

They resorted to pleading and begging, saying they wouldn't be in anyone's way, and would just sit quietly and wait.

But the policeman wouldn't budge: 'If it's not allowed, I can't let you do it! And anyway, what are you doing out on the street? There's still a curfew!'

'Well, in that case why don't you just arrest us for a bit, constable?' asked the young woman. 'Then we won't be breaking the rules by sitting inside!'

But the policeman didn't go for this suggestion either. Instead he shut the door in their faces, leaving the two of them standing on their own again in the dark street.

They looked at each other, their faces pale and bewildered. Suddenly they noticed that it was getting light, that it was nearly daybreak.

'Then it must be getting on for six. We'll just carry on walking. Maybe a tram will come along soon.'

Later on, they were sitting in a bus that was taking workers to a factory for the first shift. The bus wasn't passing very close to where they lived, but it did take them to a station on the city rail network, where the first train of the day was due to leave soon. But then they encountered a fresh obstacle: the woman in the ticket office had overslept, and the ticket collector on the barrier refused to let anybody through without a ticket: it was against the rules!

'And what if there's nobody on the ticket counter for another hour?'

'Then nobody goes through in the next hour! Rules are rules!'

'But we've got to get to work!' protested many of those waiting.

'That's not my problem! I have to stick to the rules!'

'We'll see about that!' cried a local. 'You lot, come with me!'

They all followed him through a side entrance, over a fence, across the tracks in semi-darkness, the electrified rails, and then another climb over a wall. The Dolls brought up the rear — she suddenly had pains in her leg, and he was still hurting all over from his tumble. They arrived on the platform out of breath, just in time to see the red taillights of the early train receding into the distance.

Then came more waiting in the freezing cold, sitting in the moving train feeling utterly exhausted, changing trains and waiting some more … How they longed just to get home at last! They went all dreamy at the mere thought of their couch! Just to lie there quietly, feeling warm again and falling asleep! Blissful oblivion! Dead to the world!

At last they were there: they got off the train. 'We'll be home in five minutes!' he said, jollying her along.

'At the rate we're going, it will take us another twenty minutes', she replied. 'I wish I knew what was wrong with my leg. It was only a little sore that had opened up a bit because I scratched it … Oh Lord, the bridge has gone, too. It was still there in March!'

And as they struggled along for what seemed an endless distance, forced by the destruction of the bridge to make a lengthy detour, suddenly all they saw was the destruction all around them — some of it from before that they already knew about, and some that had happened since they left Berlin. They fell silent, rendered speechless by the sight; so much more had been destroyed in the meantime. Doll thought: *What am I going to do with her, if the apartment has gone? She is ill and completely demoralised.*

Then they turned the last corner and peered intently. This time he was quicker off the mark: 'I can see the window boxes on our balcony! And the glazing bars are back in the windows! Alma, our apartment is still there!'

They looked at each other with a weary smile.

They had no keys, so had to go and see the caretaker first. Bad news—very bad news! The little caretaker had not been seen since April. Perhaps he had been killed in the fighting, or perhaps he'd been taken prisoner; his wife didn't know. Not a thing.

'Run off, you mean, done a bunk? No, my 'usband isn't the sort of man to run off and leave his wife and children, my 'usband's never been that way, Mr. Doll! And anyway, why should 'e? 'E never harmed anybody, 'e didn't! The keys to the apartment? No, I don't 'ave 'em any more. Somebody turned up from the 'ousing office a few days ago, a dancer or singer or something to do with the theatre, I don't rightly know. With mother and child—oh yes, there's a little one, too! She got the front room tidied up a bit. And the old lady's still livin' out the back, Mrs. Schulz, the one you used to let sleep there from time to time, when you went out to the country, so there'd be someone there to keep an eye on things. Well, you'll see for yourself 'ow well she's kept an eye on things, Mrs. Doll, I'm not goin' to speak out of turn. Anyway, your big cooking pot 'as gone, the 'ome Guard people came and fetched that. And if your vacuum cleaner 'as gone and your books and all your buckets and if the pantry is empty, then I know nothing about that, Mrs. Doll, and you'll 'ave to ask Mrs. Schulz—if you can get to see 'er, that is. She says she is livin' 'ere, but what do I know where she lives! I often don't see 'er for the 'ole week, and she's never paid a penny in rent!'

Slowly, ever so slowly, the Dolls climbed the four flights of stairs to their apartment. They hadn't said a word in response to all the bad news, which washed over them like a tidal wave, nor had they spoken a word to each other. It was just that their faces had turned a shade more pale, perhaps, than they were already from illness, a sleepless night on the train, and hours of sitting around in the freezing cold ...

They had to press the doorbell for a long, long time before

anything stirred in the apartment—in their own apartment! And they had to be very patient before they were eventually let in by a swarthy young woman, who was scantily clad (but then it was only around eight in the morning).

'Your apartment? This here is *my* apartment, officially allocated to me by the housing office. I'm afraid there is nothing you can do about it, madam. The three rooms at the front belong to me, and I've already spent a few thousand marks to make the place more or less habitable. The other two rooms have been completely gutted by fire—but then you'll know that for yourself, madam, if this is your apartment! The big room at the back is occupied by Mrs. Schulz, but she's away at the moment, and I don't know if she'll be back today. But anyway, she's locked everything up. I'm sorry, madam, but it's very cold in here, and I'm standing around in my nightshirt, and I need to get back into bed. I suggest you go and talk to the housing office, madam. Good day!'

And with that the door closed, and the Dolls were left standing in the hallway on their own. He took his wife and led her slowly, leaning very heavily on his arm, into the interior of the apartment. But everything was locked up, and they couldn't get into any of the rooms. So he led her into the kitchen and sat her down on the only kitchen chair (surely there had been three there before?) between the gas stove and the kitchen table.

His young wife sat there, but she didn't look young right now, staring blankly ahead without seeing anything, her face a sickly, yellowish colour. Doll took her cold hands between his own, stroked them, and said: 'It's not a good start, Alma, I know! But we won't let it get us down, we'll find a way to get through it somehow. People like us don't give up that easily!'

At these words of encouragement, Mrs. Doll attempted a smile, but it was the feeblest, most pitiful, and heartrending smile Doll had ever seen from his wife. Then she lifted her head and gazed around the kitchen for a long, long time. She studied every single object, and then wailed: 'My kitchen! Just look around and see if you can see a single thing in this kitchen that doesn't belong to us! And now this female just gives me the brush-off in the hall and doesn't even offer me a chair to sit down on in my own apartment!' Alma seemed on the verge of tears, but her eyes were dry. 'And did you see? Through the open door I could see our radiogram parked there in her room, and the big yellow armchair you always liked to sit in! Just you wait—I'm off to the housing office right now!'

But she didn't go. She stayed sitting where she was, looking blankly into the distance again. She had always been a pampered, radiant woman. And now she was sitting there in her cheap little coat, which didn't remotely suit her, and which was borrowed anyway, her stockings were all snagged and torn from the mushroom baskets, and her hands and face still bore traces of the long, dirty train journey ...

Everything lost—drained and spent—like the rest of us! thought Doll bleakly, and went on patting her hands mechanically. But then he reflected that it was now up to him to do something; they couldn't just carry on sitting in the kitchen. A little while later, he took her downstairs again to the kindly caretaker's wife, and even if they were still sitting in the kitchen down here, at least this kitchen was warm. The last of the Dolls' coffee beans were roasted in a little skillet. Bread was sliced, and the remaining meat taken out of the tin and arranged neatly on a plate. With a spot of breakfast on the table, the future suddenly looked more hopeful.

But his young wife seemed not to share the feeling. She said that Doll should go now, right now, and seek out her friend Ben, the German who was half-English, and when Doll resisted, saying he would rather go after breakfast, she became very impatient: she knew for a fact that Ben was an early riser, and always left for work in good time. If he didn't go immediately he would miss Ben, and they wouldn't be able to reach him for the rest of the day — and she needed to speak to him *now*!

Doll could think of good reasons for refusing, but his young wife seemed so feverishly agitated and desperate, and he himself was so exhausted and keen to avoid an argument, that he did actually set out to find Ben's apartment. 'I'll expect you back in under half an hour!' cried the young woman, now quite animated again, 'and bring Ben with you. I'll have breakfast waiting for you!'

It was not possible to do the journey in under half an hour, because the trams that used to run there were not yet back in service. Doll had to walk the whole way — though 'crawl' would be a better word.

The house he was looking for was still standing, at least, but there was no nameplate on the apartment door, and when he rang the bell, nobody came. He finally discovered from the porter that the gentleman had moved out, just a few days earlier. (*Somebody moved into our apartment a few days ago, and now Ben has moved out: a promising start to our time in Berlin, I must say!*) The porter claimed not to know Ben's new address. *I can't go back to Alma with this*, thought Doll, and with some effort he managed to find an elderly gentleman in the building who knew where Ben was now living, somewhere way out in the city's smart, new west end. It would take hours to get there, and he had no intention of going now. Back to Alma, then — and breakfast!

She really had waited breakfast for them, and had even managed to drum up a few cigarettes, albeit at a cost of five marks apiece, which Doll, who had previously been kept well supplied with tobacco by the Russians, found staggering. The news that Ben had moved was received by Alma with composure. 'We'll go and see him after breakfast, even though it will be hard for me with my leg. Believe me, my instinct about this is right: Ben will help us in our hour of need, he'll never forget that business with the concentration camp! You'll see', his wife went on, growing steadily more animated, 'he's done very well for himself. The fact that he's moved out to the expensive west end proves it. He'll have a villa there, for sure. And he'll be pleased that he's able to help us!'

And so, refreshed by the breakfast and a good wash, they took their leave of the friendly but ever-despondent caretaker's wife. 'I'll be back again in the next few days', promised Mrs. Doll, 'and I'll go down to the housing office and sort out this business with that cheeky cow upstairs. Doesn't even offer me a chair in my own home—she's out on her ear!'

And how are we going to compensate her for the 'few thousand marks' she's spent on doing the place up? thought Doll. And anyway, they'll never grant us the right to the whole seven-room apartment, not even if we include Petta and grandmother.

But he didn't talk about any of this with his wife. Events would just have to take their course now. There was no point in getting worked up over anything, or making plans for the future. Things would turn out one way or the other—though hardly ever for the best.

The refreshing effects of the wash and the ground coffee had not lasted long, and his wife's leg must have been in a really bad way, because their progress was painfully slow. Time and time again, Doll resolved to hold back and walk with his sick wife, but before he knew it he was ten or twenty paces ahead of her. When he then turned round and went back to her, feeling guilty, she would give him a friendly smile. 'You go on!' she said. 'I'll whistle if I think I'm losing sight of you. It must be a pain to have to slow down for me — I'm like a snail today. You go on ahead!'

After the cold night, the sun shone warmly, with that pleasantly autumnal warmth that has nothing oppressive about it, but just feels good. Here in the streets lined with villas the trees had not yet lost their leaves. The foliage was paler and changing colour, but it was just good to see healthy trees again after all the ruins. Many of the villas here had also been destroyed, but nestling among shrubs and trees, and surrounded by green lawns and flowers, it didn't look so bad somehow.

Mrs. Doll said to her husband, who had just turned back again to rejoin his 'snail': 'Ben will have his own car by now, for certain, and I'm sure he'll take us out for a drive from time to time. Now we've got the whole of the lovely autumn ahead of us — let's just enjoy it for ourselves at last, without having to worry about anything. I expect Ben can arrange a truck for us, too, so we can pick up the furniture and your books from the sticks and set up house again properly. You wait and see what a wonderful home I'll make for you! We're sure to have lots of English visitors through Ben, and then you can invite your writer friends, too ... I'll mix the most marvellous cocktails for you — I mix a mean cocktail, me! Ben will be able to supply the ingredients!'

Ben this, Ben that, Ben the other! What a child she was, the way she just pinned all the hopes of her innocent, child-like heart on a friend she hadn't thought about for weeks and months! A child in her faith and trust — so far, no disappointment had been able to eradicate this capacity for belief and hope from her heart.

Eventually, they really were sitting in the large drawing room of a huge villa, and from the windows they could see across the garden to the garage buildings, where a chauffeur was busy washing the car—Ben's car, and in that regard at least, Alma's expectations had been fulfilled. Her friend Ben had done surprisingly well for himself, and official plates on the garden gate indicated that Mr. Ben already held a senior position.

So far he had not yet appeared, having been detained for a few minutes by an important meeting on the ground floor. In the meantime, three interior decorators were busying themselves around the Dolls as they sat there amongst the antique furniture, looking lost in the magnificently appointed room; whispering among themselves, they were arranging diaphanous curtain fabrics in folds, climbing up and down ladders, and pulling on cords. And when Doll saw all this new splendour around him, such as he had not seen intact for months and years now, he felt his own down-at-heel appearance twice, ten times, as keenly. He looked from the snow-white tulle to the pale summer suit he was wearing, which showed dirty marks and streaks from the overnight train journey; and Alma's cheap little coat and torn stockings looked even worse against the rich brocade of the armchair in which she sat.

The truth was they had become beggars, and here in this house, which even in the best of times had been the villa of a *very* rich man, Doll felt this very acutely. It wasn't so long ago that he had thought of himself as a pretty prosperous man. But now he and his wife, as he suddenly saw very clearly, were no different from all those refugees whom he had only recently—when he was still mayor—had to direct through his little town in endless, wretched, starving columns. Now the Dolls, too, were down-and-out, with only a small suitcase to their name, homeless, dependent on the help of friends, strangers, maybe even public assistance. Mayor, property owner, an abundance of possessions, a bank account always in the black, decent food—and now suddenly nothing, zero, zilch!

Oh Lord! thought Doll. *Don't let Alma say too much! Please God she doesn't ask these two women for anything—I couldn't bear it, we're not reduced to begging just yet!*

The two women who had just entered the room were the wife of Alma's friend Ben and a woman friend of hers; they had eyed the two visitors with some surprise, but then Alma had started to explain …

There was no risk of her saying too much. She didn't get a chance for that. What happened next was something that Doll was to observe quite often over the coming weeks and months. Alma had barely got into her stride before the two women became very restless and fidgety, and the reason was obvious: they were dying to tell their own story!

As soon as Alma paused in her tale, the other two jumped in immediately. In a breathless gush of words, taking it in turns to speak, they now told the story of how badly they had suffered, how they had nearly starved, how they had lost so much … Sitting in this magnificent house, in an antique armchair covered in fine brocade, the Dolls learned what an awfully wretched time the owners had had of it, and indeed were still having.

Then the master of the house entered the room in a hurry; he could spare them just five minutes between two important meetings. He kissed Alma's hand, and said how sorry he was that life had become so very difficult. He could not even offer his guests a cigarette—that's how bad things were in his house! Mrs. Doll's leg really did look in a bad way; his guess was blood poisoning. He advised Doll to take her straight to a hospital.

A quarter of an hour later, they were both standing out on the street again, having got through the visit to Alma's truest and most grateful friend—thank God! The sun was still shining brightly and cheerily though the sparse foliage of the trees, the lawn in front of the villa was a deep green, and the Michaelmas daisies were in flower. Doll linked arms gently with his wife—she had such an alarmingly pale, ill-looking face—and said gaily: 'And you know what we're going to do now, Alma? Now we are going to look after our nerves, we're going to live the good life—and your poor leg will get better in the meantime. So where are we going? Well, it occurred to me, when there was mention of a hospital just now, that only a quarter of an hour from here there's a sanatorium where I have stayed a couple of times for my nerves. They know me there, and they'll admit us for certain.'

'Do what you want with me', answered Mrs. Doll. 'Just as long as I get to lie down soon!'

And so they set out for the sanatorium, but instead of a quarter of an hour it took them nearly an hour, because the woman found it such a struggle to walk. There was no more talk of best friend Ben during this veritable *via dolorosa*; deep in thought, Mrs. Doll merely observed once in passing: 'I'm never going to be decent and generous to people like I was before! Never again!'

'Thank God', he said, and gave her a tender look. 'Thank God, Alma, that's not something that depends solely on you. You'll always be a decent person, no matter how badly you've been let down!'

The sanatorium, a large, ugly building of red brick and cement, was still standing—it would have been almost unbearable if this had turned out to be another disappointment. They sat in the consulting room. 'Turn on all your charm, Alma', whispered Doll. 'They've got to take us in here. Where else are we going to go?'

Mrs. Doll quickly applied powder, rouge, and lipstick, intent on making the most of her charm. 'Of course we'll admit you, my dear!' said the white-haired lady doctor, and stroked Alma's hair. 'As far as your husband is concerned, we'll have to consult the privy councillor. But I've certainly got a bed free for you in my section.'

The privy councillor appeared. He looked a lot more jaundiced, wrinkled, and careworn, and a lot more intelligent, too, than before—or so it seemed to Doll. 'I've got a room free for Mr. Doll', he announced after brief reflection. 'But unfortunately not for the young lady at present—perhaps we'll be able to do something in three or four weeks.'

Having only just been relieved of their worst cares, the Dolls looked at each other in disbelief, then at the white-haired lady doctor, who now looked at her boss with a tight-lipped and submissive expression. Pointing out that she had just said something different was clearly a waste of time: fate was against the Dolls—end of story. Protest was futile. One disaster after another—they were headed for the streets ...

'I'm not leaving my wife now', said Doll after a protracted silence. 'Come on, Alma. Goodbye, Councillor. Goodbye, Doctor!'

This time, out on the street, they didn't notice that the sun was shining, that the trees still had their leaves. The pressing question 'What now?' overshadowed everything else. They had other friends, of course, and they still had relatives living in the city, too, but with the young wife in her present condition, how could they think of walking halfway across Berlin only to find a bombed-out shell instead of a house?

'What now? What now?' And turning suddenly to look back at the sanatorium: 'How I hate that man with his polite weasel face! Of course they had spare beds—beds for both of us. But he knew your first wife—I could tell straightaway that he was comparing me to her, and took against me. But where are we going to go now? Dear God, I've got to lie down somewhere, just a couple of hours, and then I'll be all right again.'

'I think we'll just go back to the dear old caretaker's wife for now. She's sure to have a sofa or some sort of couch where you can lie down. And in the meantime I'll find something else.'

And since at that moment they couldn't think of any alternative, they decided to do just that. The endless return trek began: travelling in overcrowded underground trains, where it didn't occur to anybody to offer the sick woman a seat, toiling up and down stairs, being pushed, shoved, and berated because they were going so slowly. He had the little suitcase in his hand, with their last crust of bread inside—the meat and the coffee were all gone now. It was lunchtime, they had no apartment and no ration cards, and no immediate prospect of getting any. And after Alma's extravagant purchase of cigarettes, they had less than two hundred marks left to their name.

We're facing utter ruin, thought Doll. *How would we do it? We don't have access to poison. Water? We both swim too well. The noose? Couldn't face that! Gas? But we don't even have a kitchen with a gas stove any more.* And then aloud to his wife, who was leaning against him: 'You've nearly made it! We're nearly home!'

'Home', she answered with a smile, and just a hint of irony. Then she added with a sudden rush of remorse: 'But you'll see, I *will* make a wonderful home for us!'

'Of course you will', said he. 'A wonderful home—I'm already looking forward to it.'

CHAPTER SIX

A new burden to bear

And then it really was almost as if they were at home. Alma Doll lay on a couch that belonged to the caretaker's wife, covered with a duvet, because she suddenly felt very cold. Her teeth were chattering. He sat on the edge of the couch, held her hands, and gazed anxiously into her face, which had become so thin.

Then the shivering attack abated, and she lay still for a long time, as if utterly drained. Now she opened her eyes. 'Dearest', she said, 'will you mind very much if I send you off on another errand? I think I need a doctor ...'

'Of course I'll go', he replied. 'And I don't mind one bit. I'll go and find a doctor right away.'

She pulled his face down to hers and kissed him. He felt her dry, cracked lips coming to life again under his kiss, filling with blood again, and becoming soft and pliable.

'I'm such a burden to you', she whispered. 'I know I am, I know. But I'll make it up to you — you know me. Just you wait till your Alma's back on her feet again, and I'll pamper you like before, you know that!'

'My wonderful pamperer!' he said tenderly. 'Yes, I know, I know you will.' He kissed her once more. 'And now I'm going.'

'You don't have to go far', she called after him. 'There are six or eight doctors living right here in this street.'

They had indeed lived there, or were living there still, but it turned out that none of them had time for a house call right now. One of them could not come until the late evening; another, not before the following day. He couldn't possibly leave his wife lying in pain for all that time. He went on further, trudging up and down stairs, semi-stupified with fatigue and hunger, his feet hot and sore ...

He did eventually find a doctor who was prepared to come with him immediately. Not exactly the right kind of doctor—this one specialised in dermato-venereal diseases—but right now he couldn't care less. All that mattered was that she was seen by a doctor. *I can't go back to her having failed again! We've had enough failures already today. Our whole life is just one long series of failures.*

The doctor had a face that appeared to be covered not with skin, but with thin parchment paper, stretched so taut that it looked about to tear. He had a ghostly air about him, with slow, careful movements, as if he might shatter into pieces at any moment, and with a soft, almost soundless way of speaking, as if he was speaking into fog ...

They walked along the street side by side. The doctor was carrying his case containing some medical instruments. Suddenly he asked: 'You are a writer, Mr. Doll?' Doll said that he was. 'I'm a writer myself', said the doctor, still speaking in the same soft, impersonal manner. 'Did you know?'

Doll tried to remember the name on the doctor's nameplate. But all he could remember was the reference to 'dermato-venereal diseases'. 'No', he replied. 'I didn't know that.'

'Oh yes!' the doctor insisted. 'I was even a very famous writer once. And it's not all that long ago.' He paused, and then added out of the blue: 'My wife killed herself out on the highway, by the way.'

What a spooky character! thought Doll, shocked by this revelation. *Of all the people I had to bring to Alma's sick-bed! I hope she doesn't find him too scary!*

But the doctor behaved quite normally at Alma's bedside. Something like a smile even flitted across his parchment features when he saw the pretty, childlike face of the young woman. 'Now then, what seems to be the trouble, my dear child?' he inquired gently. He examined her briefly, and then said, speaking more to Doll than to the young woman: 'The early stages of blood poisoning. The best thing would be for the young woman to go straight to hospital. I'll write you a referral.'

'And what's to become of my husband in the meantime?' cried Alma. 'I don't want to go into hospital. I'm not leaving my husband alone now!'

Doll tried to persuade her: 'You know our situation, my dear. It may be the best solution for the time being. In hospital, you will at least have a bed. And meals. And rest. And proper care. Please say yes, Alma!'

'And what about you? What about you?' she kept on asking. 'Where are you going to be, while I'm having rest and meals and a bed and proper care? Do you think I'm going to live a life of ease while you're struggling to get by? Never! Never!'

During this exchange, the strange doctor had sat with bowed head, not saying a word. Now he picked up his bag and said in a flat, toneless voice: 'I'm going to give you an injection for now, which will take away the pain and let you sleep for a bit. I'll call in again this evening.'

'But we have to vacate this couch before tonight!' countered

Doll. 'This is where the caretaker's wife sleeps. By this evening we might be sleeping on the street!'

The doctor didn't answer, but carried on with the injection. The effect was immediate: no sooner had the needle gone in than Doll saw the relaxed, almost happy, expression spread across his wife's face. (It wasn't her first morphine injection, of course. She'd had them before—for her bilious attacks.) She suddenly smiled, stretched herself out at her ease, and snuggled down into the sheets. 'God, that feels good', she whispered, and closed her eyes.

In the space of just five seconds, she had forgotten her husband, her pain and disappointments, and her hunger. She had forgotten a lot more besides. She had forgotten that she was married and had a child. She was completely alone with herself, in her own world. A smile played about her lips, and there it stayed. Doll watched her breathing gently, and understood that the very act of breathing was pleasurable for her now.

The doctor had packed his syringe away again. 'I'll walk a little way with you, Doctor', said Doll. For the moment, it seemed to him impossible to sit with this woman who was now so far away. Through all their differences over the past weeks and months, he had never once felt so alone as he did now.

'I'll call in again this evening', said the doctor, exactly as before, as if he had not heard a word Doll had said. 'Between eight and nine. Please make sure that the street door is not locked.'

Doll didn't bother to object again; there seemed no point with this doctor, who didn't listen anyway. For a while they walked along side by side in silence. Then the doctor started up again: 'It seems a very long time ago now, but back then I really was a very well-known writer.'

There was no hint of vanity; it sounded more like an observation from a train of thought that haunted him obsessively. And the observation he now came out with appeared to belong to the same train of thought: 'The injection I gave your wife came from my suicide pack. It contains scopolamine, around 30 per cent. She'll be asleep when you get back.'

And again after a further pause: 'Yes, I'll be committing suicide, maybe tomorrow, maybe in a year's time.' He extended a limp, damp hand to Doll. 'This is where I live. Thank you for walking with me. Of course, I didn't have a large readership like you. Anyway, I'll call in again this evening—don't forget about the street door.'

And as they took their leave of each other: 'I definitely won't be committing suicide today. You know, of course, that your wife is a real addict?'

Doll sat by his wife. She was sleeping soundly. Her face now looked carefree and happy; she was sleeping like a child. Through the open window came autumn sunshine and fresh air from the street, and the happy sound of children playing outside. Doll was not a happy man; he was feeling very tired and utterly despondent. He was also suffering the pangs of hunger. The last piece of bread had been eaten a long time ago. They had nothing left.

Why on earth, Doll thought to himself, *didn't I get him to give me an injection too? To forget it all for a while, just for once! That half-crazed doctor would have done it. So he's called Pernies. I remember, he* was *famous once. I don't think I've ever read anything by him; he was probably more someone who wrote about art than an actual artist himself. And now he's talking about suicide, and his wife killed herself out on the highway!*

Doll started up on his chair. He had nearly fallen asleep, and yet something had to be done. It would be dark in less than three hours, and the night afforded them no shelter.

He stood up. Even as he was leaving the apartment, he had no idea where he was going. So he climbed the stairs again to their old apartment.

This time, the door was opened as soon as he rang the bell. And it was not the snippy dancer who opened it, but Mrs. Schulz, the woman whom Alma had asked to look after their things while they were away, and whose honesty had now been called into question by the caretaker's wife.

The white and rather podgy face of Major Schulz's widow lit up when she saw Doll. 'There you are, Dr. Doll! I fought like a lion for your apartment — if only you had come two weeks earlier! Now you'll have trouble with the housing office and with that woman living at the front. So where is your wife? She's sleeping? That's good — if she's sleeping, that gives me time to get the room sorted out for you. You'll have to manage with *one* couch for the first night — the other one has gone, but you only need to go and ask for it back. Would you like a cigarette? What, you haven't got any more? Here, take the whole pack! Don't be silly, I can get as many as I want, even American brands, for five marks apiece, German money ... Look, I was just brewing up a pot of coffee when you arrived, so you must have a cup of coffee with me. Not the artificial stuff, but real coffee! I got some for four hundred marks a pound. That's cheap, my dear, I only buy things cheap. We'll have some white bread with it, and I've also got a tin of cheese here, and I think there's a bit of butter left.

'You can talk! You say you've lost everything? Well, my dear, you've no idea what it's like for me, I literally don't have a thing! Just the clothes on my back. No, no, today you're my guest! Should we perhaps wake the young lady up? No, you're right, we'll put something back for her. But you eat up everything that's here; I'll be getting more later today. They all spoil me ... And I never have to pay extortionate prices. Yes, the quilt has gone, stolen. I know who took it, too, but I can't prove it, so I'm not going to speak out of turn.

'You've heard that her husband has gone, I suppose? They came and took him away, of course—paid-up Nazi that he was. They should come and get the wife as well, she was worse than him! I've had the wall put up and plastered a bit—I've made a note of the cost somewhere, I'll let you know later. It wasn't much, a tradesman did it for me more as a favour. The two window frames with the cellophane and plywood are just borrowed, but there's no hurry, they can stay in the wall for the time being.

'But of course the room is available for you to use—it is your room, after all, and it's your furniture, too. The crockery and kitchen utensils belong to you as well. I can always sleep at a friend's place, and you'll get the housing office to evict the little singer and her family. They're decent enough people—but so what? These days, everyone has to look out for themselves. She's so scared of you! They've got nothing at all of their own, not so much as a spoon or a cup ... By the way, the teapot I've just made the coffee in doesn't belong to you—all your teapots got smashed in the air raid. An old lady gave it to me; she doesn't want any money for it, of course. I thought I might give her a pound of sugar and a loaf of bread. That's not much, my dear: sugar is now going for a hundred, and a loaf of bread for eighty—and you must have a teapot! I can discuss it with your wife later.

'You can eat all of the white loaf, if you like; it tastes nice, but it doesn't fill you up. I'll go and get some fresh now. I might get some jam, too. If you'd come yesterday I'd have been able to offer you cake—proper butter cake with lots of sugar on the top. Pity. But I know what, I'll have a cake baked for you for Sunday. My baker will do it for you very cheaply …'

She prattled on. And on. All Doll had to do was sit there and listen. An occasional 'Yes', 'I see', or 'Thank you' were quite sufficient. He had found a safe haven; at long last, when he was on the point of giving up hope, a safe haven had been found for them both. He sat at his ease in an armchair, his weary legs and aching feet stretched out in front of him. He ate one slice of white bread to begin with, then three slices, then seven slices, drank coffee, smoked a cigarette, and started to eat again. Meanwhile, Mrs. Schulz was still in full flight.

There she sat before him, a woman in her forties, just starting to lose her looks — though she was in denial about it — her clothes a little crumpled and scruffy, but unquestionably a lady. Or someone who had once been a lady — for who today was still a 'lady' in the traditional sense of the word?

Then it got dark outside, the big electric standard lamp by Doll's bed was switched on, and dance music played softly on the radio. The doctor, that spectral figure with the papery skin, came and went again. He did say again that the young woman ought to be in hospital, but he didn't press the point, and gave them both an injection instead. Now they were both relaxed and calm, the morphine making them believe that all their difficulties were now behind them.

On the table next to the couch are plenty of cigarettes, a pot of real tea, condensed milk, and sugar — and a loaf of white bread, too. They are well provided for, with a home, choice music. On the walls are pictures, originals, nothing to get excited about exactly, but of decent, middling quality.

The Dolls are not yet asleep. This time it was pure morphine that the doctor gave them. They are chatting quietly, making plans for the future ... Plans? Now they have completely lost touch with reality: these are just flights of fancy, and every hope that springs to mind is immediately fulfilled. The apartment belongs to them, they have ration cards for food, a truck and trailer will fetch their child Petta and their things from the little town. Tomorrow he will begin to write books again, his head is suddenly full of plans, he will become an international bestselling author ...

The young woman's salon will be *the* salon in Berlin. The 'sea surf' talks of dresses she will have made, dresses that she once owned; he hardly needs to say anything in reply, and can pursue his own fantasies instead. Yes indeed, now he will travel the world with her and their child, just as he dreamed of doing before this war. Now the ghastly slaughter is ended, a few more months and they'll be able to leave this city of ruins behind and journey to brighter climes, where the sun always shines and southern fruits ripen on the trees ...

They lie there in a semi-waking dream, experiencing the euphoria, the rush; at last they have managed to escape the bitter reality. Both of them cherish a thousand hopes; no more obstacles bar their way. They gaze at each other and exchange tender smiles, not like a married couple, but as young lovers or children do ...

Sometimes the wind makes the slackly fitted cellophane chatter in the window frames, and a door slams in the burned-out courtyard building. There are all sorts of mysterious noises coming from outside. Trickling debris? Rats, looking for something unspeakable in the basements? A world in ruins, which will take everyone's determination, everyone's hands, to rebuild. But instead they are lying on their backs and dreaming. They have no love for anything any more, and they don't really have a life to live. They have nothing now, and they are nothing now. The smallest setback could tip them into the abyss and finish them off for good. But they are dreaming ...

'Give me another cigarette! Don't worry, we'll soon get some more. I have a feeling that from now on things are going to go our way.'

But then—it is not yet midnight—they grow restless. The effect of the injection has worn off; the sweet illusion has vanished.

'I can't sleep!' And: 'I can't bear the pain any more! We must get the doctor back.'—'Too late. Curfew! We can't go out on the street any more!'—'It's crazy! What if I was having a baby? Or I was dying?'—'Well, it's a good job you're not! I'll go and fetch the doctor first thing tomorrow!'—'Tomorrow? I'll never last that long with this pain—I'll go and see him now!'—'What, *now* Alma, and with that leg of yours? Let me go instead!'—'No, it's better if I go. If a patrol does show up, they won't do anything to me, for certain!'—'But the houses are all locked up now!'—'I'll get in somehow. You know me! I'll find a way!'

And she went off, leaving him alone. The music was still playing, the lamp beside the couch was still burning brightly. But now the high was past, and he saw their situation for what it really was: without means, ill, lacking in energy, with no desire to work and no hope ... a paper-skinned spectre and a dubious lady had made them forget for a few hours what their real situation was like, but now he knew again. Yes, for the moment they had a roof over their heads, but in the greater scheme of things nothing had changed for the better, and if anything it had changed for the worse: now his wife was running around on the streets at a dangerous hour looking for a shot of morphine! He remembered how, the night before, she had insisted on leaving Gesundbrunnen station to find a first-aid post. She had talked about bilious attacks, but now that she had this pain in her leg she hadn't mentioned her gallbladder trouble again. All day yesterday she must have been thinking only about getting this shot. An addict—so one more burden to bear, therefore!

One o'clock. She said she would be back straightaway, and now she had been gone a whole hour. He should get up and go and look for her, make sure she was all right. But he didn't get up. What could he do, after all? Perhaps she had been arrested and was sat in some guard post. Or she was with a doctor in one of these dark houses—how was he supposed to find her? All he could do was wait, all he ever did was wait, time after time—a whole life whiled away in waiting, with only death awaiting him at the end.

His thoughts wandered. Extreme exhaustion, and perhaps also the after-effects of the injection, caused him to fall asleep. Or rather, he fell into sleep as into some deadly abyss.

Later on, he was aware of her lying down on the couch beside him again. She was in excellent spirits. Yes, a patrol had stopped and detained her, but they had behaved very gallantly. 'Go and see your doctor', they had said. 'Hold a white handkerchief in your hand, and nobody will bother you!'

No, she had not been able to get into the house of the strange Dr. Pernies, but she had found another doctor, a most accommodating playboy type, who had opened the door to her in his pyjamas and given her a shot of morphine straightaway. She laughed merrily. And for him she had brought tablets—no, of course she had not forgotten her husband, never! He was to take these tablets right away, the doctor had said; they were as good as morphine, and very strong. She laughed again. 'Look, I've even got a few cigarettes. One of the soldiers in the patrol gave them to me. Let's see, eight, ten, twelve—wasn't that kind?'

This isn't right, Doll wanted to protest. *This is all heading in the wrong direction. We shouldn't be doing this kind of thing, getting hold of cigarettes like this, or the morphine. That business with Mrs. Schulz was already way out of order. We can't be doing this, even if I have thought to myself a hundred times that I'm all played out. We can't be doing this, otherwise we are completely finished. No more begging for cigarettes, no more running around after a shot of morphine ...*

But he said nothing. A leaden weariness had descended upon him, and the feeling of apathy had come back with renewed force. There was no point in talking to her: Alma would always do exactly as she pleased. She was so far away. It was as if he perceived and heard the world, and her, through a curtain; everything seemed somehow unconnected to him. Nothing mattered to him any more; as hard as he tried to be 'there', he couldn't do it. He had also taken the tablets, of course, the ones that had the same effect as morphine and were said to be very strong. Perhaps they would blot out these thoughts that haunted him, and transport him from this earthly abode for a while ...

He remained in this state for days on end—how many days? Later on, he couldn't say, and nor could she. At some point he awoke from an artificially induced deep sleep, and gazed at the little cellophane window. Then it was light or dark outside, day or night, but it was all the same, whatever it was—he stayed in bed anyway. What was there to get up for? He had nothing to do out there; he felt no sense of duty or responsibility.

He struggled to collect his thoughts, and then turned over slowly and looked beside him. Sometimes she was sleeping there next to him; sometimes she was gone. Sometimes he was gone, too (it sounded strange, but that was exactly the right way to put it!), and then she had nagged him to go and see a doctor. Yes, he did that, too, since she absolutely insisted, but the truth was that he stayed in bed and did nothing because he had no purpose or goal any more, was completely drained and empty ...

But generally she went herself, even though her leg was now constantly weeping pus, and all the doctors were saying she needed to be hospitalised immediately. They had quite a lot of doctors by now, but it was important that none of them knew about any of the others. Sometimes, when Alma had arranged for several of them to call on the same evening, she took fright in case they met up and it came out just how many shots she was getting every evening. But it always worked out all right. She usually got plenty of shots now, while he nearly always went without, but she made sure she got a good supply of sleeping pills for him. When the doctors came, he had to get dressed and play the healthy husband. In his own mind, he often felt like some sort of ghost, sitting there and making polite conversation about his sick wife's condition.

But if he was not able to get himself up and ready, he would go and hide in the little servants' toilet until they left, or else he squatted in the room that had been gutted by fire, and stared out at the ruins; their whole street consisted almost entirely of ruins. But they didn't depress him quite so much now; he and they seemed made for each other, somehow ...

When the doctors left, he went back to bed and soon fell asleep. Or else he lay there for hours, as if in a drugged stupor. And throughout this time, however many days it was, they did nothing, absolutely nothing at all. They didn't go to the housing office; they didn't apply for ration cards. They couldn't even be bothered to go and get the second couch. Their friends and relatives didn't hear a peep from them: they just lay there, as if struck down, stupefied, paralyzed, unable to think or do anything. The only thing that could rouse them briefly was the need to go and get more medicines, and maybe cigarettes …

They would have succumbed from weakness a long time ago, of course, if Mrs. Schulz had not looked after them, together with Dorle, a friend of the young wife's, who had turned up from somewhere—Doll didn't know where, or why. (Even in more normal times, he had never quite worked out who was who among his wife's many friends.)

But Mrs. Schulz would not have been Mrs. Schulz, always a dubious character even when she was doing good, if her ministrations for the sick couple had been in any way regular. She said she'd look in on them the next day, and then didn't show her face for two whole days. Not that it mattered that much to the Dolls—one day or three days or a week meant nothing to them now. If they got too hungry, Alma would sneak into the kitchen. A kind of friendship had developed between her and the little dancer—who was not a dancer at all, but an actress, and one of no small standing at that—and more especially with the woman's mother. Both parties had realised that the other was not as bad as they had initially thought. Alma usually returned from these trips to the kitchen with a little piece of bread, or even a jar of jam, but sometimes with only a plateful of cold potatoes or a few raw carrots. He no longer made any protest, but ate his share of whatever she'd got, before they both tried to sleep again and forget the world.

And now there was Dorle, this friend of his wife's. She was still a young girl, with a child and a mother. The mother had been in hospital since the fall of Berlin—she'd been shot in the leg, and the wound wouldn't heal. And the child had an insatiable appetite. So unlike Mrs. Schulz, Dorle was not able to help out with food for the Dolls; it was more a case of her sharing the food they had. But she cleaned the room, dusted, did the small amount of laundry there was, and dressed Mrs. Doll's wound as best she could. And she was always willing to go and fetch new doctors—more doctors in addition to the old ones. They could never have too many.

As for the Dolls' own financial situation, it would have been desperate without Mrs. Doll's diamond ring. Mrs. Schulz had managed to feed the Dolls for a week or two, but she couldn't keep it up for longer than that—presumably owing to lack of money. She hadn't said anything, but all of a sudden the white bread, decent coffee, and cigarettes stopped coming; instead of the mantra 'Cheap at the price!' the constant refrain that fell from Mrs. Schulz's lips now was: 'Dear me! The cost of everything these days!'

Then, one day, Mrs. Doll had said out of the blue that she intended to pawn her diamond ring—not sell it, she was too attached to it for that, but just pawn it. Doll had protested, but only feebly, because what other alternative did they have? They were just lying here, exhausted and ill; nobody was bringing them any money, but everything cost money—so there! Pawning was good, because it meant Alma could get her ring back again. One day, things would take a turn for the better, and they would be able to redeem the ring. (He knew very well that he was lying to himself and to her: there was not the remotest prospect of any turn for the better.) Mrs. Schulz was given the job of pawning the ring.

But the very next day she returned with the ring. She had found buyers for it, serious buyers who were prepared to pay handsomely, but nobody wanted to take it in pawn. Lending money was not a sound business proposition these days: you could earn more in a day on the black market than you could in a month from the interest payments on a loan. But there were people willing to buy the ring, and after a good deal of probing Mrs. Doll learned that twelve thousand marks had been offered for it. A good price, surely? But then it was a very fine ring: platinum setting, fiery white diamond, flawless, nearly one and a quarter carats.

In business matters, Mrs. Doll was always something of a surprise—not least to her own husband. She asked for the ring back. 'No', she said later to her husband, 'if they're offering twelve thousand, they can go to fifteen thousand, and they probably offered fifteen thousand anyway, and Schulz is planning to pocket the three thousand difference. No, I'll get Ben to sell the ring for me; he's much better connected than old mother Schulz ...'

Ben! The ring was unquestionably Alma's, a present from her first husband, and Doll had made up his mind to hold his tongue and not interfere in the matter of the sale. But now, briefly roused from his apathy and the stupor induced by too many sleeping pills, he expostulated: 'Ben, of all people! The man who treated us so shabbily!'

'That was just the two women!' countered Alma. 'Don't forget, he was really pushed for time that day.'

'He didn't even have a cigarette for you!' cried Doll.

'We often don't have any cigarettes', replied Alma. 'You leave it to me. You'll see—we'll get a much better price with Ben!'

'Do what you like!' And with that, Doll sank back into his apathy. 'I just hope Ben doesn't let you down again!'

As a result of this conversation, Mr. Ben turned up one day while the couple were still in bed, even though it was getting on for lunchtime. But Mr. Ben evinced no surprise; with greying hair but dark, fiery eyes, he kissed the young woman's hand, examined the ring closely, declared that he knew nothing about precious stones, but would see if it was possible to get the asking price of twenty thousand marks. At all events, he would certainly get the best price for it that he could—Alma could count on him. After Mr. Ben had handed over fifteen hundred marks he happened to have on him, to meet the Dolls' immediate needs, he disappeared again with the ring, kissing hands as he departed ...

Whether Mrs. Schulz was annoyed or not that the ring had been taken away from her again (and with it, perhaps, a substantial commission), the fact was she had an excellent nose for money. Mr. Ben's fifteen hundred marks had not been in the Dolls' possession for more than a few hours before Mrs. Schulz showed up with a little notebook, and it turned out that she believed she had a claim on the Dolls that exceeded this fifteen hundred by a fair amount. The Dolls listened in astonishment as she reeled off an endless litany of cigarettes, coffee, sugar, salt, cakes, and potatoes. Nor had the partition wall been forgotten, re-erected by a tradesman 'as a favour'—a favour for which he had charged handsomely. From the very first day, every item had been carefully recorded, including everything she had made out was a gift from her, and for which she had unblushingly received their heartfelt thanks. Now it was all listed here as goods supplied to order—and not 'cheap at the price', either! Indeed, they had a lurking suspicion that Mrs. Schulz had not only charged them for the cigarettes and coffee she had supplied, but also for quite a few cigarettes that had never been smoked, and quite a few cups of coffee that had never been drunk ...

Things might have come to a head on this occasion, with an almighty row that would at least have cleared the air, had it not been for the fact that neither of the Dolls could care less what happened to them. There was a brief eruption of anger—but even this took place only after Mrs. Schulz had gone (having dropped this bombshell, the good woman had had the good sense to withdraw and await the outcome from a distance)—and Alma swore they would never accept anything from old mother Schulz again, not so much as a single cigarette. So the fifteen hundred marks now changed hands again, and Ben was informed through Dorle that he needed to bring more money straightaway.

But this time Mr. Ben let a few days pass before doing anything. And when he did finally show up, he claimed that the ring had not yet been sold. He was very sorry to have to tell them that prices for gold and precious stones were falling, and that it was a bad time to be selling. He did have someone in prospect, however, who might be prepared to pay the asking price—maybe not the full twenty, but certainly nineteen or eighteen thousand. At all events: 'You know I'll do whatever I can for you, Alma!'

Meanwhile, he had brought two thousand marks with him, an advance taken out of his own pocket, and not without considerable sacrifice—as he mentioned several times.

But for now, the Dolls' boat was afloat again, the balance of their debt to Mrs. Schulz was paid off, and from then on Dorle took care of all the Dolls' shopping.

CHAPTER SEVEN

A parting of the ways

In terms of days and weeks, the Dolls would have found it impossible to say how long they had been lying on their couch. At all events, it seemed like an eternity, a time when they were never fully awake, never attending to anything beyond the most urgent necessities of life.

The young woman's need for injections of narcotics had increased in inverse proportion to the doctors' inclination to dispense them, and the abscess on her upper thigh, which had never been treated properly, was getting worse. The doctors were becoming ever more insistent: 'Either you get to hospital, or we stop treating you!'

The economic situation of the Dolls was also becoming steadily more impossible. Ben's visits became increasingly irregular, and he brought less and less money with him. The ring had still not been sold, he still had to 'make sacrifices' in order to advance them sums from his own pocket, and the amounts got steadily smaller—first a thousand marks, then only five hundred. The state of the market in precious stones was just too bad. It was not advisable to sell right now; one would not even make fifteen, and maybe a lot less than that. But he would keep on trying, true friend of Alma's that he was …

Until one day the young woman suddenly made up her mind

and said: 'I'm going to get myself admitted to hospital today!' And a moment later she added: 'But first I'm going to take you to your sanatorium!'

This time she really meant it. The young woman displayed an energy that she had not shown for days or months past. She sorted out some underwear and toiletries for her husband, and when he asked: 'And what about you?' she just replied: 'Don't you worry about me, I can take care of myself!'

If Doll had been a little more alert and not so apathetic, he would not have ceased to wonder at his wife's sudden new-found energy; she even managed to get hold of their district mayor, and scrounged a car from him to drive her seriously ill husband to a sanatorium.

At some point, Doll awoke there from a sleep so deep that it had been more like death, without memories or dreams or any obvious sign of breathing ... Still feeling completely dazed, he turned his head with an effort, looking around him for someone to ask where he was, and where Alma was. He had always felt her presence next to him in bed, now she was gone, and he was all alone. This discovery made him very agitated, and helped to clear the fog in his brain (from the sleeping pills) more quickly; he sat up in bed and looked around him ...

The iron bedstead he was sitting in had once been painted white, but now the paint was chipped and battered; a blue check bedcover lay across his body. The room was very small, and contained nothing apart from this bedstead. The wall was painted to head height with green oil paint, and above that it was whitewashed like the ceiling, on which, very high above him, an electric light was burning. A section of the ceiling plaster had fallen off: he could see the exposed reed lathing and the boards to which it had been fixed ...

For a moment, he sat and stared at all this. He had to think where he had seen this damaged ceiling before. Then he suddenly remembered. Suddenly he recalled the night of 15–16 February 1944, when one of the worst air raids he ever experienced went on for fifty-five minutes over Berlin. For fifty-five minutes bombs had rained down in the immediate vicinity of the sanatorium, and in the next block everything had been completely flattened by an aerial mine. They—the patients and the nurses—were sitting in a completely inadequate air-raid shelter that was half above ground, and they had seen the glow of the fires in every direction. When they emerged after the all-clear, all the glass from the windows in the rooms lay scattered across the floor, most of the ceilings had collapsed, and some time that night the piece of plaster up there on the ceiling had fallen off.

He now remembered it again very clearly; suddenly it was as if he could feel the horror and the fear of that night all over again. Suddenly he had the feeling that the siren could go off any minute, and force him down into the basement for another terrible hour of torment.

But then he remembered: it was peacetime now, peacetime … There were no more sirens going off. He could safely carry on sleeping in the sanatorium's padded cell until the morning, the padded cell that Sister Emerentia just called 'the little room'. But how had he, Mr. Doll, ended up in this little room? Had he been so disturbed? Had he been raving? Never once had he been put in here when he was staying at the sanatorium before! At least he wasn't just lying on mattresses on the floor; they had left the bedstead for him, so it couldn't have been that bad. And it was only now that he noticed they'd left the iron-lined door of the cell ajar, so he couldn't have been in a very bad way.

Doll sat up gingerly on the edge of the bed. He still felt a little shaky from the sleeping pills, but he thought he would be able to walk if he leaned against the wall now and then. He automatically looked around for his slippers and dressing gown, but then he remembered that he no longer possessed such things. So he draped the bed cover around his shoulders, stepped out into the corridor, and walked along to the lobby.

As always, sitting in the big plush armchair by the light of the little auxiliary lamp, was the night nurse. For a while, Doll observed him from a distance. No, it wasn't the nice Dutchman who had been on night duty here throughout the war, and who often enough had been dragging the last unwilling patients out of their beds and down to the basement even as the bombs were already falling. It was a nurse he didn't know. Still— !

Doll gave a small cough and walked forward. The startled nurse woke from his semi-sleep, peered into the gloom, and then leaned back, reassured, having recognised Doll. 'So, you're awake, too?' he asked. And then added: 'Mind you don't catch cold, walking around like that in your bare feet!'

'No way!' replied Doll, sitting down in a wicker chair opposite the nurse, and wrapping the bed cover around his legs. 'I never get colds. I'm a tough nut. Once I lay for half a day on the red floor tiles outside the tea kitchen back there, in winter, and it did me no harm.'

'Not my idea of fun!' said the nurse. 'What did you do that for?'

'Can't remember', said Doll. 'Probably to get some medication they wouldn't have given me otherwise. Did you come straight after Simon Boom?'

'Who's that? Oh yes, I know who you mean: the Dutch night porter. No, I didn't ever meet him. They got rid of him as soon as the war ended. I've only been here a few weeks.'

'Are any of the old staff still on the ward? I expect you've heard that I was here quite often—I'm more or less a regular on the ward.'

He said it with a touch of pride. This was a place where he had always gone when his overwrought nerves, never very strong, went completely to pieces. He'd gone through some difficult times in this place—bouts of depression when he had given up completely on himself, when he thought he was losing his mind—but always he had managed to pull himself together somehow. Suddenly, from one day to the next, he had declared himself fit again, and had gone back to his work ...

He loved the place, but especially this ward with its long corridor leading to the toilets, echoing with the footsteps of patients at all hours of the day and night; this corridor with its rust-red linoleum, onto which so many white doors opened, but all without door handles—so they could only be opened by the nurses with their keys—and with big glass windows that allowed people to see into the room from outside, windows with glass so thick that even the most agitated patient could not smash it with a chair leg.

He loved the mysterious atmosphere that permeated the place after every 'exitus', the nurses standing around aimlessly, and repeatedly shuffling all the patients back into their rooms, since they were not supposed to find out about the death. It was always 'unfortunate' when someone in the sanatorium died, because all the staff felt that it reflected badly on them: people didn't come here to die; they came to get well! And generally the management were able to smuggle a dying patient out shortly before the end, and transfer him to a city hospital.

He loved the 'shock days', when the patients were treated with Cardiazol or insulin, or given electric shocks. From his room he would suddenly hear the screams of the patients being shocked as they lost consciousness, which sounded exactly like the cries of an epileptic. And then a deathly hush would descend, as if those who had been spared didn't dare move, lest they attract a similar fate.

He particularly loved sitting around—against the rules—in the 'tea kitchen', where nobody ever made tea any more but only washed up, and chatting for ages there with the nurse who had known him for many years ... She gave him extra food whenever she could. He liked the woman, who was still quite young, still attractive, and had been living for twenty years now among these men who were slowly dying; despite the loss of all her illusions, she had retained her helpful disposition and mother wit.

And he loved the ward rounds, when the doctors came around in their long, spotlessly white coats; for them, each patient was just another case, which held no more interest for them once the illness had passed through the acute stage. He was quietly amused by these psychiatrists, who studied the slightest mood swings in their patients in minute detail, but for whom physical ailments simply didn't exist. He loved these doctors precisely because the older and more knowledgeable they became, the more they seemed to resemble their patients, because they seemed to be so disconnected from real life.

He loved the walks in the little, high-walled gardens, which looked nothing like gardens at all, being places of the utmost dreariness. He loved the sudden eruption of noise out in the corridor, when an agitated patient was being hustled into the padded cell or the bathroom. He loved the whole building with its dense, stifling atmosphere, its enveloping feeling of security, the life behind the narrow iron windows. It was like home to him.

'Tell me', he asked the night nurse Bachmann later, 'why am I in the bunker? Was I that agitated? Did I smash something up?'

'Not at all!' replied the nurse. 'You were as gentle as a lamb. But there were no rooms free when you arrived, so they put you in there.'

'Were you here when I arrived? Have you seen my wife?'

'No, you arrived before I came on duty, in the afternoon. I don't know anything about it. You were pretty well drugged up, I think, but then they gave you something more.'

'I see!' said Doll. And then again: 'I see!' But he didn't continue the conversation; he just sat there quietly, and drew the bed cover more tightly around him. He suddenly realised that he didn't even know which hospital Alma had been admitted to. He couldn't write to her, send her a message, or call her. He was alone: for the first time in ages, he was completely alone again, and suddenly he felt how weak he still was, and how unwell.

He stood up. Without even thinking about it, he began to walk up and down, the bed cover draped around his shoulders, just as he had spent many previous nights wandering up and down this long corridor, getting through the endless hours of insomnia.

And that was how the old night sister found him. She called out to him in her high-pitched old woman's voice, with no regard for the other patients who were sleeping: 'And here's our very own Dr. Doll again! So how are you, Doctor? How do you like it in our little room?' And with a little giggle: 'Sister Emerentia has been having a little joke, putting Mr. Doll in the little room, our old regular! Well, you needn't worry, Mr. Doll, we'll get that sorted out. It's just that we've had over two hundred notices of admission, and not a single bed free for weeks. So when someone turns up without any notification ...'

'But they did notify you', grunted Doll. It wasn't strictly true, but ...

'Of course they did!' cried the sister, becoming more and more animated and high-pitched. 'It's no disgrace to be put in the cell if you're as good and well-behaved as Dr. Doll, is it, Mr. Bachmann?'

The night nurse grunted in agreement. 'But now it's time to get back into bed. It's much too early to be running around like this—it's only half-past two ... You'll catch cold otherwise!'

'Never get colds—'

'Of course you do; of course you catch cold! And if you can't sleep, I'll give you a little something to help you. What would you like to help you sleep?'

If he hadn't already been thinking it, this question was all it took to transport him back immediately to the old game they used to play there, namely to inveigle as many sleeping tablets out of the staff as they possibly could. He said dismissively: 'Look, just let me walk around for a bit! You're not going to give me anything that does any good—you're all out to cheat a poor, wretched, sick man!'

Night nurse Trudchen uttered a horrified shriek. 'Doctor, how can you say such a thing, an educated man like yourself! When have I ever cheated you? But of course', the night nurse went on, 'if someone constantly misbehaves and is always kicking up a racket, then I sometimes give him scopolamine instead of Luminal. But that's not cheating by any stretch—that's a medical procedure!'

'Aha!'

'But such a thing has never been necessary in your case, Doctor! I tell you what, I'll give you some paraldehyde. You always called that your tipple—you always liked taking that!'

'Well, yes, but how much are you going to give me?' asked Doll, now suddenly very interested. Paraldehyde was not a bad suggestion from Trudchen; she'd got the measure of her patients, having done night duty in the sanatorium for over thirty years now. She took the place of a fully qualified night-duty doctor, so the privy councillor gave her a free hand when it came to prescribing and dispensing drugs.

'How much am I going to let you have?' asked the night nurse, and gave Doll a quick, searching look to appraise how much he needed. 'Well, I'll give you a three-line dose of paral …'

Doll yanked the bed cover around his shoulders again and made as if to carry on pacing up and down. 'You can keep your three lines, Sister Trudchen!' he replied contemptuously. 'I'd rather carry on walking all night than be fobbed off with kiddy portions.' And as he turned away, he said insistently: 'I want eight lines, at least!'

Squeals of protest, much babble, and earnest entreaties: 'You know very well, Dr. Doll, that five is the maximum dose!' But Mr. Doll was not a bit interested in such absurd made-up notions as a 'maximum dose': he was immune to poison! He'd had sixteen once (a complete fabrication). The negotiations began, with Sister Trudchen imploring and pleading, Doll acting like some stiff-backed Spaniard spurning beggarly gifts, ready to walk away at any moment, but inwardly pumped up with the excitement of the chase. He thought to himself: *You lot are pretty dumb! I'd sleep just fine without a sleeping draught—I'm still full of the stuff from before. But I'm not letting on!* In the end, they settled on a six-line dose. Doll promised to go straight to bed, and the sister agreed not to dilute the paraldehyde with water. 'And if it burns your throat, Doctor, it won't be me who's hurting!'

Doll lay in his bed again, in the little room. This hospital was all right; in its way, it was a terrific hospital. He lay in bed at his ease, hands clasped behind his head, waiting for his bitter-tasting sleeping draught. He thought briefly about Alma, but now without any sense of yearning, without feeling an urgent need to rush off and see her. That wasn't necessary. Alma was also lying in a hospital bed, her wound was being treated and dressed every day, so she too was in good hands, just like himself—no need to worry!

As always in this place, the sleeping draught was a long time coming. This was a ploy by the staff to make the drug seem like a really precious commodity—either that, or they were just slow and disorganised. The patients weren't going anywhere, after all: they could wait. Doll heard Sister Trudchen talking to the male night nurse in the nurses' room, making no attempt to keep her voice down. In the past, he had sometimes kicked up a fuss about this lack of consideration, which showed no regard for the patients' need of a good night's sleep. But now he just smiled. It was just part of life in this place. And kicking up a fuss only created problems for the management: it just meant that even more sleeping draughts had to be administered.

For a moment, Doll saw clearly that this had been a stupid conclusion to draw: it wasn't bad for the doctors if the patients were given too many drugs to make them sleep; it was only bad for the patients, who then went around all next day in a semi-stupor. In terms of Doll's case, Sister Trudchen couldn't care less whether Doll received three, eight, or sixteen lines of paraldehyde. In actual fact, he didn't need any more at all, and he felt very relaxed in bed. His limbs, which had been icy cold, were gradually warming up again; he only needed to turn over in bed and fall asleep.

But no, it was better to be knocked out all at once, to not be there any more.

There was a poem that was printed at the front of a collection of short stories by Irene Forbes-Mosse. It was called 'The little death', and began something like this: 'The little death, how gladly would I die, the little death as stars light up the sky …'

The poet was undoubtedly talking about a very different kind of death, but Doll called this sensation of being knocked out quickly by drugs his 'Little Death'. He loved him. Recently he had thought so much about his big brother, 'Big Death': he had lived with him, cheek by jowl, so to speak; he had grown used to seeing him as the last remaining hope, which would surely not disappoint him. He just needed a little more resolve than he could summon up at the moment, and then it was done. And until he could muster that little bit more resolve, he had 'Little Death'. Right now, he was waiting for his six grams of paral, and as soon as they were inside him, he was done with all this reflection and analysis. He didn't have to torment himself any more, he didn't have to justify anything to himself any more, why Dr. Doll did this and didn't do that, because there was no Doll any more …

All the same, it was high time they showed up with their sleeping draughts. Doll leapt out of bed and went across to the nurses' room. The door was open, and the night nurse had already seen him. 'Here's Dr. Doll again! Come on, Sister, give him his stuff now!'

The sister had already picked up the brown bottle, and said (still smarting from Mr. Doll's unwarranted suspicion): 'The Doctor can see for himself that I'm not cheating him! As if I ever would! I'm more likely to give you too much than too little!'

And she poured it out. The characteristic smell of paral wafted through the room—and a vile smell it is, if truth be told. But to Doll it smelt good, wonderful! He watched closely as she poured it out, and even nodded in agreement when the sister exclaimed: 'You see that, you've nearly got seven there! Now, aren't I good to you, Doctor?'

But he was no longer in the mood for talk. He had the little medicine glass in his hand; at last, at long last, he had deep sleep, Little Death, in his hand, and was completely enveloped by the scent. He was done with talking now. His face had taken on an earnest, almost sombre, expression: he was by himself now, just him and his sleep. He tipped the entire contents of the glass into his mouth at once. It burned his throat more fiercely than the strongest schnaps, it felt like it was eating into the lining of his mouth, and made it impossible to breathe. Much as he didn't want to, he had to take two little gulps of water to dilute this—wonderful—taste of death. Then he looked at his two companions again, murmured a brief 'Night!' and went back to his cell, into his bed. He lay there for a moment, hands clasped behind his head, gazing up at the light.

His head seemed to fill with moving clouds, he tried to focus his thoughts on this and that, but already he was gone from this world, into the arms of his beloved Little Death …

At some point he would wake up again, and each time his mood was different. Sometimes he would lie sullenly in his cell for hours, hardly speaking at all, and when the doctor came on his ward round he refused to volunteer any information. Or else he would cry quietly to himself for hours on end; at such times, he felt full of pity for himself and his wasted life, and felt as if he was going to die. On days like these, he wouldn't eat or drink anything: let them watch him croak in his stinking cell … And then on other days he was in a sunny mood, and with his bed cover wrapped around his shoulders he would scoot around all over the place, talking to the other patients.

The young ward doctor was friendly with him, tried to help him, and wanted to understand where this mixture of apathy and despair in Doll came from. But Doll didn't want to talk about it; maybe he would never be able to talk about it, not even to his wife, to Alma. Maybe he would be able to write himself free of it one day—but only when it was all behind them. Sometimes he believed he would get well again, that there would be something there again to fill up the emptiness inside him. But those times were the exception.

Mostly he tried to throw the young doctor off the scent; he would tell him something about his life, talk about books, encourage the young doctor to talk about himself—about the bad pay, the even worse food, the long hours he had to work, the arrogant way the privy councillor treated his staff. Or else he tried to winkle information out of the young doctor about the different ways of committing suicide. He was very clever at doing this: he found out about cyanide, morphine, scopolamine, about dosages that were guaranteed to be fatal; about how to inject air into the veins to cause an embolism; about insulin, which enabled someone to commit suicide in a way that was virtually undetectable later. He was gathering information: he wanted to be ready when the time came and he felt strong enough to do 'it', to take the only way out that was still left to a German today.

PART TWO

Recovery

CHAPTER EIGHT

Voluntary discharge

While Doll was leading a life of idleness up on 'Men's Ward III', albeit forced to be a little more wide-awake each day as the dosage of sleeping drugs was progressively reduced, it could not escape his attention as the ward's resident patient that the other patients on the ward were now a very different bunch from before. The paralytics and schizophrenics had given way completely to a relatively transitory clientele, which appeared to be neither mentally ill nor emotionally disturbed.

These patients generally arrived in the evening, and were rarely accompanied by relatives. There was often a kind of strange, unreal hilarity about them, and they were very ready to engage in conversation and to dispense the most expensive English and American cigarettes with a generous hand. Later on, they would be taken off to the bathroom, with some gentle persuasion, by two male nurses, and while they were sitting in the bathtub the ward sister and the female nurse would go through their belongings very thoroughly. Doll sometimes watched them, and saw how they checked every corner of the pockets and every envelope with meticulous care, whereas earlier they had been content just to remove anything with a blade or point, and perhaps the dressing-gown cord as well, which some depressives used to commit suicide.

When the new arrivals emerged from the bath they were put to bed immediately, despite all their protests. There was no more chatting with the other patients. A nurse stood guard by their bed, the young doctor appeared, usually an intravenous injection was given, and the patient fell asleep. He was usually kept in this comatose state for a week. But sometimes there would be a lot of noise coming from the room—shouting and screaming, and the sound of feet dragging across the floor—and through the window in the door, Doll would catch a glimpse of a figure in pyjamas, wrestling with the sister and a male nurse, and hear him saying: 'You're driving me crazy! I want to …' And the soothing voice of reason: 'If you could just hold on for a moment, Doctor!' (Nearly all these patients were addressed as 'Doctor'.) 'The doctor is on his way …'

And sure enough, the doctor summoned by telephone quickly arrived on the scene—quite often it was the privy councillor himself—fresh injections were given, different sleeping drugs administered, and everything quietened down again.

Once this first week was past, the patient appeared from time to time, leaning on the arm of the nurse. Puffy-faced and drugged up to the eyeballs, he would make his way to or from the toilet, and it was not uncommon for him to stop part-way, lean his head against the wall, and groan: 'I can't go on, I just can't go on! What an idiot I was to come here!'

Idiots or not, it was obvious even to a layman that these patients made rapid progress. By the third week, most of them were wandering up and down the corridor fully dressed, leaning against the window, gazing outside and declaring impatiently: 'It's high time I got out of this place!' And for the most part they did disappear again quite quickly, especially the ones who were actually entitled to be addressed as 'Doctor', and new patients of a similar sort moved into their rooms.

Even someone less familiar with such places than Doll would have worked out after three days what was going on with these patients. So when one of these 'Doctors' spoke quite openly to Doll one day, he wasn't telling him anything he did not already know: 'It's all right for you, my dear fellow, you can stay here as long as you like. But I've got to get out again as soon as possible. I don't want anyone outside to know that I'm here, or why I'm here.'

Of course they didn't want anyone to know. They were medical doctors, after all, doctors who'd become addicted to morphine, who came here to be cured of their addiction in complete secrecy, and in particular without the knowledge of the feared public health authority. The fact that most of them were doctors was due to the circumstance that they had ready access to morphine at a time when it was in very short supply. If the drug had been more widely available and easy to buy, then doubtless three-quarters of the German population would have used it to anaesthetise themselves against the malady of the age—a mixture of bottomless despair and apathy.

So it was mainly doctors or other people with plenty of money who could afford the black-market prices for morphine. They began with one or two injections. These were enough to take away their cares, so that cold, hunger, the pain of loss—whether of people or of things—no longer troubled them. But gradually they had to increase the dose. What had worked a week earlier no longer worked now. So it was a case of step up the dose, and then step it up some more. In the beginning, they had only injected themselves at night, before going to bed, and then the afternoons began to drag, and another shot was just the thing to help them get through that, and eventually they could no longer get up in the mornings to face an endless grey day. In the end, they had used so much morphine that either the chemists had become suspicious or they had completely lost their zest for work. Or else their wives, relatives, or friends began to distrust them, and their marriage, their whole social standing, and their livelihood were put at risk: a man addicted to morphine was no longer a doctor who brought healing, but a sick man who was a danger to others. So they quickly disappeared inside a sanatorium. To the outside world, they were suffering from angina, and a friendly colleague stepped in as a locum—just as long as the public health authority, the body to which they were answerable, didn't find out about it.

Doll looked upon this endless succession of addicts as companions in suffering, people just like himself, who despaired of themselves and of Germany, who had broken down under the weight of all the humiliations and obscenities, and sought refuge in some artificial paradise. Just like himself, they were all seeking their own 'Little Death'. Maybe they all still cherished a tiny hope that kept them from taking the ultimate step; maybe they all still needed—just like Doll—that last, final push. Everywhere people were escaping from the present, refusing to shoulder the burden that a shameful war had laid upon all Germans.

But behind his own person, behind all these transient visitors up on Men's Ward III, loomed a dark and menacing multitude: the entire German nation. There had been a time, a time of illusion it had been, but during this time Doll had known that he was not lying all alone in that huge bomb crater: the entire German nation was in there with him. As the morphine-addicted doctors had cut themselves off from this nation, so too had Doll. Walking up and down the rust-red linoleum of the corridor at night for hours on end, lying in bed in his cell for hours on end, staring up at the ceiling light, he reflected and pondered, looked back over the road he had travelled to get here, deeper and deeper into selfish isolation—running away like a coward from the job they were all called upon to do …

But the German nation was out there. It could not be denied or argued away; it was there, and he belonged to it. While he was sitting idly in here, featherbedding himself, living off the charity extended to him by this place, in consideration of the times he had stayed here before, the German people were hard at work. They had cleared away the tank traps and the rubble from the streets, and were now repairing roofs and winter-proofing people's homes. They retrieved burnt-out machinery and got it working again. They were hungry, they were cold, but they repaired the railway tracks, dug for potatoes in the icy October rain, and hiked along the highways in endless columns, making do with next to nothing.

While Doll was gazing enviously at the extra rations of the other patients, the milk was drying up in the breasts of mothers and children who were starving to death. While Doll was arguing with the night-duty nurse over an extra sleeping draught, old women and men, exhausted beyond endurance, were lying down in roadside ditches or in the rain-soaked forest to fall asleep for the last time. While soldiers returning home were looking for everything—their old home, their wives and children, food and work, week after week, never giving up hope—it was too much effort for Dr. Doll to go and speak to some official about their apartment and their ration cards. While Doll lived the life of a freeloader, supported by the proceeds from the sale of his wife's jewellery, and complained bitterly that the money wasn't falling into his lap fast enough, money that he promptly squandered anyway, frail girls were doing hard, physical labour, so poorly paid that they couldn't afford to buy a cigarette—at prices that Doll had long since come to regard as normal.

The fact of the matter was that he had lost his way completely, and had lapsed into a shamefully useless and idle, parasitic existence. He saw clearly the path that had led him to the padded cell in this place, sinking deeper and deeper into the swamp and quagmire since that day, 26 April. And yet he had no idea how he could have gone down this path. How had he got himself into such a state over a harmless schmuck like Piglet Willem? And how come he had let himself get so worked up about the beer wholesaler Zaches? He'd always known what these Nazis were like, after all. All this pointless running around after doctors and sleeping drugs and injections, which didn't change anything, and just made every decision that had to be taken even harder!

And then there was something else as well. This Dr. Doll who had just come to his senses a bit, this writer of books who had thought he had nothing more to write, this brooding self-doubter, who had thought himself completely empty and drained, this ex-mayor who had not been up to the job, this father and husband who had forgotten all about his wife and children—suddenly he thought about his children, and, full of concern, he thought about his wife, too. Now that Doll felt he was getting better, and that there might still be some sort of work for him to do in this life, in the midst of a population that was labouring with grim determination once more, he suddenly remembered his wife, and felt fearful on her account.

By this time, Doll was getting some news of his wife. She hadn't written, of course, but one day Dorle turned up to see him, his wife's loyal friend, and she had brought him a brand-new nightshirt, and cigarettes, and half a loaf of bread. Yes indeed, his wife was thinking of him, she never forgot him, she was worried about him, and she took care of him. She loved him, and he loved her—once more.

He'd just forgotten the fact while he was ill, that was all.

Doll smoked, and wolfed down half the white loaf at a single sitting. Dorle sat on the edge of the bed and talked. She told him that Alma was the darling of everyone at the hospital, even the strict, devout nuns, and that everyone there spoiled her, including the doctors. Her wound had been really bad; the infection had gone quite deep because of the delay in treatment. But now it was looking better; they had sprinkled sugar in the wound, an old home remedy, and since then it was a lot better ...

And Alma had a bit of money again. Ben had eventually—after many phone calls—turned up at the hospital and had brought money with him, though only two-and-a-half thousand. Apparently he had said that with the continuing fall in the market for diamonds he had only been able to get eleven thousand in total, and he just hadn't been able to make any more. Alma had been furious with Ben, and she had forbidden her, Dorle, to mention the matter to Doll; Dorle implored him not to let on to Alma that he knew. A woman who shared the room with Alma, and who was very knowledgeable about the black market, had apparently told Alma that a ring like the one she had described would easily fetch twenty-five thousand marks, maybe even thirty thousand. 'So you can just imagine how angry Alma was', said Dorle, and added that she was done with her good friend Ben once and for all.

Doll shared her anger, but his anger was mixed with mild gratification, since no husband can avoid feeling a little jealous of his wife's former men friends, and is always glad to see the back of them. He listened patiently, therefore, when Dorle diffidently, but understandably, sang her own praises—how she was such a good friend to Alma, willing to do anything for her, through thick and thin. And as he listened to her prattling on, he thought to himself:

My dear, good, stupid Dorle! You, too, will only be such a good friend to Alma for as long as you can still get something out of her. And Alma must know this herself. Do you think I haven't noticed that there you are, all innocent and unassuming, already lighting up the third of the ten cigarettes you brought me? I bet you do the same with Alma, even though she's very willing to share — much too willing, in fact, and quite extravagant; she wants to share rather than have her things pilfered from her. And one day it will be all over with her as far as the friendly feelings are concerned — and that includes you!

Such were Doll's thoughts, but he kept them to himself, asking instead how it was going with his wife's painkilling injections. Here again, Dorle had all the answers. To begin with, Alma had had quite a few injections, but then the senior consultant had laid down the law, and now the patient was allowed just one small shot at night, and not every night at that. So she had to stage an elaborate little routine first with the young night-duty doctor, which usually achieved the desired result, the young doctor readily succumbing to her charms when she begged, pouted, cried, wailed, laughed, turned her face to the wall, and sulked — then immediately leapt out of bed when the doctor turned to leave and clung on to him, only to go through the whole rigmarole all over again. And if that failed to do the trick, the doctor was very amenable to foreign cigarettes, which he could not afford on his small salary. So Alma usually ended up getting her evening shot — according to Dorle.

Having reflected on this news for a couple of days, Doll decided it was time for him to go and check on Alma for himself. And anyway, it would be very nice to see the look of joy and surprise on his young wife's face when her seriously ill husband suddenly appeared in the door of her room. Doll knew the privy councillor, and rightly doubted whether he would give him permission at this stage to go out on his own into the city. Doll was right in the middle of coming off his sleeping medication, and his moods had not yet quite stabilised; so the doctors were likely to suspect that if he went off into the city on his own, he would try to get hold of additional sedatives or other, more powerful drugs. That's what these doctors were like, or so their patients thought—and therefore Dr. Doll, too: always distrusting their patients, and never able to distinguish the goats from the sheep.

But if Doll was acquainted with the privy councillor and his suspicious ways, he was also familiar with the routines of the establishment, and it was around them that he now constructed his plan to slip out of the locked-down Men's Ward III for a city visit. After lunch, when one shift of nurses was going off for their break and the next shift was returning from theirs, in that moment of transition when nobody was really in charge on the ward, Doll audaciously claimed that someone had phoned through to say that he should report to the office briefly to discuss his account.

'Well, you'd better get along to the office then!' said the male nurse with casual indifference, and unlocked the door for him.

Doll descended the stairs. The stairs reminded him that he was still very unsteady on his feet, and that this outing into the city was really quite a bold undertaking. Steps now struck him as a funny sort of arrangement; they were never quite where you expected them to be. His knees wobbled, and a light sweat immediately broke out on his brow. But he had successfully got past the first obstacle, and now it was time to tackle the second one, the main door out of the building. Sitting in the porter's lodge was a girl who was always alert, and she would never press the button to open the door without good reason.

Doll tapped on the window of the lodge and then said amiably to the face that peered out: 'The privy councillor phoned through to the ward—he wants me to go and see him in the spa house.' (This was the main building of the sanatorium, where the privy councillor also resided.) 'I'm Doll, by the way, from Men's Ward III upstairs.'

The girl nodded, then gave him a searching look. She said 'I know', but this 'I know' was in reference only to Doll's name and ward number.

Doll smiled again. 'Maybe you should call the privy councillor', he said softly, 'just to check that it's OK.'

But even before he finished the sentence she had made up her mind. She pressed the button, and the door lock buzzed. Doll said 'Thanks!', and he was standing outside in the grounds. The gate to the grounds was unlocked, and beyond that the street was just a few steps away.

But he said to himself: *I mustn't go out into the street here—the girl might be watching me through the window. I must go through the grounds to the spa house, and use the exit there. She was a little bit suspicious, I thought. It's good that I'm only wearing my suit, and don't have my hat and coat. Nobody goes out dressed like this in late November. Lucky she doesn't know that I don't own a hat or coat!*

He smiled to himself. He strolled through the grounds, hands in pockets, expecting any minute to run into a doctor or nurse who would not be taken in so easily. But he was in luck, and he managed to get past the main villa unchallenged and on to the street, where he now quickened his pace and headed off towards the underground station.

It was damned cold, though. Hopefully, Alma would soon be up and about, and the first thing they needed to do was to go back to the small town and fetch some different clothes more suited to the time of year. Well, no, the first thing was to sort out the business with their apartment and the ration cards. They had a lot to do before he could settle down to work in earnest again!

It was really too cold for the summer suit he was wearing, and he was glad when he was finally sitting in the underground train, where it was a little warmer. Now his teeth weren't chattering quite so much. People couldn't stop staring at him because he was so lightly clad, but let them take him for a fitness fanatic if they wanted to ...

He sat on a bench, his hands between his knees, his face leaning forward slightly so that it stayed in the shadows. He felt dreadful, overcome with nausea, and the sweating he had experienced on the stairs started again. Those damned dried vegetables he'd had for lunch! It made him feel sick just to think of it. Had they gone through the whole war eating dried vegetables, just to have them dished up now in peacetime, with a helping of mouse droppings?! *It's outrageous—the noble privy councillor can't get rich quickly enough!*

But a moment later, Doll had to admit that it was not the dried vegetables that had made him feel ill. He did get two second helpings from the male nurse Franz, after all—and the mouse droppings may not have been mouse droppings at all, but perhaps a bit of burnt turnip. The truth is, it was just too soon for this little jaunt. He wasn't properly well again yet. And it was too cold!

He felt this especially keenly as he made his way slowly from the last underground station to the hospital. It was not very far—a ten-minute walk normally—but today it took him half an hour. He was no longer feeling cheerful, and not especially looking forward to seeing Alma again. Tripping over a granite paving slab that had been dislodged by a bomb, all he could think about on the wearisome trek to the hospital was the even more wearisome return journey afterwards—that, and the reception that awaited him at the sanatorium. They'd be looking for him by now. The male nurse and the girl in the porter's lodge who had let him out would be getting it in the neck. There would be big trouble when he got back! Well, he was already in the little room, so they could hardly put him anywhere worse by way of punishment. Was this endless road going to go on forever? And then it began to drizzle—just the sort of weather you wanted for a little jaunt like this!

But when he was taken to Alma by one of those nuns whose smile, like something lifted from a painting of the Madonna, always has a mysteriously unsettling quality about it, and he found himself standing in the door of Alma's hospital room, and saw her lying there in bed—her back turned towards him, her face to the wall, probably sleeping—and when the lady in the other bed said: 'Mrs. Doll, I think you have a visitor …', then all that he had been through was suddenly forgotten.

He placed a finger on his lips, took three quick steps forward to her bed, and said softly: 'Alma! Alma! My very own Alma! My darling!'

She slowly turned over, and he could see that she literally doubted the evidence of her own eyes. But suddenly her face shone with joy, she beamed with delight, stretched out her arms towards him, and whispered: 'Where have you suddenly sprung from? I thought you were in the sanatorium!'

He was already on his knees at her bedside, and threw his arms around her, his head resting against her breast. He smelt the old familiar scent of his wife, which he'd been deprived of for so long, and whispered: 'I've run away from them, Alma! I was missing you so much, I couldn't stand it any more, so I just took off …'

What bliss to be together again, and to feel that there was a place for him somewhere in this icy-cold world of loneliness and destruction! Bliss and happiness, he had found them again—when for so long he had thought that he could never be happy again! To hear how she introduced him with pride to her roommate: 'This is my husband!' And he knew he was just an ageing man in a crumpled and far from pristine summer suit, looking crumpled and anything but pristine himself. But she didn't see any of that, because she loved him, quite simply, and was blind to the rest.

Later on, he sat with her on the edge of the bed and they told each other what they had been doing—dear God, they had so much to tell! They talked about the doctors they had, and about the other patients and the nurses, and about the food, where Alma had had much better luck than him, the poor man! She made him eat some bread that she still had, and also the soup that she got instead of afternoon coffee. She waved some money in the air, and a nurse went off to fetch cigarettes. Oh yes, the money: the two-and-a-half thousand, the balance owing from Ben and the last money she had received, it was nearly all gone already. Money didn't last long with her. He needed a nightshirt, after all (five hundred marks!), she needed a nightshirt (seven hundred!)—and now these cigarettes! *The crooks around here charge her fifteen marks for American cigarettes! They know she is confined to a hospital bed, and can't do anything for herself.*

But she laughed about it, laughed about the extortionate prices, laughed about the money that was draining away: live for today, that was her motto! It would all work out somehow. She was twenty-four years old, and somehow it had always worked out so far, something had always turned up. And something would turn up now! Once they were back together again, they would do things differently this time. They would fetch their belongings from the small town; they still owned many things of value, so they could live on their hump for a whole year. They would set up home in a lovely apartment, and she would open a shop on the Kurfürstendamm, selling men's ties. Only very expensive merchandise, mind you, preferably from England! She knew a thing or two about the business—she'd once worked in the most exclusive men's outfitters, as he surely remembered? She would see to it that she only attracted a clientele with real money; she had a nose for such things.

Meanwhile, while she was earning money in this way, he would write a great book that would make him a household name again overnight. But he wouldn't only write, he would also spend some of his time looking after their child, Petta. The child must get used to being around him a lot more; she must learn to love him properly, and never to think of him as her stepfather.

She chattered on. She saw no obstacles anywhere, and could only imagine everything turning out well. He listened to her, and nodded or looked reflective, but none of it signified. She was a child; today's plans would be forgotten tomorrow, and tomorrow there would be other plans, other hopes. He was happy to let her concoct the most outlandish plans, because they would never come to anything. And yet he felt himself infected by her spirit and energy, by this bubbling youthful vitality: breaking out of the sanatorium like this might have been premature, but it was a first independent step, a nod to the future!

So they sat and chatted tenderly about the past and the future, until the light was switched on in the room, which by now was in darkness, and a nun was standing in the doorway, her hand resting on the switch; as their startled faces quickly drew apart, she smiled her Madonna's smile and said: 'Supper is about to be served! I think it's time for you to go home, Mr. Doll.'

They had been so absorbed in their long conversation that they were quite oblivious to everything around them. They hadn't noticed that the light was failing and that it had now become dark. The dance music on the radio had ended a long time ago, and now some man or other, speaking with a lisp, was giving a speech about the necessity for paying taxes. Even so, Doll didn't leave straightaway. He would be getting back to the sanatorium much too late now anyway. Maybe they wouldn't even save his supper for him, just to annoy him, but right now he couldn't care one way or the other.

The last cigarette, the very last one left, they now smoked together: 'You take three puffs, then I'll take three, then you take the next three. But hey, no cheating in my favour—that was only two puffs!'

'You must come back tomorrow!' insisted Alma as he was leaving.

'Tomorrow?' he replied with a smile. 'I doubt if I'll be able to come again tomorrow. They'll want to keep me under lock and key for a while as punishment.'

'Oh, you'll find a way!' she opined confidently. 'You can do anything if you put your mind to it.' He just smiled at this compliment. 'And', she added quickly, 'if you can't come tomorrow, then come in three or four days' time! Just keep thinking to yourself that I'm lying here just waiting for you to come.'

He kissed her. 'Bye for now, my dear! As soon as I can!'

'As soon as you can! Bye! Get back safely—oh you poor thing, you'll be frozen out there!'

And he was indeed chilled to the bone on the way home, and glad when he finally reached the sanatorium. From the moment he pressed the bell and the door lock started to buzz, all he could think about, despite the cold, was the reception that awaited him, and he fervently hoped they would go easy on him.

The girl who had opened the door for him, and who was now looking through the lodge window, was the same one who had opened up for him in the afternoon after he had told her a bare-faced lie. She was about to open up her little window, but then thought better of it. Doll climbed the stairs with a sigh of relief, and thought: *Well, I've got over the first hurdle ...*

But what am I like? he thought to himself as he was going upstairs. *I'm acting as if I've been summoned to the headmaster's study for playing truant at school. Am I a boy of thirteen, or a man of fifty-two? It's exactly the same feeling I had back then, and now it even smells the same as it did in the Prinz Heinrich grammar school in Grunewaldstrasse! That tingling, expectant sensation of fear, that smell of dry, dead dust warmed by the sun ... It's true: we never leave school for the rest of our lives. Not me at any rate. I am and always will be the old grammar-school boy, and I'm still doing the same stupid things I did back then!*

Now he pressed the bell button for Men's Ward III. As always, he had a long wait before somebody opened the door. The old senior nurse looked at him for a moment, as if about to say something, but then let him in without a word. *So that's hurdle No.2,* Doll thought to himself.

Many patients were sitting around in the lobby, as always during the hour between supper and bedtime, while others were marching up and down the long corridor with angry impatience. This was the time when even patients who had lain listlessly in bed all day now got up. Driven by a vague sense of restlessness, perhaps impelled by an unconscious yearning for freedom, they stood or wandered around aimlessly, hardly speaking, until sleep came — generally dispensed by the night nurse in the form of potions, tablets, or injections.

Doll made his way without a word through this gathering of fellow sufferers, and they in turn paid very little heed to him. That was the big advantage of this ward for 'difficult' patients, that you could behave just as you wanted: talking to all and sundry today, not saying a word to anybody tomorrow, being cheery today, and smashing the place up tomorrow. Nothing came as a surprise, and the staff took everything in their stride.

Doll found his little room, the cell, locked up. Not only the inner door with its little glass spyhole was shut, but also the padded, sound-absorbing outer door. This was an awful lot of trouble to take over the possessions of a man who owned next to nothing. All right, so they had secured a very small piece of soap, a nightshirt, and a comb against possible theft by a kleptomaniac colleague; but now he needed to get into his room! He was dead tired and hungry, and hopefully they had left his supper there in the cell for him, so that he wouldn't have to go off and find it.

'Mr. Ohnholz', said Doll politely to the male nurse who was then walking past obliviously, 'could you please unlock my cell for me?'

'Your cell?' replied the nurse with a faint grin, and proceeded to do nothing of the kind. 'Bartel from Room 14 has been in there since this afternoon. He was a bit agitated, if you follow me.'

'And where am I supposed to live now? In Room 14?' inquired Doll, and still couldn't quite believe what now seemed the most obvious inference.

'I couldn't tell you!' replied the male nurse with a shrug of his shoulders, and was already walking away. 'As far as I know, no other arrangements have been made.'

Very nice—just what I wanted to hear! thought Doll, and carried on to the tea kitchen. *Well, we'll see about that—time will tell...*

Sitting in the tea kitchen was his old friend, Nurse Kleinschmidt. They'd sat together trembling with fear in the air-raid shelter a few dozen times, and shared the last cigarette and the last of the real coffee between them when the raid was over.

'Well?' inquired Kleinschmidt, as Doll sat down without a word on the wooden chair on the far side of the kitchen table. 'Well? I thought you'd discharged yourself, Mr. Doll?'

'Just a little unauthorised visit to see my sick wife', replied Doll. 'And in the meantime they've occupied my bunker! Just like the boss, playing God Almighty!'

'God Almighty is always right!' said the nurse, nodding in agreement. She had as little time for the privy councillor as Doll, and she had known her boss for nigh on twenty years. 'You know what, Mr. Doll', she went on, and looked at him meaningfully through narrowed eyes: 'If I were you, I would settle for voluntary discharge ...', and then after another pause: 'I wouldn't wait until they kick up a fuss and chuck me out of a place that has made so much money from me. I'd rather chuck myself out!'

Doll thought hard about this for a moment. It was getting on for eight o'clock. 'Have I still got time to catch a train into the city?' he asked.

'Plenty of time!'

I'll get into the house somehow. Mrs. Schulz won't be very pleased to see me again, but I'll straighten things out with her somehow. It's all happening a little faster than I had planned, my return to the world, to an active life, but Kleinschmidt is quite right: it's better to be doing than to get done!

'Well?' asked the nurse again, and gave him a searching look.

'Right you are!' he replied, and got to his feet as he spoke. 'I'll see you again, my dear, or rather I won't see you again — not in this place, anyway!'

'Hang on a moment!' cried the nurse, and didn't take his proffered hand. 'You haven't had your supper yet! Wait, I'll get you something!' And from the warming cabinet she took out a dish of potatoes with carrots. She added some bread, four or five slices.

'I can't take that!' protested Doll. 'That's more than my bread allowance. I don't want you to stint yourself on my account.'

'Don't talk such rubbish', said Kleinschmidt. 'I'm only giving you what's going spare.' And by way of explanation: 'Old Bartel had a little turn earlier, and now we've given him an injection that he won't wake up from before tomorrow. So he won't be needing any supper—that's why!'

'Well, in that case, thanks very much!' said Doll, and fell to eating like a ravenous wolf. While he was eating, the nurse slowly and deliberately rolled herself a cigarette from various butt ends, lit it from the gas flame in the warming cabinet, and began asking Doll questions about his wife's condition, where he planned to live, what sort of possessions he still had, and above all, what his prospects were ...

'Well, there now', she said when he had finished, clearing away the plate and replacing it with a mug of milky coffee and a plate of bread and jam, 'now you can start all over again, like the rest of us. It can't do you any harm. And it'll put paid to any silly ideas!'

Doll protested: 'But this bread and jam don't come from here. Someone else has brought them in—they don't serve jam butties here. And anyway, I'm completely full up.'

'For a grown man, you don't half carry on!' she said in a gently teasing tone. 'Just be glad that you can eat your fill before the lean times come! Eat up, man!' she cried, now sounding piqued. 'Did I say anything when you gave me the last of your coffee and your last cigarette on the morning of 16 February 1944?! Well then', she went on, calming down now that he was eating, 'why do you men always have to make such a fuss? You're worse than a bunch of old maids!'

Later on, as he was getting ready to leave, she pushed a 'proper' cigarette—as opposed to the home-made variety—across the table towards him, together with a twenty-mark note. 'Now I hope', she said sternly, 'you're not going to act all coy again! And I won't object if you bring me back two cigarettes instead of one. I'll expect the money back by the end of the month—point of honour, okay? And now get the hell out of here! I've put your things in a cardboard box; there's still room in there for more. And by the way, the last underground train must have gone by now. But the walk to Wilmersdorf is nothing for a strong young man like yourself—especially at this time of year. You may catch pneumonia—which is no bad thing! The way things are, you'll save yourself a lot of trouble!'

CHAPTER NINE

Robinson Crusoe

The last underground train really had left, and the walk in the dark through a bombed-out Berlin was no bad thing—just as Kleinschmidt had said. Sometimes Doll, who knew Berlin like the back of his hand, actually had no idea where he was. There were hardly any people on the streets to ask, and those he did see hurried on past him so fast, as if they were afraid of him—which they very probably were. Sometimes Doll himself felt a kind of horror creep over him, so monstrous did this nocturnal stone jungle appear, across which a November wind was blowing dark storm clouds. And yet something had changed inside him. When he arrived in Berlin, he had thought: *I'll never be able to work in this city of the dead!* But now he thought to himself defiantly: *But I will work here, even so! In spite of everything! Or because of it!*

He had to wait a long time outside the locked building. The doorbell was disconnected, and nobody seemed to want to go inside. It was very cold, and Doll's teeth were chattering. But he steadfastly resisted the temptation to revive his spirits by choosing this moment to smoke the cigarette that Kleinschmidt had given him: he had decided to save it until he was lying in bed, when he was really 'at home', in the house that was actually going to become a home for them—if he had anything to do with it. He also dismissed the fear that he might be waiting all night for someone to turn up with a key to the front door, because everyone who lived there had already come home: *No,* he told himself, *I won't be standing here all night; there'll be someone still to come. Any time now—I can feel it in my bones!*

For a long time, it seemed that his bones were playing tricks on him. Then a tall, lanky young man came round the corner and said with surprise: 'Ah, Dr. Doll, it's you! Forgotten your front-door key? And here you are, standing in the freezing cold without a coat!'

They knew each other, the way Berliners got to know each other in the air-raid shelters—in passing, exchanging names, telling each other what they did for a living, and trying to decide whether the other was a rabid Nazi with whom one needed to guard one's tongue. Doll was about to respond with some pleasantry or other, but then said, since the young man was known to be 'a decent sort': 'To tell you the truth, I don't have a front-door key as yet, nor a coat. We arrived here in Berlin pretty much cleaned out—like so many others today!'

The stairwell, where all the broken windowpanes had been replaced with cardboard, felt pleasantly warm to him after standing outside in the cold and wind. 'Ah!' he said, 'it's nice to be in the warm!'

His companion murmured his slightly surprised assent, and inquired after his 'good lady wife'. Mr. Doll informed him that she was in hospital, unfortunately, but that he hoped to have her home again soon. The young man said that he hoped so, too, and looked forward to seeing the young lady again soon—she had always helped to boost morale in the air-raid shelter. He—along with all the other residents of the building—had always admired her steady nerve during the worst of the air raids. Her carefree cheeriness had been an example and a comfort to many—including him, as he freely confessed.

The two men parted with a handshake that was unexpectedly hearty. Then Doll climbed up the next flight of stairs and rang the bell by the door of Mrs. Schulz's apartment—or rather, his own apartment. He pushed the doorbell hard and repeatedly. He had the cardboard box with his things under his arm, and, despite the 'pleasantly warm' stairwell, he still felt a chill running down his back.

Eventually, the door was opened, just as he switched on the emergency lighting in the stairwell for the eighth time. And again it was the young actress who opened the door to him for this, the start of his second life in Berlin. Alma had since discovered, of course, that this young woman was not at all as mean-spirited and snippy as she had appeared that first morning. On the contrary, she had often displayed great generosity in helping out the Dolls when they were short of food.

Having opened the door, she said: 'Oh, it's you, Mr. Doll! And at such a late hour! Come into the kitchen with me for a moment; I'm just heating up some food for the baby on the stove, and anyway it's a bit warmer in there with the gas on!'

Doll sat down wearily on the kitchen chair between the gas stove and the table, the same chair on which his wife had sat so forlornly that September morning, and the bit of warmth from the gas stove really was very pleasant. Miss Gwenda stirred her pan of puréed food, and said: 'Are you really feeling better now, Mr. Doll? You don't look all that well, I have to say, and if I was going to collect firewood in the forest I wouldn't be taking you along, that's for sure!'

'Oh yes, I'm quite well again', replied Doll, not entirely truthfully, for at that precise moment he was feeling particularly wretched and low. 'It's the hospital air that's made me look so poorly', he added by way of explanation, not wishing Miss Gwenda to get the idea that their shambolic way of life, lying around and going without food and sponging off others, was going to start all over again. 'All these weeks I haven't been out in the fresh air at all until today. I also went to see my wife, and it was probably all a bit too much for me on my first outing.'

Miss Gwenda inquired solicitously after the health of his young wife, and so it was quite a while before Doll was able to ask about his room. Was Mrs. Schulz there today? Was she already in bed? Was it possible to speak to her?

Yes. Miss Gwenda reckoned 'yes'—Mrs. Schulz *was* sleeping here today, as far as she knew. But she couldn't say if she'd already switched her light off. So Doll crept along on tiptoe to the door of 'his' room and peered through the keyhole. Everything was in darkness. He listened at the door for a long time. He could hear someone breathing in their sleep—a soft, wheezing sort of sound followed by a gentle whistle—and he knew now for certain that tonight he could kiss goodbye to a good night's sleep. As for a warm bed … It looked like he wouldn't get to enjoy that nice, quiet smoke, courtesy of Nurse Kleinschmidt.

When he got back to the kitchen, Miss Gwenda and her purée were gone, and the gas was turned off. Here, too, things had shut down for the day without him. He stood there for a while, looking round the kitchen. It was indubitably his, her, the Dolls' kitchen; every item in it belonged to them, not just the furniture, but also every spoon, whisk, pan, and plate. But when he went to look inside the big, wide kitchen dresser, he found every door locked and the keys removed.

It's a funny old world, he thought. *They really ought to ask us, at least, and they ought to be paying us a bit of rent, too. What is the position with the rent on the apartment?* he suddenly wondered. *Miss*

Gwenda and her little family have only been living here since the end of August, but as for old Mother Schulz, who's so good at keeping accounts, I'll be putting the screws on her first thing in the morning for the rent, electricity, and gas. That'll bring some money in, and even if it's not a lot of money when you're paying black-market prices, even a little money is a lot of money to those who've got no money at all.

While he was thinking these thoughts, he had a look at the locks to the pantries, of which there were two in this rather grand kitchen — one on the right of the window and the other on the left. But they were both locked. *Of course,* he said to himself with a gentle sigh. *One is for Mrs. Schulz, the other for Miss Gwenda. They haven't reckoned on the Dolls. That'll have to change, too. Tomorrow morning, I'm going straight down to the housing office to clarify our rights here. Ah, no, the first thing I need to do is go to the Food Office and get our ration cards; we simply can't go on as we are, begging and borrowing, and buying stuff on the black market.*

Now Doll was standing by the kitchen table, gazing at it thoughtfully. But it looked too short and too hard to spend the night on. Then he remembered the bathtub, but the chill that still lay in his bones made him shiver at the mere thought of sleeping there, so he dismissed the idea immediately. There was carpeting on the floor of the little lobby, and in the hallway he had seen some sort of woman's coat hanging on the coat stand. He could use these as blankets.

But he still wasn't quite sure this was what he wanted — and then he remembered that the apartment had six-and-a-half rooms, and the half room was for the maid. He went inside and flicked the light switch, but the light didn't come on, either because the wiring was broken or because there was no bulb in the socket. So he went back to the kitchen, fumbled around with the lighter to get the gas stove lit again, found a newspaper in the waste bin, and rolled it up to make a torch. He used this to light up the maid's room.

Yes, the bedstead was still there, with the mattress on top and even the wedge pillow, but nothing else—no bed linen and no bed cover. And it was damned cold in this poky little hole! He used the last of the torchlight to light up the window, and saw that there were only a few shards of glass sticking out from the frame. There was nothing to keep the cool night air out. But he decided to make this his bedroom anyway—a bed was a bed. And, like a typical man, it never occurred to him that a bed could be moved somewhere else, into the kitchen, for example, which was warmer, and protected from the weather. But no, the thought never even occurred to Doll, for the simple reason that he was a man—or so Alma said later, after she had heard about this first night of his.

And now Doll suddenly felt qualms about just taking the woman's coat to use as a blanket. He spent ages taking up a threadbare runner in the back passageway, pulling it free from the tacks that held it down. He managed it eventually, but it was clear that this runner, now completely frayed and tattered along its edges, could never be relaid. In the kitchen, Doll quickly stripped off his suit, lit his cigarette on the gas stove, dragged the runner along behind him, and moved into his overnight quarters, folding the old, dusty carpet over and over on itself to cover him. He used the remains of a dressing gown that he had found in the bathroom to wrap around his feet, which were stiff with cold.

He lay like this in the dark, the tip of his cigarette glowing red from time to time; with the fiery glow so close to his face, he could no longer see the pale window opening, with the black silhouette of the courtyard building roof and the grey sky above it. When the red glow subsided, he could see the light of the sky again, and the air felt cooler on his face.

At first, despite the cigarette, he couldn't really relax because he couldn't get warm; the runner was heavy, and smelled unpleasantly of dust and all kinds of other things he couldn't quite identify, but it certainly wasn't warming. But when he had finished the cigarette and only the night sky above the black roof cast its pale light over Doll's face, he suddenly found himself, in that bitter cold, in an imaginary world between waking and sleeping, in a place to which he had always resorted ever since his earliest childhood at times when he was feeling particularly vulnerable.

In this imaginary world, he was Robinson Crusoe on the desert island, but a Robinson Crusoe without Man Friday, and a Robinson Crusoe who dreaded the arrival of white people, and felt only fear at the thought of being 'saved' by them. This latter-day Robinson Crusoe did everything possible to hide away completely from his fellow creatures. The vegetation around his cave could never be sufficiently dense, or the pathway through it sufficiently overgrown and concealed. His favourite fantasy was a deep valley basin between steep, towering cliffs, only accessible through a long, dark tunnel cut into the rock, which could be blocked up easily with stones. The valley basin itself was lightly planted with trees, but the tree cover was dense enough to ensure that this Robinson could not be detected from the air.

Even as a boy, Doll had sought refuge in such fantasies of hidden solitude, whenever the world and other people became too frightening, or when he had failed to grasp a proof in geometry, or when he had told a lie and been found out. As a grown man, he had taken refuge in the same escapist fantasy in times of depression, and in the last few years it had assumed a special importance for him, of course, during the constant heavy bombing raids over Berlin.

At bottom, though—and Doll knew this very well since reading the works of Freud—this rocky cave or the sheltered valley basin signified his mother's womb, to which he wished he could return when danger threatened. There and only there had he been safely at peace, and the southern sun that he always pictured shining down on Robinson's island was in fact his mother's great, warm heart, which graciously and tirelessly streamed its warm red blood down upon him.

With these and similar thoughts, Doll finally fell asleep, and when he woke, the fading night was still a dirty grey light in the empty window opening. But Mr. Doll leapt out of bed with alacrity and still feeling all warm, eager to begin the first real day of useful activity after the collapse of all his hopes. In the kitchen, under the electric light, he got a shock when he saw how filthy he was from the dusty old carpet runner. But there was nothing he could do about it, not having a change of clothes with him. Instead he took time and trouble over his ablutions in the bathroom, and felt fresh, if also very cold again, as he inspected himself in the large mirror in the hallway. It seemed to him that he was looking fresher and healthier than he had in a long time. He hurried down the stairs and through the front door, which was already open; but around the corner, the shop run by Mother Minus was still closed.

He could see a light inside, and began to knock, and he carried on knocking so persistently that eventually the familiar, big, white-haired head of Mother Minus was pressed up against the glass in the door; but she was shaking her head vigorously, to indicate that it was not yet opening time. Whereupon Doll knocked all the harder, so that the sound echoed through the empty street in the pale grey light of dawn, and when dear old Minus finally opened the door to get rid of the importunate caller, with all the irritation that only she could muster, he immediately grasped her hand in both of his, and said: 'Yes, it's really me, Dr. Doll! We last saw each other at the end of March, and I'm so glad you've come through it all safely, as have we. My wife's in the hospital at the moment, but I think she'll be back home again soon. And the reason I was kicking up such a terrible racket just now was that I absolutely must speak to you alone before your first customers arrive!'

While Doll was chatting away so cheerily to Mother Minus, he had been gradually inching his way forward, forcing her to take little steps backwards into her shop. Now he closed the door of the shop behind him as a precaution, in case anyone else might be cheeky enough to take similar liberties.

'Yes', said Mother Minus, no longer angry. 'Yes, I'd heard that you were both back again, and someone did tell me that you were not well. So what's on your mind now, Doctor?'

But before Doll could tell her about his needs and his prospects and promises, she broke in: 'But what am I even asking for? Why would anyone call on Mother Minus at this early hour, insisting on speaking with her alone? You want something to eat, don't you? A nice, tasty morsel, eh? Well now, Doctor, just this once, I'll do it without ration cards — but just this once, understand? Never again!'

'That's fantastic, Mrs. Minus!' cried Doll, delighted that it had been made so easy for him. 'You're an absolute star!'

'Get on with you!' replied Mrs. Minus, and she was already packing things up and filling bags, weighing, slicing, and slapping stuff onto greaseproof paper — while Doll's eyes grew steadily wider, since the best he had been hoping for was a loaf of bread and a bit of coffee substitute. 'Don't talk so much — and don't make any promises! But don't forget, I said "just this once", and I mean it. I know everyone says I'm too soft-hearted and can't say "no", but I can! You know it's not allowed, and they can shut me down just like that for such a thing. But just this once, I say: you've got to do right by people, and I've heard what the two of you have been through. So here you are, just take the stuff and shut up. It comes to twelve marks forty-seven, and if you've got the money, you can pay now; otherwise you can leave it. I can put it down in the book, and in your case I'm happy to go on doing that for a while—that's different. But not without ration cards!'

And having said this for the third time with as much emphasis as she could muster, as if she was trying to harden her soft heart, she pushed Doll, who was really touched by her generosity, out of the shop and back onto the street. He heard the key turning in the lock, and nodded vigorously in farewell, since his hands were full and he couldn't wave. Then he went home, feeling that he'd suddenly become a very rich man.

When he had left, he had taken the key out of the apartment door and kept it with him, which was a good thing, because when he got back, nobody was stirring as yet. This suited him fine, because now he could unpack his spoils undisturbed and unobserved. When it was all laid out before him on the kitchen table, he really did feel like a rich man who'd been poor Lazarus just a little while ago. Arrayed before him now were three loaves of bread—one white, two brown—a bag of coffee substitute, another bag containing sugar, one with noodles, another with white flour, a twist of paper with coffee beans, a parcel of greaseproof paper with butter and another with margarine, and a cardboard plate piled with jam.

If I'd had to buy that lot on the black market! thought Doll, and put some water on to heat in a pan—for the coffee substitute, of course: he was saving the real coffee beans for his reunion with Alma.

He found it quite difficult to scrape together enough crockery for his breakfast, since they had locked up his kitchen dresser. But he finally found what he needed in the sink, washed it as best he could with cold water, and said to himself once again: *All this has got to change—as of today!* And then he sat down to a veritable feast.

He was disturbed only twice. The first time, Mrs. Schulz came wandering into the kitchen like a ghost, albeit a distinctly unwashed ghost, looked aghast at the early-morning guest and rushed out again, with a cry that was more of a croak: 'Dear God, you might have told me, Dr. Doll!'

And she was gone again, with her untidy, tattered nightdress and her tousled head, her short locks in curlers. Doll hurried after her. 'Mrs. Schulz!' he cried beseechingly. 'Hang on a minute. I won't look, really I won't!'

The door was slammed in his face, and he was reluctant to barge into her room. So he called to her through the keyhole: 'Mrs. Schulz, I'm just going to pop down to the ration card office—can I speak to you later?'

A sigh, followed by an 'Oh Lord!', came back by way of reply.

'I absolutely must speak to you today! It's about something that's important for you, too!' A sigh, deeper than the first one, was the only reply. 'It wasn't that bad, you know', Doll whispered, piped, through the keyhole. 'I've got an attractive young wife myself, after all! So: we'll speak again later, Mrs. Schulz—in peace and friendship! Until later, then!'

Another sigh of 'Oh Lord!', but at least now it sounded like something that Doll could take for a 'Yes'. *You old bat!* he muttered under his breath. *Just you wait, I'll have you out of here so fast your feet won't touch the ground! Do you think I've forgotten how you rejoiced over the divine deliverance of your beloved Führer after the 20th of July?*

He hadn't been sitting eating his bread and jam for long before he was disturbed for the second time: somebody rang the bell to the door of the apartment. When he opened the door, there stood the tall young man from the previous evening—the one who had let him into the house and thereby brought him in out of the cold.

'Oh, it's you, Dr. Doll!' he said, momentarily wrong-footed, then quickly collected himself. 'I thought you'd still be asleep, and I just wanted to drop this off ...' He produced a large package. 'It's a coat', he explained quickly. 'Only a summer coat, I'm afraid, but there's a hat, too. I'm taller than you, but it might just fit. It's just a loan, of course—I hope you don't mind. But I thought you could wear it until you get something else ...'

'But Mr. —', Doll started to say, quite overcome. 'See, I've even forgotten your name ...'

'Oh, never mind the name! Anyway, even though it's only a summer coat, it's better than nothing ...' The package had meanwhile changed hands, and the two men had exchanged a vigorous handshake ...

'That is really so kind of you, Mr —', began Doll, but then interrupted himself again. 'Look, you really must tell me your name—'. Doll felt as if he couldn't really thank the man properly unless he knew his name ...

'Grundlos', he replied. 'Franz Xaver Grundlos. But look, I really must be going—I have to get to work. The underground—'

The last words echoed from the stairwell. Just when Doll could have thanked Mr. Grundlos properly, he was gone.

For the second time this morning, Doll found himself unpacking gifts. It was as if Christmas and his birthday had come on the same day. How wrongly he had judged the Germans in his depression! *Decency, plain old-fashioned integrity—they haven't died out yet;*

they will never die out. They will flourish and grow strong again, overwhelming and choking the rank weeds of Nazi denunciation, envy, and hatred!

Only a light summer coat, and too big for him—the man was right on both counts. But it was a smart, blue-grey cloth coat, partially lined with silk. *So people are helping each other out again, nobody is completely alone in the world, everyone can help, everyone can be helped.* The coat was a bit too long, certainly, but what of it?

He kept the coat on, and put on the hat as well—a little velvet number in the Bavarian style. There was a time when he wouldn't have been seen dead with such a thing on his head. But it wasn't so stiflingly warm in the kitchen that you couldn't wear a summer coat while eating your bread and jam. And he did not sit down to resume his meal. He suddenly felt a pressing need to get down to the ration card office. He'd put it off for months, but now he would show the major's lady wife that he too had ration cards, that he was no longer dependent on her! And today was the day he would show her!

There was one problem, though: where was he going to put his groceries while he was out? He didn't trust anyone. In the end, he crept along to the fire-ravaged front room, which was filled with rubble and general clutter, and hid the bags in a drawer of Petta's scorched changing table.

He inspected himself one more time in the mirror. *Good!* he said to himself. *Or at any rate, a thousand per cent better than I have looked in the last few months. And now it's time to get down to the Food Office with all guns blazing! I hope to God that some of the people down there are as decent as the three I've met in the last twenty-four hours. But this is my lucky day, and I can't go wrong!*

It was well before eight when Doll left the house, and it was way past noon when he returned—a very different Doll. He sat down without a word on the kitchen chair next to the gas stove. He was utterly exhausted. Miss Gwenda, who was keeping an eye on her potato soup on the stove—it had been sitting there for four hours, and should surely have come to the boil by now, but the gas pressure was so feeble—asked him for the key to the door of the apartment, which she assumed he had taken. Doll stood up without a word. He saw at a glance that the keys to both pantries and the kitchen dresser were now back in their locks. He took them out, put them in his pocket, and made to leave the kitchen.

The two women—Gwenda and the widow of Major Schulz—exchanged a quick glance and came to a mutual understanding: they should just let the poor lunatic have his way for now. Mrs. Schulz was all dolled up now, her hair in coquettishly tight little curls, and she said in honeyed tones: 'If you want to speak to me, Dr. Doll, I am at your disposal. I have come specially to see you.'

But he was not at her disposal. He went along the passageway to Mrs. Schulz's room. He entered, locked the door behind him, and sat down in an armchair. He was feeling really under the weather, dead tired and pretty desperate. The morning had been too much for the feeble strength of a man who was still convalescing. All he wanted to do now was rest ... He leaned back and closed his eyes. But he opened them again immediately. He felt cold—really, really cold! He was still wearing the coat, but ... He struggled to his feet again and moved the electric fire right next to his legs. He fetched the quilt from Mrs. Schulz's bed-settee and wrapped it tightly around him ...

He closed his eyes for a second time. Before nodding off, he thought to himself: *I mustn't sleep later than four o'clock. I need to be with Alma by five. Though I don't know what I'm going to tell her about my brilliantly successful brush with officialdom ... But I mustn't think about that now, otherwise I'll never get to sleep!*

He slowly drifted off. But he hadn't been asleep for more than five minutes before there was a knock at the door and Mrs. Schulz was chirping: 'Dr. Doll, have you got a minute? I thought you wanted to speak to me?'

He pretended not to hear. He was sleeping. He had to get some sleep.

'Be a dear, Dr. Doll, and open the door just for a minute, so that I can at least get my hat and bag! I have to go out!'

Doll slept on. But when she had pleaded with him for a third time, he jumped up, knocked the electric stove over, lunged towards the door, turned the key in the lock, flung the door open, and shouted angrily: 'Go to blazes! If you don't get away from this door right now, I'll move you myself, down all four flights of stairs—do you understand, woman?!'

This angry outburst was so effective that Mrs. Schulz fled before him down the passageway. 'I'm going, I'm going!' she shrieked in terror. 'I'm sorry I disturbed you! It won't happen again, I promise!'

Doll then slept soundly, falling into a deep, peaceful sleep immediately after his angry outburst, as if this storm had cleared the air. When he woke again, it was already getting dark in the room. He felt wonderfully rested and refreshed—better than for a long time. His first healthy sleep without any kind of sleeping aids! He stayed sitting quietly in the armchair, and was now able to reflect more calmly on the outcome of his morning visit to the ration card and housing offices.

He pictured himself again, standing along with so many others in a long line at the ration card office. Even though he had arrived early, there were nearly a hundred people there before him. Once again, he saw how the other people waiting with him were

177

constantly bickering and needling each other. He saw people nearly come to blows over a single word, which was often just a simple misunderstanding, and the unbelievable outbursts of fury when they thought someone was trying to jump the queue. Waiting for three hours in this hate-filled atmosphere inevitably put paid to Doll's early-morning conviviality. He tried to fight it, but this depressing mood was all-pervasive.

Eventually, he was standing in the room, at a table, in front of a girl or a woman, with people talking behind him and beside him, and now it was Doll's turn to speak, to say what he had thought about and rehearsed in his head a hundred times …

But he didn't get beyond the third sentence. 'First you need to bring your police registration form and your housing referral form', explained the girl. 'Without them we can't issue any cards here. You'll have to go to the housing office first!—Next, please!'

'But Miss!' he cried. 'It's always been our apartment, we were never de-registered, so why do I need to go and register again? You can check in your card index!'

'Then you'll have to get confirmation from the housing office! And anyway …' She gave him a dismissive look. 'Next, please!'

Doll was wasting his breath. One thing she had learned at work was the knack of not hearing. His words were like the buzzing of a fly to her. He had to leave, and he'd wasted more than three hours and a lot of energy just to be told that!

He went off in search of the housing office, and found it. This time he didn't have to queue for so long. He was only waiting an hour and a half. But he got nowhere at the housing office either. Once again a lady listened to his story, and felt doubtful about his case. He should have registered before the 30th of September, and now it was almost December! The lady passed him on to a male colleague, a very excitable gentleman, who, as Doll noted from his treatment of a man before him in the queue, was not a great listener, and preferred to do the talking himself.

Doll placed various pieces of paper in front of this man: old rent receipts for his apartment, proof of his appointment as mayor of the small town, written confirmation that the Dolls had spent time in hospital in the district town …

The man behind the desk blinked briefly, then pushed all the papers together in a heap and said quickly: 'I'm not interested in any of that. You can put it all back in your pocket, though you might just as well toss it into the wastepaper basket! Next!'

'And what about my certificate of residence?' persisted Doll, now quite angry.

'Your certificate of residence? That's a good one!' cried the excitable gentleman, now in full flight. 'On what grounds? I can't think of any! I've no intention of issuing one of those! Next!'

'So what kind of documents do you want, then?' inquired Doll doggedly.

'I don't want anything! You're the one who wants something! Next, please, and quick about it!' This 'Next!' appeared to be a kind of linguistic tic, the way other people end every sentence with '… you see?' He added quickly: 'Bring me a sworn statement from your landlord that you've occupied the apartment since 1939. Bring me a notice of departure from your last address in the town you were evacuated to, plus confirmation that you are signed off the ration card register.'

'I was never evacuated. And there was nothing to sign off from, because they haven't got ration cards there.'

'Ridiculous!' cried the official. 'Stuff and nonsense, a bunch of excuses! You just want to worm your way into Berlin, that's all! But you're not getting anything from me, nothing at all, and I don't care how many certificates you produce!' He slammed his hand down on the table. He was getting more and more worked up. 'I know your sort as soon as I clap eyes on them—you'll never get anything from me. Next!'

Suddenly his tone of voice changed. Now it was just sullen: 'And anyway …'

It was the second time this morning that Doll had heard the words 'And anyway', and it sounded like some kind of dark threat against him. After these absurd rantings and accusations, Doll's own blood was up now, and he asked sharply: '"And anyway"? What's that supposed to mean? What are you getting at?'

'Oh, come off it!' said the official, suddenly acting very bored, 'You know very well. Don't pretend you don't!' He studied his fingernails, then looked up at Doll: 'Or are you going to tell me what you and your family have been living off here in Berlin since the 1st of September?' He ploughed on triumphantly, and all the other people in the room were looking at Doll and enjoying his discomfiture as he got it in the neck. 'Either you didn't move here on 1 September, but only just now, in which case you have missed the deadline, and there is no way you are going to get a certificate out of me! Or you've been living off the black market since the 1st of September, in which case I have to report you to the police!'

Doll flared up angrily, failing to see in his agitation and his uncritical self-regard that the man was at least partly right: 'If you had looked at the paperwork properly, instead of just binning it without even reading it, you'd have seen that I was in hospital until yesterday—so I got all my meals there. And my wife is still in hospital, you can get written confirmation of that any time …'

'I'm not interested in any of that! It's got nothing to do with me! Next! I've told you what paperwork I need from you. Right: next!'

This time, his final word was not just a verbal flourish tacked on to the end of a sentence: he really did turn his attention to the next man in the queue. Doll walked slowly out of the office. He could feel the other man's disdainful, taunting gaze in his back; he knew that he was relishing his triumph and thinking: *I gave him what for! He won't be back again in a hurry!* And Doll knew with equal certainty that the next man in line would have no trouble getting what he wanted, no matter how shaky his case might look. He would even receive friendly treatment, because the official was now keen to demonstrate to himself, his office, and the waiting public that he really was a decent sort of fellow. But he wasn't: he was one of the millions of petty tyrants who had wielded their sceptres in this land of commissars and corporals since the beginning of time.

On the way home Doll completely forgot that he was shielded from the November cold by a coat that had been generously given to him only a few hours earlier, and that his belly was full from a breakfast that had come to him the same way. Once again, he despaired completely of his fellow Germans. His buoyant mood of the morning had evaporated. Robinson felt very much alone on his island.

And so it was that Miss Gwenda, and more especially Mrs. Schulz, had to atone for the sins of the housing office. And so it was that Doll fell asleep feeling completely depressed. But now he was no longer the Doll of the recent past. An hour and a half of sleep had restored his confidence and spirits. *I'll get there!* he thought to himself. *And if I don't, Alma will succeed where I have failed. Maybe it would have been better to send her down there in the first place. She knows how to handle men much better than I do. And anyway, Alma is Alma ...!*

He had to grin, because here he was, resorting to 'And anyway ...' himself. Then he crept along quietly to the burned-out room to fetch his food supplies, and sat down to a late lunch.

CHAPTER TEN

Robinson at large

As quietly as Doll had crept along, the widow of Major Schulz had heard him anyway. He had hardly cut the first slice of bread before there was a gentle tapping on the door, and when he said, 'Come in', Mrs. Schulz's mop of curls appeared round the door. 'Oh, Dr. Doll, would it be all right if I fetched my things now — if I'm not disturbing you?'

'Take them, take them!' replied Doll. Then he remembered the angry outburst with which he had punished this woman for the sins of the housing office, and he said: 'By the way, I'm sorry I got so worked up earlier. They gave me a really hard time down at the government offices, and my nerves were in shreds. The fact is, I'm still not well again yet.'

The words were hardly out of his mouth before he regretted them. He could sense, indeed he could positively see, how Mrs. Schulz, all meekness just a moment before, now perked up again. It had been particularly unwise to mention the 'government offices', because she immediately asked: 'And what did they say down at the housing office? What did they decide about the apartment?'

'How the apartment will be divided up between me and Miss Gwenda', said Doll, rather more guarded now, 'has yet to be decided.

But you will understand, dear lady, that I cannot give up the use of this room.'

Mrs. Schulz grimaced. 'But Mr. Doll!' she cried plaintively, 'you can't put me out on the street at the start of winter! I'm happy to look for another room, but until then ...'

'Until then we'll be living here together, and when my wife comes there will be three of us ...' She made as if to speak. 'No, no, dear lady, it's out of the question. I know you've only ever made occasional use of this room ...'

'That's a lie!' shrieked Mrs. Schulz, and her podgy white face quivered with anger and indignation. 'You shouldn't believe a word of what that Gwenda says! She's an actress—she tells lies for a living!'

'I've never said a word about you to Miss Gwenda, Mrs. Schulz!'

'No, of course you haven't. Please forgive me. I know who it was—that snake in the grass, the janitor's wife, that Nazi bitch! She's always trying to pin something on me! But I'll see her in jail yet! I can't tell you all the stuff she lifted from your apartment before I took the key away from her! Buckets and pans and pictures—your wife ought to take a good look round her rooms downstairs; there's enough stuff there to furnish half a house! Of course I've always lived here, every day!'

'So', said Doll, 'you've been using the room on a regular daily basis?'

'Yes, always! I've told you, since last year.'

'Then you'll agree that it's high time we settled up for the rent, etcetera. I haven't kept a written tally of everything, like you, so I'll make it very reasonable. Shall we say, for the rent and the furniture and use of the kitchen throughout that time, two hundred marks, and for the gas and electricity, another hundred, making three hundred marks in all? So, if you wouldn't mind, dear lady …?'

And he held out his hand.

Mrs. Schulz had involuntarily sat down, probably not so much because she wanted to get comfortable, but because the shock had made her unsteady on her feet. She hadn't been expecting such an assault. 'I've got no money!' she mumbled, holding on very tightly to her handbag. 'Barely twenty marks …'

'Oh well!' said Doll in a soothing tone, 'that doesn't matter. Give me the twenty marks for now. I'm quite happy to take instalment payments. And in the meantime, while you're getting the three hundred together, perhaps you could leave the quilt here for me! I could really use it at the moment.'

'No! No! No!' Major Schulz's widow was positively screaming now. 'I'm not paying that! That was never agreed! I arranged with your wife that I would look after your things here, and in return I was allowed to live here.'

'But you've just told me that so many of my things have been removed! How could that happen, if you were supposed to be looking after them? No, Mrs. Schulz, the three hundred marks have got to be paid. Maybe you recall that I didn't quibble when I settled your accounts for so and so many cigarettes, for this and that loaf of bread, for so many pounds of potatoes—no, my demands are very reasonable. And I'm quite certain my wife would take a different view; she would demand a lot more …'

'Your wife expressly told me I wouldn't have to pay anything here!'

'No, dear lady, that's not something she would have said. There's no point in discussing it further. That's how it is, and the money must be paid, and the sooner, the better!'

'And what about my quilt?' cried Mrs. Schulz. 'Doctor, dearest

Doctor, I've been bombed out of my house four times now, and all I've managed to rescue is this quilt. Doctor, you can't be that hard-hearted! I've got nothing left, I am a poor woman, and I'm getting old!' She had grabbed hold of his hand, and was looking at him with tears in her eyes. 'It's the cigarettes!' she whispered as if to herself. 'He's holding the cigarettes against me. I really didn't overcharge you — or only a tiny bit. You surely don't begrudge me my livelihood — the cigarettes are my living, after all, and I need to live, too! What was the point of struggling to survive for the last few years, only to die of hunger now? No, you can't hold the cigarettes against me, and you have to let me keep my quilt! You're not as hard-hearted as you make out. There is no way I can pay the three hundred. It would be a different matter if they paid me my pension. But nothing, not a bean! And yet the Führer said ...'

By now she had got herself into a complete state, and just looked imploringly at Doll with tears in her eyes. She was squeezing his hand in both of hers, which were unpleasantly warm and moist.

'Dear lady!' he said, and freed his hand with a sudden pull that was not polite. 'Dear lady, tears don't work with me; in fact, they generally just make me more annoyed. You've just admitted that you didn't charge me the correct amount for the cigarettes, so when you plead poverty I don't believe a word of it. You can keep your quilt if you pay me the three hundred. If you don't, the quilt stays here.'

'No!' said Major Schulz's widow, and her feverish agitation was gone in a flash. 'No, I'm not paying the money. You can take me to court if you want. Your claim won't stand up. Your wife expressly told me ...'

'We've been through all that, Mrs. Schulz. So the quilt stays here!'

'Fine', said Mrs. Schulz drily. 'In that case, you'll see where that gets you, you and your wife! Morphine addiction is against the law!'

'Not as serious as fraudulent trading in cigarettes.' But then he felt sickened by the turn this conversation was taking. 'Thank you, Mrs. Schulz, we have nothing more to discuss. Kindly remove your things from the kitchen dresser and the pantry. And give me your house keys.'

'I'm not giving you my keys! I won't be turfed out on the street like this!'

'Your handbag!' shouted Doll. He was suddenly angry again, to his own surprise. He snatched the bag from her hand. She squealed a little. 'Don't worry, I'm not going to take your things!' The bag was stuffed full of letters, all manner of toiletries, and cigarette packs. 'Where are the keys?' asked Doll, and burrowed down further into the bag. He came across a bundle of money—blue notes, hundred-mark notes, at least thirty of them, maybe even forty. He put them into her hand. 'Here are your twenty marks, you poor woman with nothing to your name, who has to wait until the Führer pays her pension …' Finally he found the keys. 'Is one of these a private key of yours?'

She shook her head. 'I've got nothing …', she whispered, holding the bundle of notes in her hand and still looking utterly bewildered.

'So I see!' said Doll, and gave her bag back to her. 'Thanks very much. Now if you could be on your way— ?'

She stood there for a moment, undecided, then suddenly placed three hundred-mark notes on the table—without looking at him, without saying a word. (Was she ashamed after all? Unlikely!) She walked out of the room …

'Your quilt!' Doll called out after her. 'You've forgotten your quilt!'

She walked on down the passageway, past the kitchen. 'And your things in the kitchen dresser!' shouted Doll. But to no avail. The apartment door banged shut. Mrs. Schulz was gone.

Doll shrugged and went back to his loaf of bread. Despite the money, he was not really happy about the way their conversation had ended. The sight of the three hundred-mark notes made him feel a little uncomfortable, and in the end he put them in his pocket. Based on the prices that Alma was now paying in the hospital, they would only buy fifteen cigarettes or one pre-war mark. But they were worth a lot more than that to him, and not just because he had had to fight for them.

By now it had grown quite dark. He put the light on to eat his bread, and marvelled yet again how small a loaf of bread is when a man does indeed live by bread alone—and how quickly it is gone. He kept on saying to himself: *Now this really is the last slice!* And every time, after a moment of indecision, he cut himself another one. He ate the bread dry, keeping the jam and margarine until Alma came home.

Then he took his supplies, and was about to take them back to Petta's scorched changing table. Then he remembered that he'd had the keys to the pantry in his pocket since lunchtime, and went along to the kitchen.

There he found Miss Gwenda. She was now wearing a silver-grey fur and make-up, as if she was going straight from the kitchen to the stage. It turned out, however, that she had only been invited out by friends. Miss Gwenda started to moan about how cold it was now, and said that in the winter it would be so cold in the apartment that they wouldn't be able to stand it. So she had bought herself a little stove on the black market, and in the next few days she planned to get some briquettes on the black market, too, costing two-fifty apiece. She assured him that was cheap, incredibly cheap;

some people were paying four marks for a briquette. And what was he planning to do in the winter, she asked. He couldn't possibly run the electric fire all the time, otherwise they'd cut off the electricity, and they'd all be sitting in the dark!

'Listen, Miss Gwenda!' said Doll, interrupting her tale, which wasn't exactly gladdening his heart. 'Listen, Miss Gwenda, I've given Mrs. Schulz her marching orders and taken her keys away. So she's got no business here from now on. Just so that you know …'

Miss Gwenda promptly twisted her painted face into a grimace that was doubtless an attempt at laughter, and she said: 'Ah, so you've rumbled her little game, too, have you?! I thought she wouldn't be able to keep it up much longer. Well, I won't be shedding any tears on her account.'

'So you've had problems, too', noted Doll. 'I think we'll leave the kitchen dresser open from now on, and each can take what he or she needs. There should be enough crockery for both of us. But we'll keep our supplies in separate pantries, and both hold on to our own keys. Which one would you like, the right or the left?'

Miss Gwenda preferred the left, and otherwise she was happy with the new arrangements. 'Well, let's both of us check what supplies Mrs. Schulz still has left, so that she can't accuse us of anything later on …'

'Oh, you won't find much of hers here', said Miss Gwenda disdainfully. 'She always lived from hand to mouth, and just bought what she needed.'

Which must have been true, because they found nothing apart from a few spices, two onions, and a handful of potatoes. So Doll moved his things into the pantry, which was now considerably better stocked than during Mrs. Schulz's time.

Then he locked the door. Meanwhile it had grown late, and

it was already dark outside. The weather had turned rough; the wind pressed hard against the cellophane in the window, and squalls of driving rain rattled against it from time to time. But Doll was determined to go and see Alma in hospital anyway. He'd been thinking about this visit all day long. He pictured himself sitting on the edge of her bed again, with the radio playing softly in the background, and perhaps she'd have some smokes again ... (Although, given their financial circumstances, it was a shocking waste of money!)

It would be best not to tell her that he had been discharged from the sanatorium, since that would only unsettle her. She would worry about how he was coping in the apartment on his own. She would then demand to be discharged herself, despite the fact that her leg was still not right. So he would act as if he had just given them the slip again at the sanatorium. He'd think of some little story he could tell her.

Turning these thoughts over in his mind, Doll went down the stairs and stepped out into the icy November wind, his face lashed by heavy rain. He shivered. *It's only a light summer coat*, he thought to himself. He came to a halt. Summer coat or not, he couldn't go to the hospital wearing that coat, because it would immediately give away the fact that he was no longer staying in the sanatorium. He would have to go in his thin summer suit, and the thought of this made Doll shiver even more. *I could drop the coat off at the porter's lodge*, he mused. But that wouldn't work either. Then she would feel sorry for him, and admire him for coming to see her in such weather — only to discover suddenly that his suit was dry, while outside it was pouring with rain.

No, he'd never get away with it — he would have to go in his jacket. Then he had a further thought: *I could say that somebody in the sanatorium had lent me the coat. But that's pretty darned unlikely — sneaking out on the quiet, and borrowing a coat to do so. And anyway, Alma might recognise the summer coat of Mr. Franz Xaver Grundlos — women have an eye for such things. No, there's nothing for it — I'll have to go in my jacket.*

The weather was really foul, wet and cold, and when Doll retreated into the stairwell, out of the wind, the still air once again felt pleasantly warm — just like the previous evening. But it was only when he got back to his room and saw the comforting red glow of the electric fire that it occurred to him he didn't really need to go at all. Alma would certainly not be expecting him. It was suppertime in the hospital now, so she had probably given up any hope of seeing him today. So there was no need to go out into the dark and the wet and the cold, and freeze half to death. He could just stay at home, climb into a warm bed, read for a bit, and then do his visit the next day, in the daylight, when hopefully the weather would be better.

But straightaway Doll shook his head and even stamped his foot, so determined was he. He'd planned to do this visit, and he did not want — did not ever want — to fall back into the old ways of the last few months, sinking into an apathetic stupor and letting himself go because he just didn't care. And quickly, as if he feared he might change his mind again, he tore off the coat, threw it over the armchair, and ran back down the stairs, out into the stormy blast and the ice-cold rain. And he ran on so fast that he didn't really notice how cold he was, or that he tripped over the same loose granite paving stone as before: all of this pretty much passed him by. All he could think about was the soft light of the hospital room, with the faint sounds of music on the radio, and in his mind he heard himself, still out of breath from running so fast, saying 'Good evening, Alma!' and saw her face light up with happiness.

And as he ran on, propelled by this joyous expectation, he felt as if he were escaping from his own broken, godless past, in which he had lived with a false and foolish pride in his solitary ways and his desert-island existence. And it felt as if this poor, bare man that he had become was now running towards a better, brighter future.

And so he entered the doors of the hospital as if effortlessly wafted there by the wind. He paused for a moment, dried his face off with his handkerchief, and wiped the rain off his glasses. Then he smoothed his hair with his hands—he'd forgotten his comb, of course, as he always did. Then, when he was breathing a little more easily again, he slowly climbed the stairs, reached the door of her room without anybody stopping him or even seeing him, knocked, and quickly entered.

He saw her face light up with joy, just as he had expected, and yet a thousand times lovelier than expected, and heard her cry: 'It's you, my dear, it's you! Have you run away from them again? I've had a feeling all day long that you would come!'

He went across to her bed at more of a run than a walk, bent down and kissed her, and whispered: 'No, Alma, I didn't run away this time. They kicked me out last night. I didn't really want to tell you, but when I saw your happy face, I knew straightaway I couldn't lie to you!'

He sat down beside her and told her everything that had happened to him since he had left her the day before, including his wasted trip to the government offices, which had almost dashed his spirits completely again, and his battle with Mrs. Schulz, and at the end he told her the tale of the coat he had so foolishly left behind. 'And now I've got myself frozen for nothing! Or maybe it wasn't quite for nothing. I don't know yet—the whole thing feels like some sort of conversion. And anyway, I wasn't actually all that cold, or at least I didn't have time to notice.'

He gazed at her as he spoke, in a way that made her reach up and pull his head down to her and whisper: 'What's that look on your face, you! You know that I love you terribly much, and that you suddenly look thirty years younger! If I had my way, I'd be out of here right now myself, and I'd come back with you this evening to our darling little home!'

In the instant that she spoke these words, he saw from the change in her expression that the sudden notion of coming home with him there and then was taking shape in her mind, and that the fleeting wish had quickly turned into a fervent desire and then, seconds later, into a firm intention. She had forgotten all about her leg wound. She murmured: 'I'll manage it somehow! And if they won't let me out, then I'll do what you did, and discharge myself!' She beamed: 'Think how nice that will be: this evening we'll be together again!'

He replied with some annoyance: 'Don't even think about it, Alma! Think about your bad leg, which still needs to be treated and dressed every day. You need to get properly well again first. I can manage by myself until then. The main thing is not to start lying around in bed all day again!'

She told him defiantly that she still had a mind of her own, and did what she wanted. And she would *definitely* be getting out of here this evening now!

He knew how stubborn she could be, so he had no choice but to change tack and try and win her over with soft words. But he got nowhere for a while, and she stuck to her decision to get herself discharged the same day. 'I'll soon talk that young doctor round …!'

They carried on arguing, with no end or resolution in sight. The nun, with her Madonna-like smile, had already said a couple of times that it really was time for Mr. Doll to be leaving. Alma's supper had now been sitting on the bedside table for some while. In the end, when he did eventually leave, he got her to concede that she would not leave this evening at least, and that she would in any event check with the senior consultant first. The evening that had begun so happily ended on a sour note: neither of them had got what they wanted, and both were feeling upset in consequence.

As Doll was crossing the hallway, he looked through the open door of a room and saw a youngish man standing there in a white doctor's coat. *Aha*, he thought, *let's go and see about this!* He entered the room and made himself known. It turned out that the young, jaundiced-looking man was indeed the night-duty doctor. Doll, who had taken an instant dislike to the man, said: 'My wife has just told me she wants to be discharged immediately. I've managed to talk her out of it. I assume that meets with your approval? The condition of her wound—'

'Is excellent!' the doctor promptly chimed in, finishing Doll's sentence. He seemed to feel much the same about Doll as Doll felt about him. 'She no longer needs to be in hospital. Outpatient treatment is all she needs. If your wife comes to have her wound dressed twice a week, that will be quite sufficient.'

'I have asked my wife, and made her promise, to discuss her discharge with the senior consultant first', continued Doll undeterred, though there was a note of irritation in his voice. 'Apart from the wound, she needs a morphine injection more or less regularly every evening, surely? And before she is discharged, these injections would need to be discontinued completely, wouldn't they?'

There was no doubt about it: the young doctor had wilted under this assault, and his jaundiced face now looked pale and ashen. But he quickly collected himself and answered, laying it on thick as the medical professional who knows better than the ignorant layman: 'Oh, the injections—your wife has told you about those? Well,

I can put your mind at rest on that score, too: your wife *thinks* she has been getting morphine. In actual fact, I gave her harmless substitutes to start with, and more recently she's only had distilled water ...'

The doctor smiled so unpleasantly as he said this that Doll was tempted to reply: *And you let her give you expensive American cigarettes in return for distilled water! How very decent of you! Anyway, I don't believe a word of it. Alma can tell the difference between the effects of water and morphine. That's all just a smokescreen, to cover your back with your boss!*

But he said none of this, for what could be gained by turning it into an argument? Instead he observed: 'As far as I understand these things, she'll still need to be weaned off her faith in the water that she thinks is morphine, won't she?'

The doctor smiled unpleasantly again. 'Oh', he said, with a dismissive wave of the hand, 'these things are not as complicated as all that. I suggest we both go to your wife's bedside now, and I'll explain the necessary to her. You'll see that it won't come as a shock to the system — on the contrary, it's likely to produce a certain sense of relief.'

'No!' said Doll with a look of fury in his eyes. 'I haven't the slightest intention of going along with such a suggestion. All that would achieve is to make my wife angry with me instead of you. We'll do as I said: I'll discuss the matter first with the consultant, and I must insist that you don't mention this conversation to my wife in the meantime!'

Now the man in the white coat gave a superior smile. 'Don't worry, Dr. Doll!' he said, full of sardonic solace. 'I won't show you up in front of your wife — you won't get to feel the full force of her wrath! Needless to say, it was only a suggestion of mine that you should be present when I tell her. I can of course quite happily do it on my own ...'

'I don't want you to tell her anything this evening!'

'Well', said the doctor vaguely, 'I'll have to hear what your wife has to say about your visit. I will, of course, be guided entirely by the condition of the patient at the time.' He looked at the other man as if pondering what else to say. Then he reached into the pocket of his white coat and took out a little pack of American cigarettes. 'Please', he said to Doll, who was taken completely by surprise, 'do have one—'.

And Doll, defeated, wrong-footed and utterly taken aback, took the proffered cigarette ... An instant later, he could have kicked himself for this act of stupidity, this lack of presence of mind. Yes indeed, this cunning little schemer had got the better of him in every respect, and by accepting a cigarette he had cut the ground from under his own feet, making it impossible to speak of the matter again.

So the two men merely exchanged a few courteous pleasantries, and Doll went home filled with rage—rage at himself and his chronic inability to think on his feet and display presence of mind.

The only consolation was that Alma had given him a firm promise not to request her discharge today, but to wait until he or she had spoken to the senior consultant. But as Doll pondered the matter further, he could draw little comfort from this. For while he was sure that Alma would keep her word, it seemed to him entirely possible that the young doctor would talk, and thus bring about the very thing that Doll most wanted to avoid at the moment: Alma's premature discharge.

On his way to the hospital, the feeling of joyous anticipation had made him impervious to the cold and rain; on the way home, it was his gloomy thoughts that stopped him noticing the rain on this stormy November night. He was only shaken out of these thoughts when he ran straight into a man not far from his apartment, knocking him over. He promptly helped him up with profuse apologies, resigned to the prospect of being showered with abuse and threats by the man. But, to his surprise, this didn't happen; instead, the other man, who was completely unrecognizable in the dark, inquired in tones that were almost apologetic: 'Have you done anything about re-establishing yourself in the literary world, Mr. Doll?'

He was so startled by this completely unexpected question in the middle of the night that it took him a long time to work out who it was talking to him, and who it was he had knocked over in the dark: namely, the doctor with the papery skin, the first one to have attended his wife in Berlin. Eventually he said, somewhat fatuously: 'Oh, it's you, Doctor! I do beg your pardon. I hope I didn't hurt you …'

'I think', said the other, still a past master in the art of not hearing something that didn't interest him, 'I think one will have to move quickly now if one wants to play a real part. All sorts of complete unknowns seem to be jostling round the trough again now …'

This sounded not so much envious as simply disembodied, spoken into the fog, like everything else he said, without resonance for himself or those around him. They walked side by side towards their neighbouring homes. The spectral doctor went on: 'And there are all sorts of clubs and associations, leagues, chambers, groups being formed again—but not a single one has invited me to join. And yet at one time I was quite a well-known writer; not as well-known as you, Mr. Doll, but still, a well-respected figure.'

While he was talking, they had been approaching their

destination, and it seemed the obvious thing for Doll to accompany the doctor into his building and into his apartment and then into his tolerably warm surgery, where they sat down, again without preamble, on adjacent sides of his desk. The white-painted treatment chair with its stirrups for the legs looked just as spectral as its owner. There was something unreal about all of it, as though Doll were trapped in a dream from which he was about to awake.

The doctor went on: 'It's as if everyone thinks I'm dead—that's how forgotten I am. But I can't be entirely forgotten, because I'm reading the names of old friends in the newspapers. I haven't forgotten them, so they *can't* have forgotten me. But nothing! Not a peep! As if I were already dead—but I'm not dead, not yet!'

He fell silent for a moment, and gazed at Doll with his expressionless brown eyes, in a blank, unblinking stare. Thinking to make him feel better, Doll said: 'Nobody's got in touch with me either ...'

'No!' said the papery spectre, with a forcefulness that was quite unlike him. 'No! I have nothing to reproach myself for!' He answered a question that hadn't been asked: 'No, I was never a Nazi. Of course, I was a doctor in the Wehrmacht for a while, that was something that nobody could get out of. But I was never in the Party—and now this silence, as if they thought I was a Nazi. How do you deal with that?'

He looked at his companion with feverishly blinking eyes, and the paper-thin skin over his cheekbones appeared almost flushed. 'How do you deal with what?' inquired Doll. 'Being ignored? Why don't you get in touch with one of your old friends? They may not even know that you're still alive. So many people have perished in recent times ...'

'I've written letters, lots of letters!' replied the doctor. 'Look—half a drawerful! He opened a drawer in his desk, and showed Doll a little pile of letters, sealed in envelopes, addressed, and already franked with Berlin Bear stamps. The doctor quickly went on: 'A letter is like putting out a call—just by writing it, you are calling out to your correspondent.' He was silent for a moment. Then: 'Nobody can reproach me! Not when I was never a Nazi! Never! Really not!' He blinked even more fiercely.

Doll felt certain that this Dr. Pernies still partook sufficiently of this world to be tormented by something, and that he was even capable of lying in order to avert this torment. The reiterated assurance that he had never been a Nazi seemed suspicious, at the very least. It reminded him of that beer wholesaler, who had repeatedly sworn to his mayor that he honestly hadn't hidden a thing—until the hiding place was discovered.

Doll stood up. 'I would send the letters', he said.

But the doctor had become quite impenetrable and remote again. 'Of course!' he said in a toneless voice. 'Only, which one shall I send? And to whom? All those people are incredibly vain, and anyone I haven't contacted will feel ignored. I thank you for your visit!'

Doll stepped out into the night. Maybe Alma had talked to the young doctor in the meantime about her discharge, and was already at the apartment? He quickened his pace.

But when he entered the room, it was empty. There was no Alma; he was on his own again this evening, and it might be that for some days to come he would have to labour alone at building their future life together. His intention was to get back to his work, and thus to a meaningful life, as soon as possible. To do that he would have to seek out the people who were in the know today, and find out what sort of publishing opportunities there were now, and what there was in the way of newspapers, magazines, and publishers. But who could he turn to? He'd been in the city of Berlin for two months, but he knew nothing, absolutely nothing of what had happened here since Germany's collapse and defeat. He'd never looked at a newspaper—shameful as it was to have to admit it to himself!

While Doll was thinking these thoughts he had been tidying up his room and getting it into some sort of order. He had also laid out everything for his supper, and brewed up some coffee. Now he knocked softly on Miss Gwenda's door, which was opened by her mother, and he asked her politely if they had a few newspapers to hand—it didn't matter if they were out of date. He promised to return them the next morning.

He was given a whole stack of newspapers, and retired to his room with them. That evening he ate his bread and drank his coffee without even noticing, because he was reading—reading the newspapers, new ones and older ones, totally absorbed in the words on the page, the way he had been as a fifteen-year-old reading his Karl May adventures, without a thought for anything else. He read everything: domestic and foreign politics, letters to the editor and the features section, arts reviews and small ads. He devoured the newspapers from the first page to the last.

And as he did so, the world in which he had hitherto lived with his eyes closed now opened up before him, and everything became clear to see. He had walked through the streets of this city without once stopping to think who had removed the anti-tank barriers, cleared away the mountains of rubble, and got the transport system running again. He had seen them working in the streets, and his only thought at the time had been that it was a little odd to see people working again—what was the point? Or else he had thought: *These people are former Nazis, who are being* made *to work. The rest of us, who don't have to work, will just wait and see for now, the situation will change somehow …*

Yet these workers were people in the same situation as himself, no better and no worse; but while he had been lazing around and busily making himself ill, these people, who were just as disillusioned as he was, had got stuck in, and through sheer hard work had overcome their despair and disillusionment.

He read about theatres that were putting on plays again. About art exhibitions and concerts, about new films from all over the world. He read about the self-help initiatives for fetching timber from the forests, rebuilding homes that had been destroyed, repairing roofs, and getting burnt-out machinery working again. He read small ads where people were offering items for sale that for a long time had simply been unavailable. There weren't many of these, but at least it was a start—and that's all that could be expected for now.

He'd dismissed Berlin as a 'city of the dead', a 'sea of ruins', in which he would never be able to work: but just look how much work was being done in this city now! Anyone who wasn't doing their bit should feel ashamed of themselves. They had been living in a state of blind selfishness for the past few months—a parasitic, self-centred existence. All they had done was take, take, never stopping to think how they might give something back.

When Doll had put down the last newspaper that evening, that night, laid down on the couch and turned out the light, he didn't need to resort to some pathetic Robinson Crusoe fantasy in order to get off to sleep. Instead, all the things that he had read were going round and round in his head, and the more he went over in his mind all that had been achieved so far, the more incomprehensible it seemed to him that he had stood idly by, resentful and blank, while all this was happening. These reproaches pursued him into his dreams at dead of night.

CHAPTER ELEVEN

A stormy start

In spite of his tormenting dreams, Doll woke feeling fresh and rested, and, like the day before, he took a great deal of trouble over his toilet so that he wouldn't be distracted by thoughts about his unkempt appearance. He hoped very much that his planned errand would be successful, and that he wouldn't have his spirits dashed again by some other petty little tyrant like the one at the housing office.

Reading the newspaper the night before, Doll kept coming across the name of a man whom he remembered from pre-Nazi times. He had not had a great deal to do with him personally, but as publishing editor for a large publishing house, this man—Völger by name—had overseen the publication of several of his books. Doll now planned to track him down, and hoped that he might even find him at the editorial offices of that very newspaper.

Doll was just slipping his arms into the sleeves of his borrowed summer coat when the doorbell to his apartment was rung repeatedly, five or six times; and when he opened the door to see who was so impatient to be let in, who should it be but his own wife, Alma! She had a bulging shopping bag in each hand, her arms were festooned with items of clothing—dresses and skirts or something—and it was clear from the expression on her face that she was not in the best of moods.

Doll, who had been worried the night before that his wife might turn up, was now nonplussed by her sudden appearance. His newspaper reading and his planned visit to the publishing editor Völger had so preoccupied him that he had barely given a thought to his wife this morning, and certainly not to her arrival at the apartment. 'Alma, it's you!' he said, sounding genuinely flabbergasted.

'Yes, it's me, Alma!' she said, mimicking him with angry sarcasm. 'And if it was left to you, I certainly wouldn't be here—I'd be stuck in hospital for weeks on end! (Can you just shut that door and take some of these things from me? You can see I've got my hands full here!) That's a great way to keep a promise, turning that young doctor against me! And then you go and accept cigarettes from someone like that—well, thanks very much!'

As she spat out these words, she marched ahead of him into the room. Here she dumped her bags, tossed the armful of clothes over a dining chair, and sat down in an armchair. But she was on her feet again straightaway, dug a pack of cigarettes out of her pocket, and lit one up. Despite her anger, she showed that the spirit of comradeship was not something acquired or artificial with her, because she immediately proffered the pack and invited him to take one: 'Here!'

Doll, who the evening before, to his own annoyance, had not declined the offer of a cigarette from the young doctor, chose to do so now—another mistake!—with his wife, and said angrily: 'I didn't turn the doctor against you! And anyway, I didn't ask for cigarettes from him; he pressed them upon me and I took one, just one, just to be polite!'

'Is that so?' she replied angrily. 'But you won't take one from me? Then again, why be polite to your own wife? That makes it easier to go behind her back and persuade the doctor, contrary to a solemn promise, to keep me in hospital for God knows how long!'

'I didn't promise anything of the kind! But you promised *me* solemnly that you wouldn't leave there until you'd spoken to the senior consultant!'

'See—you've said it yourself: we were going to talk to the consultant, but you go and hide behind the ward doctor! Typical! All you were interested in was making sure I stayed there! Presumably you don't need me here!'

'Alma!' said Doll quietly. 'Alma, let's not quarrel. Let's think about the future instead. And I can't imagine a future without you. But you need to get well again first, that's all I care about here. I was reading the newspapers last night—Alma, there's so much been happening in the world during the two months we were lying around here doing nothing! From now on we need to do our bit again. When you arrived, I was just about to go and see Völger, my former editor, who always spoke up for my books. They've discharged you, all right; what's done is done. But now you need to lie down and look after that leg ...'

Her face had relaxed and become friendly, now that he had dropped the combative tone. But at his last suggestion she shook her head like a sulky child, and replied: 'I can't see why I shouldn't come with you. My leg is fine—or nearly. I don't want to lie around here and get bored!'

When he answered, his tone was still gentle: 'It's because we don't want to end up lying around again the whole time that I'm asking you to take care of yourself. If we go back to a life of idleness, there'll be no more getting out of bed in the mornings and going to work—or only to go and fetch morphine, and then Mrs. Schulz and Dorle will be running our lives again. Have a care, my dear, and look after yourself, before we end up like that again!'

But she shook her head and repeated stubbornly: 'I've looked after myself for long enough; now I want to do my bit again, too. Whatever you're doing, I want to be part of it!'

'You've been confined to bed the whole time until just this morning—you can't just start running around again as if nothing has happened!' he persisted. 'You've no idea how scared I am that we'll fall back into our old ways. And this time we have no reserves, no more diamond rings to sell. You've got to get used to the idea that we are poor now, Alma, and that there are lots of things we can no longer afford, such as doctors and expensive American cigarettes, and maybe not even white bread, which gets eaten much too quickly and doesn't fill you up anything like brown bread.'

'Is that so?' she cried, growing more heated herself. 'Is that why you wouldn't take a cigarette from me just now? So now you want to play the pauper? And then I won't be allowed to smoke cigarettes either, and I'll have to eat brown bread all the time, when you know it always plays havoc with my gall bladder! If that's how you want to live, be my guest, but you can count me out! For a start, I've still got lots of things I can sell, and when they're all gone I can still think of a better way out than rotting away in misery.'

He was now equally fired up with anger: 'Oh yes, it's easy to say you're not prepared to make any sacrifices and threaten to run away every time the going gets a little bit tough. But I'm not going to be threatened, even by you, and if you want to run away, then the sooner the better! I'll go my own way, on my own!'

'See!' she cried triumphantly. 'That's just what I thought—there was a reason why you tried to persuade me and the young doctor that I should stay in hospital as long as possible! I'm just a burden to you, and you want to get rid of me. Well, fine, I don't want to make things difficult for you, I can go whenever you like! I'll get on much better without you!'

'What rubbish you talk!' he cried. 'I haven't said anything about you being a burden and me being better off without you! You brought the subject up, not me! But that's not what it's all about! The question is simply whether you're prepared to be reasonable now and look after your health. Yes or no?'

'No—obviously!' she replied scornfully. 'If you'd asked me nicely, I might have done it. But not like that!'

'I asked you nicely enough at the beginning, but you just don't want to. So if you really don't want to ...'

He looked at her expectantly, but her anger, if anything, was mounting.

'How many times do I have to tell you that I don't want to! And I'm certainly not going to be bullied by you! See, I'm lighting up another cigarette now, just to annoy you!'

And she lit a fresh cigarette.

'Fine, fine!' he said. 'At least I know now where we stand!'

And with that he walked straight past her. Her eyes had grown black with anger; but he walked out of the room, shut the door behind him, put on his coat in the hallway, put on his hat, and left the apartment.

It wasn't blowing a gale outside today, and it wasn't raining either, but never had the street they lived in, with its burnt-out ruins and huge piles of rubble, seemed to him so dark and menacing. Which is just what his life looked like: the war had destroyed everything, and all that was left to him were ruins and the ugly, incinerated detritus of former memories. And that's how it would probably always be; in this respect, it might even be that she was right: there was no escape from this scene of devastation. What he had just been through with his wife was enough to discourage anyone from going on. And he was right, but she was wrong. Reason was on his side, and everything she'd just been saying about not being prepared to do without was utter nonsense!

Yes, she was young, yes, she was pampered and spoilt, and he needn't have come down on her so hard; his comments about the cigarettes and the white bread would have kept until later. He could have been a bit more patient and circumspect. But he was only human, for heaven's sake, and these troubled times weighed heavily upon him, more heavily than they did on her, who lived free as a bird and forgot all her cares from one day to the next! Why did he always have to show consideration for everybody else, when nobody ever showed consideration for him?

No, it was probably just as well, the way things had turned out. The manner of their parting just now showed how things really stood between them, when infatuation didn't make them blind to their differences: at odds about everything; strangers, complete strangers; apart and alone. And now he would go his own way, alone; he wouldn't be telling her what to do any more—she could smoke and sell things off to her heart's content! Not another word! But nor would he be telling her anything about the outcome of his visit to the publishing editor Völger.

Absorbed in these thoughts, he had reached the underground station, bought a ticket, and was waiting for the train with other travellers. The train arrived, and the alighting passengers elbowed their way through the narrow gap grudgingly created for them by the people waiting on the platform. Then he squeezed into the overfilled carriage with the others.

Suddenly a voice beside him inquired in a mocking tone: 'Perhaps you'd care for a cigarette now?'

He spun round and gazed with bewilderment into the face of his wife, who eyed him with cool disdain. He didn't answer, but declined the proffered pack with an ill-tempered shake of his head. This was the last straw, and anger rose within him again. To have her follow him in secret after such a quarrel and now make fun of him in public—it was more than he could bear.

He was furious that she was coming along with him to what might be a crucial meeting, as if she really belonged there. She was a distraction. He wanted to reflect on what he needed to say to the publishing editor Völger, but all he could think about now was this wretched woman!

He had to change trains from the underground to the local commuter network, and then take a tram, but there was no shaking her off. He had to admit that his behaviour was not exactly gallant—as when he jumped onto the tram at the very last moment, when it was already moving. But she wasn't going to be caught out, and managed to jump aboard after him; enjoying her triumph at his expense, she even paid his fare. He put up a feeble protest, but neither she nor the conductor took any notice.

But it wasn't just about *schadenfreude* for her. Twice she had tried to let bygones be bygones and engage him in harmless conversation. But he had remained tight-lipped, and refused to say a single word.

Now that they had alighted from the tram and had to walk the last part of the way, she tried a third time. They were just crossing a temporary wooden bridge; alongside it, the broad iron bridge with its tarmac-covered carriageway lay in the water, dynamited by Hitler's minions in a futile gesture of defiance. She looked intently at the smooth roadway, which, still in one piece, dropped down steeply from the river bank to the water—which covered it to a depth of less than half a metre—and then rose steeply again to the other bank. Dreamily she said: 'It's a pity I'm not a child any more: I'd slide down there on the seat of my pants! I'd still do it now—you could do it on a sledge or a bike, too. Tell you what—for a hundred American cigarettes, I'd give it a go here and now!'

Her last words spoiled the impression made by her initial remark, at which he found himself smiling inwardly, despite himself. He could clearly picture her sliding down the slope, laughing and flashing her white teeth, her strawberry-blonde hair streaming out behind her. And she would have done it, too—she was quite capable of something like that. But her last remark about the American cigarettes promptly soured the mood of levity.

But her words had had the opposite effect on her. She took the pack of Chesterfields from her pocket, looked inside, and offered it to him: 'Well, how about it? The last chance! There are just two left—shall we share?'

He pressed his lips more tightly together and shook his head, even though his fingers were itching to reach out and take one, so badly did he crave a smoke.

'Have it your own way', she said evenly, and took out a cigarette for herself. As she lit it, she went on: 'If you insist on being silly and stubborn like a little child, be my guest! But I'm still going to enjoy my cigarette!'

She had drawn the smoke deep into her lungs with a sensual relish, and blew it out again in his direction, doubtless not entirely unintentionally. With the same mocking superiority as before, she said: 'You'll come round. You'll introduce me to your editor fellow, and you'll have to talk to me, however silly you're acting now!'

The whole time he had been thinking that her remark had struck home at the heart of his frustration. Stung by her words, he now broke his silence and said angrily: 'Instead of trotting along beside me and distracting me when I need to think, you'd have done better to get down to the housing office and the ration card office!

You were full of talk about how you could get it all sorted out in no time! But it never occurs to you to take the initiative, of course—it's so much easier just to leave it all to me!'

She replied scornfully: 'Don't you worry about the apartment or the ration cards! You think, because you didn't get anywhere, I won't do any better. Well, I'll go down there myself this afternoon, and I'll see that we get what we need!'

Full of feigned pity for her preening ignorance, he said: 'The offices are closed in the afternoons.'

And she shot back, even more sure of herself: 'Not for me, my friend, not for me! You'll be surprised!'

To which he replied: 'No I won't—because you won't get anywhere.'

And with that, this fresh argument was ended for now. They had arrived at the big publishing house, which had once been one of the largest and most imposing buildings in Berlin. On the outside, the towering building still looked impressive and, apart from the window openings—some with shattered glass, others empty or patched with cardboard—untouched by the war. The great heaps of rubble around the building were the only indication that it had probably not escaped unscathed on the inside.

And indeed, when they entered, they found themselves in a cavernous, smoke-blackened space, still reeking of fire, which had been created by the collapse of internal walls.

They then went through a low iron door, and suddenly the smell of burning was gone, and they breathed in the damp, acidic smell of fresh lime. A broad, dimly lit staircase rose before them, the paint on the walls seemingly only just applied by the decorators. Everything smelt new, though it had the smell of a rather cheap job. At any rate, this part of the building had only just been patched up.

On the second floor they entered the editorial office, where Doll hoped to find the publishing editor, Völger, or at least learn his whereabouts. His voice almost faltered as he inquired after the man who had formerly overseen the publication of his books; suddenly he felt as if he had been pressing towards this moment ever since the collapse of the regime, the moment that—hopefully!—would enable him to reconnect a broken past with a new and happy future. Suddenly, in the intervening second between question and answer, he trembled in fear of a 'No', or a 'No one of that name here', as if such an answer would definitively slam the door on a better future.

So he breathed a deep sigh of relief when he heard: 'I'll just go and see if Mr. Völger is free. Who shall I say is inquiring?' He felt a deadness in his limbs as he gave his name, and it was as if, overcome by vertigo, he had just been saved from falling into the abyss.

They were then led into a large, untidy-looking room, which looked more like the workplace of an engineer than a literary editor. Doll gazed into the old, careworn face of an elderly man with sparse white hair. *Good Lord!* he thought to himself in a daze, as he shook the proffered hand, *surely that can't be Völger, not this ancient old man! That can't be Völger!* And as he heard the other man start to speak, he was still thinking to himself: *Maybe he is just as shocked by my appearance. I would never have recognised him! This bloody war—what has it done to us all!*

Meanwhile he heard the other man say, visibly moved: 'Doll, I can't tell you how pleased I am to see you! You realise, don't you, that you were reported as dead? We all thought: so now he's gone, too! And now here you are, in my office! Take a seat, please, and you, too, madam! I'm sorry, it's such a mess in here ...'

And he heard himself answer, no less agitated and flurried: 'It doesn't matter if they said I was dead. As the saying goes, there's

212

life in the old dog yet, and I intend to prove it!' As he spoke he felt Alma's eyes upon him, and was glad that she was sitting quietly, not trying to be the centre of attention at this particular moment, and so, quite contrary to his original intention, he introduced her: 'This is my wife, by the way, Mr. Völger!' And then added, sensing surprise in the other man: 'We married shortly before the end of the war.'

'Yes, indeed!' replied the man, and nodded his white-haired head. 'There've been big changes everywhere — and that includes me!' He glanced at the young woman, and it sounded almost as if his own marital circumstances had changed. But then he went on: 'And yet here I am, sitting here in this building again, like I was before the start of the Thousand-Year Reich, older and more bedraggled, doing my job like before. Sometimes it feels as if everything I've been through in the last twelve-and-a-half years is completely unreal, like a distant memory of a bad dream ...'

'Not me!' countered Doll. 'I haven't reached that point yet. For me, all these horrors are still very real. But then, of course, you've got your work again ...'

'And you? Have you not been able to do any work since the surrender?'

'No, nothing! But you have to remember, they made me mayor of the town. And then I was ill for a long time.' And he began to talk about the events of the previous months, about the hopelessness, the growing sense of apathy ...

The other man grew restless as he listened to this account, and he seized the first available opportunity to tell Doll what a dreadful time he'd had of it, and what bad experiences he'd had with other people.

Listening distractedly to the other man's story, Doll immediately thought of the far worse things that had happened to him. He barely heard what the other was saying until he had finished, and then promptly launched into his own tale of horrors.

Both men paused, each looking into the other's careworn face with a wan smile as they realised what they were doing. 'We're doing it', said Völger, smiling more broadly, 'just like our dear fellow men, whose foolishness we like to make fun of. Everyone has had it so much worse than anyone else!'

'Yes!' agreed Doll. 'And yet it turns out we've all been through pretty much the same things.'

'That's right', said Völger. 'Everyone has suffered about as much as they can take.'

'Absolutely!' agreed Doll.

And then they both fell silent. Doll was in two minds whether he should get up and leave now. Völger had not offered him the prospect of any work; he had not even asked if Doll wanted to write a piece for the newspaper he now helped to edit. Even if Völger didn't see it, Alma knew with what expectations her husband had come here. Perhaps Völger thought that Doll had simply dropped by to say hello to an old acquaintance. But she knew that this visit was meant to be the start of a new life ...

And yet ...! Precisely because Alma was there, he didn't want to ask Völger straight out if he knew of any work for him. He didn't want to beg in front of Alma. No, the only thing he could do after the other's long and unambiguous silence was to get up, say goodbye, and leave. *Moriturus te salutat!* He who is about to die salutes you! Leave now, and die quietly and with dignity! And Doll was instantly put in mind of another writer, the doctor, the doctor who had once been a writer, the fellow with a head like a skull, ignored and forgotten—how had he put it? *It's as if one were already dead.* And Doll stood up, stretching out his hand: 'Well, my dear Völger, I must be going. You must have a lot to do …'

'Yes', said Völger, and took the proffered hand. 'Yes, there's always a lot to do, far too much! But it's really done me good to see you again—the man they said was dead! Granzow must have been pleased to see you, too. Do give him my regards. I take it he told you I was here?'

'No!' replied Doll, little suspecting what he was about to learn. Consequently he didn't inquire who this Granzow was, to whom Völger sent his regards. 'No, I read your name in the newspaper, Völger. I just came here on the off chance.'

'But you have seen Granzow?'

'No', said Doll, cautiously. 'Not yet.'

'Not yet!' cried the other. 'Maybe you didn't even know that Granzow has been trying to get hold of you for weeks now, ever since there was a rumour that you were in Berlin? Didn't you know that, Doll?'

'No', answered Doll again. 'And to tell you the truth, I don't even know who Granzow is.'

'What!' cried Völger, and was so genuinely shocked that he suddenly let go of Doll's hand, which he had still been clutching. 'You *must* know who Granzow is! You must know his poems, at the very least! Or his big novel, *Wendelin and the Sleepwalkers*? Well, of course …', he went on, as Doll continued to shake his head, 'of course, Granzow *was* living in exile for twelve years, and the Nazis immediately banned all his books in '33, obviously. But all the same—you must know him from the time before '33!'

'I really don't!' insisted Doll. 'You have to remember that I've nearly always lived out in the country, and I know very few writers in person.'

'But you must have read about him lately in the newspapers', said Völger, trying another tack. 'He returned from exile back in May, and founded the big artists' association. You *must* have read about it, Doll!'

'I was the mayor of a small town, working an average of fourteen hours a day', said Doll, smiling at his persistent inquisitor. 'So I barely had time to read the letters I was sent, let alone a newspaper. The truth is, I looked at a newspaper last night for the first time since the end of the war, and the only name I came across that I knew was yours, Völger. That's why I'm here today. But perhaps you can tell me', he went on, 'why this Granzow is looking for me, when I don't know him and have certainly never met him?'

'But Doll!' said Völger, 'Granzow wants you to join his association, of course! People are expecting great things of you — you're just the man to write a popular novel about the last few years ...'

'No, no', said Doll in reply, and his face had suddenly darkened. 'I'm definitely not the right man for that, and I wouldn't go near the subject.' He shook his head again and went on: 'The thing is, Völger, I started off like everybody else, of course, down in the mire. But even later on, when I had clawed my way up out of it a bit, and started to think about what I might like to do later, it seemed to me impossible to write books like before, as if nothing had happened, as if our entire world had not collapsed around us. I thought we would have to write in a completely different way now, not pretending that the Thousand-Year Reich had never existed, and that one only needed to pick up again where one had left off writing before 1933. No, what was needed was a completely new beginning, new in terms of content, certainly, but also in terms of form ...'

He paused for a moment and looked a little uncertainly at Völger, who was listening closely. He ended abruptly: 'But I don't know — so far, I haven't found a way. Maybe I'll never write another book. Everything looks so bleak. Who are we any more, we Germans, in this world we have destroyed? Who should we be talking to? The Germans, who don't want to listen? Or people in other countries, who hate us?'

'Well', said Völger, 'if I were in your shoes I wouldn't worry about it, either about finding the right form or finding a readership. I am quite sure that one day you will write again, simply because you are compelled to write! And now you should go and see Granzow—I'll give you his address. The best time to catch him is around lunchtime.'

They parted shortly afterwards. The young wife had not contributed a single word to this memorable discussion, which was highly unusual for the 'sea surf'. And now, too, as they were walking back on their own, she was silent. This prolonged silence was making Doll feel uncomfortable. Even if he did feel unable to write the novel that had been suggested, and even if he had to disappoint the hopes that Völger, and presumably Granzow, too, had placed in him, he was still gratified by the reception accorded him, and by the fact that people were actually searching for him in the great metropolis of Berlin. (Though how exactly such a search could be conducted was something of a mystery to him.)

For months on end he had felt so small and dejected that the first little bit of interest anyone showed in him, the first sunshine ray of sympathy, warmed him and brightened his life. He felt different, he walked differently, he gazed with different eyes upon the burnt-out machinery lying in the fire-ravaged hall. *Perhaps one day you'll be working for me again after all*, he said to himself. *You look burnt-out and ruined now, but that can be put right—everything in life gets back on track sooner or later ...*

He stepped out into the grey November day, making his way between the huge heaps of rubble. The wind whipped up evil clouds of dust and ash and scorched scraps of paper. But to him it felt like the wafting of a warm spring breeze, as if all the birds were singing, and the trees were just putting out their first green leaves. He was still somebody, after all! For so long he had felt like a nobody, he had let everyone push him around: but he was still somebody, after all! Völger had shown him it was so, and Granzow believed in him. He felt just like those machines: one day they would all be working again.

He looked across at his companion with an unspoken challenge. Why didn't she say something? Now would have been the time to let him know that she, too, was happy about the reception he had met with.

But she wasn't looking at him at all. Her gaze was directed at the windows of the shops and their pitiful displays, a meagre selection of overpriced substitute goods and showpiece items that were not for sale. All of a sudden, and without giving him any indication of her intentions, she had disappeared inside one of these shops, or rather not a shop but a pub.

Once again he was infuriated by her behaviour, the completely inconsiderate way she just left him standing there without a word of explanation, simply taking it for granted that he would wait for her. But she might be wrong about that: the tram stop was not far away, and when she emerged from the pub he might well be on the tram and on his way, and she would not be present when he had his crucial meeting with Granzow.

It upset him and fuelled his rising anger that his partner, of all people, had to sour this day when his luck was beginning to turn. So no sooner had her face appeared again than he strode off in the direction of the tram stop, not vouchsafing her so much as a glance or a word when she blithely took her place at his side as if nothing had happened.

She was smoking again, of course! So that's why she had gone into the pub—to buy more cigarettes! She was blowing the last of their money without a thought for the future. And now, of course, just when he might have had a cigarette to celebrate this special day, she hadn't offered him one.

The tram was not particularly full, and as luck would have it there were two free seats next to each other, on one of those benches by the door that face inwards rather than forwards. On the other side of the entry door, separated from them by the full width of the tram, sat a fat man with a pale but jowly face, and an old lady who was clearly not with him, whom Doll promptly dubbed 'the putrid baby' in his mind. This old maid, who had plainly never married, had the pink, innocent cheeks of a baby, but was so disfigured by age and the signs of approaching death that her childlike appearance had something vaguely obscene and sinister about it.

This old creature, decked out in frills, lace, and buttons, appeared to be irritated by the mere sight of Alma casually smoking a cigarette. She gave a couple of contemptuous snorts, looked at her jowly neighbour, then at the young woman again and finally at Doll, who revealed by the fact that he was now paying the conductor for himself and his wife that she was with him.

Doll returned her look with a cool, impassive stare, whereupon 'the putrid baby' began to mutter furiously. She directed the gaze of her pale-blue eyes now at Alma, now at the other passengers, as if inviting them to join in her protest. It was obvious that the old lady would not be able to contain her feelings for much longer. An explosion was imminent.

Perhaps Alma wanted to hasten the detonation, or perhaps she was simply oblivious of this entire dumb show. At all events, she suddenly took a comb from her handbag, tossed her hair to fluff it up, and began to comb her locks.

This was too much for the old lady. In a loud voice verging on a shriek, she called across to Alma: 'Kindly do that at home, young lady! You're not in a hairdressing salon here!'

The jowly man nodded involuntarily at these words, and indeed it seemed as if everyone on the tram who had observed the incident was on the old lady's side. But the young woman responded coolly and with controlled politeness: 'I'm sitting far enough away from you, madam, for it not to bother you!'

But when she saw the cantankerous look on the putrid baby's face, and the censorious or gleeful expressions of the other tram passengers, she suddenly handed the comb over to Doll. 'You need to use this, too, my dear. Your hair's a real mess.'

After a brief hesitation Doll took the comb and began to comb his hair. At Alma's impulsive action the gleeful faces of the onlookers had taken on an expectant or smiling expression. Even the jowly man sitting next to the old lady was smiling now. But the aggressor flushed crimson with rage, then her face suddenly turned a yellowish white, and she barked out a stinging reprimand: 'They're all the same, these dolled-up little tramps!' To which Alma coolly replied, while the whole tram waited silently with bated breath: 'And they're all the same, these dried-up old bats!'

Doll was not the only one who thought the term 'dried-up old bat' a priceless description of the old lady, because the whole tram was laughing. In fact, the jowly man was so tickled that he drummed his feet on the floor with glee—though he promptly shot an anxious glance at his neighbour. But there was nothing more to fear from her; she had lost the battle. She leaned back in the dark, grimy corner of the tram, and appeared to be wheezing her last, in the last stages of putrefaction, as Doll said to his wife.

After this little interlude, everything was sweetness and light again between the married couple. They chatted away as if they had never had the slightest falling-out. Doll now took a cigarette without hesitation, drew the smoke that he had denied himself for so long deep into his lungs with great relish, and even nodded in agreement when Alma said, almost apologetically: 'I've been reckless again — I wanted to celebrate today!'

An hour later the two of them were standing in a large, almost opulently appointed anteroom. The general state of the building and its furnishings were far superior to the place they had visited earlier. And just as this anteroom, with its old paintings on the walls, the deep-pile carpet underfoot, and the ordered efficiency of a well-run office, into which two female secretaries nonetheless injected a note of homely warmth, was far superior to Völger's place of work, so the reception they were given here far exceeded the one they got from Völger. Doll had only just said his name, and one of the two ladies had only just disappeared into the next room to announce him, when the door of this room was opened (it turned out to be a spacious salon, decorated throughout in white and blue) and a tall, fat, grey-haired man rushed out to greet Doll.

'Doll!' he cried, seizing his hand, and his entire body seemed to be shaking with excitement. 'Doll! You've finally come!'

Completely overwhelmed, Doll was tugged from the anteroom into the blue-and-white salon, while Mrs. Doll followed on silently behind. 'Doll! So you're not dead after all! You've no idea how worried we've been about you!'

And Doll, his hand clasped between the large, soft, moist hands of the other man, could think of nothing to say apart from the name that he had heard for the first time an hour and a half previously: 'Granzow! Yes, here we are, Granzow!'

They looked at each other with tears in their eyes. It was like a reunion of old friends. And there was nothing fake about these tears. They were overcome by emotion, and the memory of the past twelve years, spent in exile or in servitude, swept through them again. They were both survivors of a catastrophe, after all. Both felt the other's joy at seeing each other and getting acquainted. Under normal circumstances they would have got to know each other a long time ago.

Doll felt rather more conscience-stricken than Granzow, who did at least know Doll's books, and he was filled with a faint sense of guilt. As in: *I hope Völger never tells him that I hadn't even heard of him.* But this sense of guilt was quickly dissipated. Granzow was plainly quite uninterested in himself. He only wanted to hear about the Dolls, about what had happened to them in the last few years, where and how they had lived, where they were living now, and how they were doing. All Doll could see in the eyes of Granzow, who was listening attentively to every word he said, was joy, kindly joy. *And what am I, when all is said and done? A minor novelist, who had given up on himself a long time ago and gone into hopeless decline. But I can't let him see that, now I need to pull myself together again ...*

As these thoughts were going through Doll's head, the three of them were already comfortably installed on the curved blue-velvet sofa around the big table. Lying on the table were packs of Granzow's cigarettes, to which the Dolls were free to help themselves. Coffee had also been ordered and brought in—not coffee substitute, but the real thing, even if it was a little weak: 'You'll have to excuse us, Doll. Our canteen is not quite up to scratch yet. But that will soon change, things are getting better now ...'

The 'now' almost sounded like a reference to Doll being found again, as though this moment marked the beginning of a new era—which in the present context could hardly be the intended meaning.

The conversation now took a quieter turn. The two Dolls did most of the talking, describing their experiences over the preceding months. It was very different from their meeting with Völger; here, Alma spoke, too, with no thought of demurely holding back. Which was only right and proper, for while Völger had taken no notice of Mrs. Doll apart from an initial surprised look, Granzow was visibly charmed by the vivacious young woman. He divided his attention equally between her and Doll himself, his expression by turns smiling or solicitous.

Granzow knew how to ask the right questions—and he was a great listener. What happened with Völger couldn't possibly happen here—that both parties couldn't wait to talk about their own sufferings. Granzow seemed to feel no need to talk about himself; he was, as the expression goes, all ears. He nodded eagerly when they talked about their decision to leave the small town for good. He shook his head with a worried look when he heard about the state in which they had found their Berlin apartment. He slapped the table with his hand when Doll was telling the tale of the tyrannical official at the housing office. In short, he appeared to take a lively interest in every phase of the Dolls' recent life, and they had the impression that he was not just listening for the sake of it—in one ear and out the other—but that he was already drawing conclusions and reaching decisions even as he listened ...

And they were correct in their impression, because, during a lull in the conversation, Granzow said: 'I think I've got the picture, and

I know what needs to happen next.' They looked at him expectantly. He went on: 'First, you need to get a decent apartment, ideally in an area that has not been too badly damaged. Secondly, we need to sort out a truck and trailer to fetch your things from the small town. And thirdly, you need to be issued with ration cards, preferably the No.1 card, but failing that, the No.2.'

He smiled in an affectionately fatherly way when he saw their astonished, incredulous expressions. They had only wanted to get things off their chest, after all; they were quite prepared to shift for themselves. All they wanted was a bit of sympathy, a bit of encouragement. And now it looked as if they were about to get something like real, practical help.

'Yes,' continued Granzow, still smiling, 'we can sort all that out. I'll just go and make some inquiries ...' And the big, heavy man stood up, hurried from the room, and left the two of them alone.

They looked at each other, and their faces had brightened. 'It's not possible', said Doll. 'And yet it is so. Someone's really going to help us again!'

And she replied: 'I've always liked my apartment, even though it's been wrecked—but if we can get a place of our own, just for us ...'

Doll said: 'It was that simple: we just needed to talk to this one man. And we were pretty much on our last legs, Alma!'

He felt a kind of trembling in his limbs, and she too was sitting quite still, thinking back on the journey that had led them here, to the blue-and-white salon. They had got through the bad times; now things were looking up again. At that moment it did not occur to Doll to think that maybe it wasn't that easy, that it would take more than having a place to live, food to eat, and their old things around them. He forgot now that there had been a war on, the time of suffering before that, that he was a burnt-out case, an empty shell devoid of content ... That even the helpful Granzow could not give him this content, that he would have to create it for himself, finding a faith again, not only in himself, but more especially in his fellow Germans, in the entire world, in the meaning of work and perseverance, a firm belief in a bright future for mankind: he forgot that he had none of this in him.

Right now, all this was far from his thoughts. Instead he said, as he freed himself from her embrace: 'Now we have been given a chance, and God knows we'll make the most of it! We mustn't let Granzow down and make him regret it!'

'Definitely not', she agreed.

Granzow returned with a smile on his face. 'That's all arranged!' he said. 'The best thing would be to come by again the day after tomorrow, then I can tell you more. Would one o'clock, the day after tomorrow, suit you? Good, then let's say Thursday at one o'clock here!'

He looked at them both, smiling benignly, like a father who is well pleased with his children. The thought flashed through Doll's mind that Granzow could hardly be any older than him, and yet he felt so young, so boyish and immature by comparison. 'And there's one thing more I must ask you, Doll', continued Granzow after a pause. 'But you don't have to answer if you don't want to. So: how are you getting on with your work? You understand that we're all waiting for it ... Have you written anything recently? Or have you got plans for a new work?'

'Well', said Doll hesitantly, 'The thing is—'

And Granzow cut in quickly: 'No, really, Doll, if you'd rather not talk about your plans ... I'm not asking just to be nosy.'

'Oh, I understand', replied Doll, speaking more quickly. 'And it's not that I'm reluctant to talk about it. It's just that I'm afraid you'll be disappointed, Granzow. The fact is, I don't actually have any plans. It's true that in the last six months before the surrender, I started to write down my memories of the Nazis ...'

'That's great!' cried Granzow.

'I don't know. I don't think it *is* great. Nothing really terrible happened to me, you see, and to note down in such detail all the little pinpricks that came my way ... The book might have been of some interest, perhaps, because it shows how a person can be driven to the brink of suicide just by pinpricks ...' Thus far, Doll had been speaking hesitantly, almost reluctantly. But now he went on more quickly: 'But it's all so long ago. Since then the war has ended, and so much has happened to me that my hatred for the Nazis has gone completely, and been replaced by a general hatred of mankind. For me, the Nazis have ceased to exist ...'

'No, no!' protested Granzow. 'On the contrary, Mr. Doll, I think those Nazi gentlemen are still very much alive. There are times when I am acutely aware of that.'

'Well, yes, perhaps the odd one here and there, who will never learn and never change.' Granzow shook his head vigorously. 'But', Doll went on, 'be that as it may, the book is past history for me.' And when the other gestured as if to plead with him: 'I can't even bring myself to take a look at it or type it up—not for now anyway ...'

He fell silent and looked at Granzow, who replied quickly: 'Look, my dear Doll, nobody is going to force you to do anything you don't want to. All in good time. And what about your own plans for the future?'

'Nothing!' said Doll, feeling guilty. 'I have thought about writing novels sometimes, and about particular themes. But none of it seemed of any consequence. After everything fell apart—including me—I've always had this feeling that I need to start all over again, and do things differently.' He was speaking more quickly now, only repeating what he had said to the publishing editor Völger an hour and a half previously. 'No', he said in conclusion, 'I'm sorry to disappoint you, Mr. Granzow, at our very first meeting. Maybe my appetite for work will come back again, once my outward circumstances have improved a little. I need a certain inner calm in order to produce anything, as well as peace and quiet in my outward life.'

'Of course!' agreed Granzow. They carried on talking for a few minutes, but not about Doll's work. The jovial mood of first acquaintance returned once more. Then they took their leave of each other, with the promise to reconvene at one o'clock in two days' time.

But as they were leaving the building, a chauffeur in grey uniform inquired: 'Mr. Granzow has asked me to drive you home. Where would you like me to take you?'

More kindness and courtesy, more indulgence! But more of an inward obligation, therefore, not to disappoint so much good faith.

For a while they sat in silence in the back of the car behind the driver, overwhelmed by happiness. Then the woman nudged her husband gently. 'You know—!' she whispered.

To which he replied: 'Yes, what then?'

'My dear', she said, 'I'm so happy I'm going to die! To think that someone is helping us out again! I want to shout—shout for joy!' And she babbled on like a spoilt child: 'And now you must be really nice to your little Alma! Now you must give her a lovely long kiss! A thousand kisses! Otherwise I'll scream!'

'The chauffeur!' he reminded her, and yet was happy to oblige her anyway.

'Chauffeur very old man!' she babbled. 'Chauffeur only drive car! Chauffeur see nothing! You young man, you give little Alma thousand kisses, otherwise I'll scream!'

And so the Dolls exchanged a long, lingering kiss … It was so long since they had sat in a car that it didn't even occur to them that a chauffeur has a rear-view mirror, in which he can see everything that's going on in the back of the car. Just like children, they thought that nobody was looking.

The chauffeur was not a discreet man, but he was a genuine Berliner. 'And do you know what, Mr. Granzow', he said, as he was driving his employer home that evening and had finished telling the tale, 'do you know what, they didn't just give each other a little peck, like an old married couple — they were all over each other, like a pair of young things. And as for him, he's getting on a bit, he must be our sort of age, Mr. Granzow. But he's all right, he is, and if he writes books the same way he kisses, then I might take up reading yet, Mr. Granzow!'

CHAPTER TWELVE

Restored to health

In a northern suburb of Berlin, a man is sitting by the window of a small room. It is high summer, July; to be precise, it is the fifth of July in the year 1946. Although it is only around nine in the morning, the air has lost the dewy freshness of the night. It is hot, and it is going to get a lot hotter still today, unless a thunderstorm cools things down a bit.

But for now the sky does not look as if a storm is brewing. It is radiant with sunshine, completely cloudless, and not so much blue as a dull, whitish silver with just a hint of blueness. Whenever the man looks up from his writing and gazes out of the window (which he does not infrequently; he appears to be not all that absorbed by his labours), he finds himself squinting a little to shield his eyes against the glare of the summer sky. But then beneath this sky shimmering with heat he sees something that gladdens the heart, even in a suburb of Berlin: green treetops, the gables of houses, and red roofs, but not a single ruin. There's not so much as a freshly repaired roof to be seen, and even the windows of the houses appear to be all intact. A real sight for sore eyes in this city of ruins!

The writer looks up frequently from his work. He sits there, pen in hand, poised to begin writing again. But first he listens out for the voices down in the yard. The voices he hears are invariably women's voices, and almost always those of young women, and they all speak in the easy, rather throwaway manner of native Berliners. More than once, somebody says: 'It's too 'ot indoors by 'alf today!' or: 'I'll tell you what *that's* all about, so I will!'

But the man doesn't smile at this, and he doesn't feel the slightest bit superior when he hears this kind of rough, 'uneducated' talk. He has learned that he has no reason to feel superior to anything or anyone.

Although the voices sound young, and although the man only needs to stand up and step over to the window to get a good view of the women as they speak, he doesn't do so. He knows that some of these girls and women are very pretty, and they are sunning themselves out there in the most casual state of undress, but he is not curious; instead he feels old, very old, and tired. During the last year, his hair has gone very grey; but given how old he feels, it ought to be snowy-white.

As he writes, the man frequently hears another sound apart from the chattering of the women. He lays the pen down and listens, straining hard to hear. It's a very strange sound that comes to his ears, a cross between the cooing of a dove and the fluting of a slightly out-of-tune blackbird. This strange sound, which he could not identify at all during the first few weeks of his stay here, is made by a large dog, half Doberman and half Alsatian. This creature was probably driven out of its mind by all the gunfire and the flames and the crazy commotion during the final assault on Berlin, and is now chained up somewhere down there beneath the green treetops, looked after by a halfwit who lives in this building at No.10 Elsastrasse. In the evening, Hermann—that's what everyone in the house calls her, though her real name is Hermine—lets the dog loose, and the creature then guards No.10 Elsastrasse through the night; and woe to the stranger who dares to climb over the fence! The dog would tear him apart without a moment's hesitation: it is a mad dog, and nothing could hold him back, not even his keeper Hermann.

The strange thing is that this dog—called 'Mucki', a name conferred on him in happier times that no longer suits him at all—can bark at night, but during the day, when he is chained up, he can only flute and coo like a bird. He just didn't have a good war. Wounded inside, he cries out in pain, is capable of murder, and is no use for anything. The man sometimes wonders, when he hears this strange sound, how many humans are in much the same place as this Mucki.

Yes, the man finds all kinds of reasons for looking up from his work and taking a break for a few minutes from the concentrated effort of writing in his scratchy hand. From time to time, he looks across at a loudly ticking wall clock to check the time and see if it is still too soon for him to stand up and tidy his papers away. This wall clock with its faded blue face and brass-coloured pendulum is the only item of furnishing in the small, cramped room that goes beyond the bare essentials. A table, a chair, a bed, a narrow wall closet, and an ancient, completely faded velvet armchair constitute the sum total of the room's furnishings.

Except—there is one object that should not be forgotten, even though it is generally tucked away out of sight. It is a black velvet cushion, decorated with a kind of painted scene. The scene depicts a castle with three turrets, lilac-coloured roofs, and lots of windows, which are red at the bottom and yellow at the top, while the walls of the castle are formed by the unpainted black velvet. One turret has a white flag on top of a long pole, the second has a cross, also in white, and the third just has a kind of very long white lance. Also in the picture are trees with white trunks and green leaves in many shades;

rocky crags in pink, lilac, and flame-red; and dotted about here and there, for no apparent reason, are white railings. Hanging over the whole scene is a circular, yellow orb, which might equally well be the moon or the sun.

The man loathes this cushion with a fierce hatred. He curses it just because it has survived this war undamaged in all its bovine ghastliness, while so much of beauty has been destroyed. He hides the cushion at the bottom of his bed or in the little wall closet, just so that he doesn't have to look at it all the time. But the cleaning lady keeps on finding it, and helpfully pats it out flat again on the faded velvet armchair, clearly delighting in this choice work of art. The man could ask the cleaning lady to leave the cushion where he has hidden it, but he refrains from doing so. He never says a word to this woman, even though she always announces in the same friendly manner, when she has finished cleaning the room: 'Now you can get back to your work!' or: 'Now you can have a cup of coffee.'

Not that one could really blame the writer all that much for pausing so often in his labours. He is only writing out of a sense of duty, without any real enthusiasm or belief in what he is doing, perhaps in part just to prove to himself and others that he is capable of finishing what he has started. Begun six months or so earlier, this piece of work at first seemed to be going well. Then came various interruptions, due to personal disagreements, illness, or simply a lack of appetite for work, and the more he delayed final completion, the less interest the writer himself took in the work he was doing.

But the situation on this fifth of July was a little different. On this morning, the man had awoken from a sound night's sleep and had suddenly realised how to steer the little ship of his writing out of the sea of facts and into a tranquil harbour at last. He could not yet say with certainty whether he would reach this harbour in two days, eight days, or twelve days, but even a voyage of twelve days held no more terrors for him, since he now knew that a safe harbour awaited. When he paused in his work today, he was just continuing the bad habits of previous days; he was not deliberately looking for excuses to be lazy.

The man glanced again at the wall clock with the faded blue face, and saw that it was late enough for him to stop writing with a clear conscience. He gathered up pen and paper, put them away in the wall closet, and picked up a block of wood with a key hanging from it. With this key and some toilet things, he crossed a forecourt towards a door on the far side, on which was hung a sign that said in large, clear letters: 'Not to be used by gon. or syph.!'

The man made to open the door when he saw that there was already a key in the lock, attached to a block of wood exactly like the one he was holding in his hand. He muttered something about 'bloody cheek!' and was about to place his hand on the door handle when the door was opened from the inside and a girl or young woman, dressed only in a very short shirt, brushed past him, obviously feeling guilty, and disappeared through the door of a nearby room.

The man gazed after her for a moment, in half a mind to kick up an almighty fuss over this unauthorised use of his toilet. The sign was clear enough, after all. But then he thought better of it. He had never yet sounded off since he had been living in this place, and he would adopt a different tactic. He withdrew the key from the lock, went into the toilet with both keys, and bolted the door behind him.

As he was having a thorough wash in there, he wondered whether he should complain to Mother Trüller about this blatant disregard for the no-entry sign, or whether it would not be simpler just to commandeer this second key, which was supposed to be for the sole use of the nursing staff, and had only been left in the door as a result of someone's carelessness. He decided on the second course of action: Mother Trüller had enough on her plate, and the effect of even the most severe dressing-down from her would last only for a day at most. As for the so-called patients here …

Yes, as for these so-called patients, who for the most part were not actually ill at all, as for these sixty women, with whom he shared this madhouse at No.10 Elsastrasse as the only male occupant, all warnings, tongue-lashings, pleas, and prohibitions were completely lost on them. On the contrary, they were all imbued with the best of bad intentions, determined to break all the rules and make trouble wherever they could.

When the man moved in here a good eight weeks previously, and suddenly found himself in the company of sixty women who were mostly young and pretty, he had expected to be living a highly entertaining and also instructive life. Not that he had any designs on these ladies, not at all: the nature of the diseases that had landed them in this place—usually under gentle pressure from the police—was such as to deter him from any such designs. The women had picked up these diseases, the names of which were spelled out with brutal clarity on the no-entry sign on the door of his toilet, out there in the city of Berlin, recklessly, knowingly, or—in a few cases—unknowingly. They had been diagnosed by doctors and put on a course of treatment.

But these women had given up on the treatment, either failing to turn up for their appointments at the doctor's surgery or choosing to ignore the doctor's instructions, so that they posed a constant threat to anyone who had anything to do with them. That's when the gentle police pressure was applied, and they were deposited at the door of this institution, which they were not allowed to leave until they were fully cured. Some of them had proved difficult to find; they knew what awaited them. They had changed their address, avoiding their treatment by devious cunning, only to be scooped up eventually in some police raid.

Well, despite all this, or perhaps precisely because of it, the man had hoped to derive some entertainment and instruction from these ladies, and hear some colourful life stories. Instead he soon realised that all these girls were hopelessly stupid and dishonest. To hear them talk, they had all ended up in this place through the dirty tricks of the doctors, the public health authorities, and the police, and it was only when they got here that they had been infected by the immoral women they had to share a room with!

It didn't take great powers of discernment to see that they were lying, and as for their laziness, it beggared belief. Although they were not confined to bed by illness, except on the days when they were given their injections or a crash course of pills, there were many among them who hardly got out of bed during the whole eight or twelve weeks of their treatment. There they lay, young and blooming, with strong, healthy limbs, but bone idle and not prepared to do any useful work. They were so lazy that if one of them felt sick from the large intake of pills, none of the others could be bothered to hold out the sick bowl for her. For all they cared, she could vomit all over the floor—that's what the nurse was there for, to clean it up afterwards. So they would ring for the nurse, and if she didn't come at once, the mess stayed where it was. The filth and smell didn't bother them, but the idea of doing any work at all was anathema to them.

That wasn't what they were here for, living in a world where it is so easy for a pretty young girl to clean a man out, like a nicely fattened Christmas goose! And they would boast to each other of their triumphs, telling of pockets daringly picked, of their magnetic charms as barmaids, of their whole wasted, useless lives—and the more useless, the more glorious in their eyes. And then they went and stole cigarettes from each other, and tossed their medical prescriptions out of the window or dropped them down the toilet (being too 'smart' to let themselves be poisoned by these doctors!); and when their relatives came to visit them on Sundays, they complained bitterly about how bad the food was here, and how they had to go hungry. Yet according to their regular weekly weight checks, they were growing steadily fatter from idleness and gluttony.

No indeed, the man's expectations had not been fulfilled. There was nothing romantic about these women; they were not bathed in some redemptive glow. He was not very patient with them, it is true. There had been great excitement among them when this man came to live in a house of women; they had been friendly and welcoming towards him, and in the first few weeks there had been no shortage of visitors who sought him out in his room under all manner of pretexts. But he had soon given up chatting to them. It annoyed him every time that they thought him stupid enough to believe their cock-and-bull stories.

And they were greedy. He could tell from the way they looked at the food on his plate, comparing it with their own portions. As a private patient of the senior consultant, who had not been able to find room for him anywhere else but here, he did enjoy something of a special position, but by and large he was given exactly the same food as they had. Mother Trüller could hardly cook separate meals for one man! But they eyed the size of his bread slices, gauged the thickness of the topping, and said: 'It's all right for some!' Or else: 'I couldn't care less!'

And then they always wanted something from him: a cigarette, or a light for a cigarette, or a book or a newspaper or fuel for their lighter—they took it to such extremes that he would refuse them the simplest favour.

Then came a stand-off period, when they no longer visited him and hardly gave him the time of day; after that, open war was declared on him. One day, a drunken lout had tried to climb over the garden railings and get into the house, whereupon the man declared that it could hardly come as a surprise to anyone who had observed how they shamelessly accosted or taunted every passing man from the balconies of their rooms, after the manner of whores, which of course is what most of them were. This had driven them to extremes of indignation at this liar and traitor. None of them had ever called out to anyone from their balcony—not so much as a word—and when the doctor gave instructions for the balcony doors to be locked anyway, they swore to the man that they would beat him one night until every bone in his body was broken!

Well, they hadn't beaten him. In fact, they had soon abandoned the silent treatment they gave him during the first few weeks following this incident. They were unreliable in everything—even their dislikes. They started speaking to him again, every now and then one of them would come and scrounge a cigarette, and if he couldn't spare a cigarette, then a couple of butt ends would do. But the man didn't forget so easily; he was finished with them for good, even if that meant casting out a few righteous souls for the sake of the many unrighteous.

The man finished his ablutions some time ago, and now he has tidied up his room a bit and locked the two keys to the toilet away in his wall closet. He grinned a little at the thought of Nurse Emma and Nurse Gertrud, who would soon be searching frantically for this key!

He now put on a coat, despite the blazing sun: he was ashamed to be seen on the street in his stained and crumpled suit. He went downstairs and made for the kitchen. In the kitchen, Mother Trüller and her acolytes were busy preparing lunch for the eighty or so residents. Her face was flushed a deep red; her stout chest, invariably covered by a yellow or lilac lace ruffle, heaved mightily as the heavy cooking pots became as light as feathers in her hands. She was working so hard that the sweat stood out on her brow in bright little beads, but she was in an excellent mood.

She smiled radiantly when she caught sight of the man, and said: 'Mr. Doll, are you leaving so early? You want to sign out now, I expect?'

'Yes, I'd like to sign out, Mother Trüller, I'm in good health, and ready to roam! And if the truck and trailer really do turn up today, I won't be back for lunch, either. I hope they do turn up.'

'I hope so, for your sake. But I won't hear of you missing lunch. I'm glad to think I've put twenty pounds on you! If you're not back by three, I'll send out some lunch for you—and enough for the whole family!'

'No, don't do that, Mother Trüller!' said the man. And in a quieter voice, so that the others wouldn't hear: 'You know I'm already too deeply in debt to you. Who knows when I'll ever be able to pay it all off again!' And he sighed deeply.

'Oh, you'll have paid it all off in six months!' announced Mother Trüller with a broad smile. 'A man like you—healthy again, full of energy, all you have to do is sit down and start working, and you'll be rolling in money! So what is there to sigh about, on a nice summer's day like this?'

While she was administering this good-natured rebuke, she had shepherded Doll to the door of the building, stopping at the threshold that the girls and women who lived here were only allowed to cross when they were fully recovered. 'Well, all the best, Mr. Doll! Maybe the truck really will come today. And if you should hear anything—you know what I mean—you'll let me know at once?'

'But of course, Mother Trüller', replied Doll, and stepped out onto the street, into the brilliant sunshine.

That's her all over, he said to himself as he walked on, *and she'll never change. She'll never forget to remind anyone leaving the house that they must tell her at once if they hear any news. It doesn't matter what they've been talking about—she always thinks to give them this reminder as a parting shot.*

In actual fact, she is always thinking about it, even when she's having a conversation about something completely different. The worry about her missing son is constantly eating away at her, underneath it all—the thought of him, her love for him. As the director and proprietor of this somewhat crazy hospital in Elsastrasse, an institution for women run by a woman, she thinks all the time only of her son, and thinks of herself only as his trustee. She has had no news of him for fifteen months now; Erdmann disappeared at the time of the battle for Berlin. He might have become a POW, or he might be lying somewhere on the streets of this vast sea of ruins, hit by a stray bullet, crushed under falling masonry, buried under rubble. And this might have happened a while back, fifteen months ago.

But his mother is still waiting for him, and she will carry on waiting if she has to, for years on end. And many other mothers and wives are waiting with her for their sons, their husbands—waiting for loved ones who may never return. Meanwhile this farmer's daughter from Hanover, who has worked her way up in the world by her own efforts, is tirelessly busy. She keeps her female patients, who are always up to mischief, on a tight leash, she works day and night, she has a friendly word for everyone, she has a sympathetic ear for everyone's troubles, and tries to help wherever she can. She really doesn't have time to feel depressed and fed up with work. With her plain, no-nonsense approach to life, she is an example to us all.

But she never forgets to say to anyone who is going out: 'If you hear anything—about my son Erdmann, that is—you must let me know at once.'

The outside world, beyond the neighbouring streets where all her tradesmen live, is a remote, alien world for Mother Trüller, who is always in her little hospital, constantly under pressure to keep people fed and attend to their other basic bodily needs. For her, the big wide world, where miracles can happen every day, begins a leisurely five-minute walk away from her front door—a world where one might run into her missing son Erdmann in the street, and say to him: 'Look here, Erdmann, it's high time you called in on your mother again. She's been waiting for you constantly, day and night, for fifteen months. She's still living at No. 10 Elsastrasse.'

Not that Erdmann is the kind of son who needs to be told to go and see his own mother. Quite the contrary: Erdmann would have got in touch with his mother without being told.

But the world out there, this vast, sprawling, chaotic Berlin, is so weird and wonderful, so full of wondrous things. The visitor might run across someone who has heard of the son, who has perhaps seen him somewhere. He might have heard news of the repatriation of POWs, the most astonishing and incredible rumours—Mother Trüller is ready to hear anything and everything. Her stout heart is not apt to flutter at the smallest thing; she is not that easily discouraged. Her hopes are kept alive by the story of one home-comer who turned up out of the blue.

So she waits and hopes. And waiting and hoping along with her are hundreds, thousands, of women that nobody talks about. In the war they were good enough to offer up their sons and husbands, and then quietly step into their shoes in the workplace. Now they are quietly waiting, getting on with their work, wherever they are. It's just that they say to anyone who is going out: 'You will let me know if you hear anything, won't you?'

Good, capable, indestructible Mother Trüller, mother of the people, eternal mother, eternal believer, who waits and faints not, who seeks to help wherever she can …!

As he was thinking these thoughts, the man in the shabby, crumpled, stained clothes under the pale summer coat, which was not exactly in pristine condition itself, walked past quite a few pubs, where—as he very well knew—cigarettes could be bought on the black market. He was dying for a smoke, but he restrained himself. Dear American cigarettes costing eleven marks apiece had been off-limits for a long time now in the Doll household—as he had rightly predicted to his wife. But even so-called 'cheap' German cigarettes at five marks each were strictly rationed to one a day, at most; one German cigarette only in the evening after supper, the smoke drawn deep into the lungs with sensuous relish—and then that was all for the next twenty-four hours.

All? Well, not quite. The Dolls were smokers; they would always be smokers. Even now, Doll had his pockets filled with something he could smoke. They collected the rose petals from Mother Trüller's garden—not just the ones that had fallen off, but the ones that were in full bloom as well—and dried them. They reasoned thus: 'This rose will drop its petals in the next few hours anyway!' and then they would pluck them, stuff Doll's pockets with the petals, and turn his room into a drying and curing plant. So the room smelled constantly of roses. They had also smoked the leaves of cherry trees, and, when they were really desperate, even a vile-tasting blood-cleansing tea, from which they first had to pick out the juniper berries and stalks.

That's how frugal they had become, even the young wife, who was so determined never to deny herself anything. They once owned a car—one each, in fact—and money, and all the things that money can buy; such commodities, the good things of this life, were no problem for them. But now the mantra that they were a defeated nation had become engrained in their thinking. They laughed at their foul-smelling 'tobacco', they were apt to cover up their stained clothing, but they were not ashamed any more. *What do people expect? We are a defeated nation, we have lost an all-out, total war, and now we are reduced to total beggars.* The suburb through which Doll was now walking had survived the war relatively unscathed. Here and there a roof had been blown in, even the odd house reduced completely to rubble, but by and large everything appeared intact and not too run-down amidst the abundant summer greenery. It was just the people on the streets: they could all have done with twenty pounds more weight on them, and fifty fewer wrinkles on their faces. They were still enduring unimaginable poverty, wearing rags instead of clothes, and shoes that were forever falling apart and being mended, held together with string, shoes that looked as if they had trailed the length and breadth of Europe.

For quite a while there was a young girl walking ahead of Doll, who had none of the charm that youth confers on even the most unprepossessing; she walked with difficulty on bloody, festering, dirty legs, as if barely dragging herself along. Her dress appeared to have been made from a couple of flour sacks. When the wearer made it, she still retained a little bit of hope, despite her wretched circumstances; she had added some crudely embroidered decorative trims and a little white collar, as if to say: 'I'm young, you can still look at me, even if I am only wearing a dress made from old sacking!'

But all these additions were now looking battered and crumpled, and so dirty that the white collar looked almost black, or at any rate no lighter than the sacking. In the course of her long travels she had lost all hope, given up on herself a long time ago. *These people I see walking the streets with me can be divided into two groups*, thought Doll: *the ones who cannot hope, and the ones who dare not hope.*

But all of them, whichever group they belonged to, were carting something around with them: a few wretched twigs snapped off the trees; burst suitcases, whose contents one would really rather not know; handbags stuffed full; and mysterious briefcases whose locks had long since broken because they had been overfilled too often, and which were now held together with a piece of string.

We're all going to perish anyway, thinks one group. *But first, let us eat our fill again! Eat until we are replete with good things, and contentment flows through our veins along with the bright blood, which has at last received some decent nutrients!*

Meanwhile the expressions on the faces of the other group are saying: *We have to gather our strength for our daily toil, so that we can survive these times in one piece.* But all of them were scarred by the war, and all of them shared a tendency to caution, a lingering doubt: *Maybe something terrible will suddenly happen to us, too — so it's good to have had our hopes, at least!* Doll himself was moderately pessimistic: he didn't believe that he or his family would perish, but he thought it entirely possible that the future could get extremely unpleasant.

He now turned off from a main thoroughfare into a quiet, green side street lined with villas. But his access to this street was blocked by a red-and-white barrier pole, with a sentry box next to it painted in diagonal red-and-white stripes, where a Russian sentry and a German policeman were standing guard to ensure that no unauthorised persons entered this area, where only officers of the occupying power were allowed to live. Doll had the necessary identification papers on him, and was let through without difficulty, but he still didn't like going through this barrier. Anything that reminded him too much of the war and the military was unwelcome. The sense of impatience he felt at the sight of this red-and-white sentry box could be more or less summed up thus: *It's time to be done with this kind of business—not just here, but across the whole world!*

At the same time, he knew very well that such feelings were foolish. All of this was still necessary: the world, and his fellow countrymen in particular, were not yet ready for a life without constant supervision, without the threat of force. For too long had reason been cast down from its throne. Especially as his dear fellow countrymen would doubtless smash each other's heads in if they were left unsupervised …

By now, Doll was only twenty paces away from a pretty, yellow-painted villa, which looked very well maintained, with its flowerbeds out front (though they had potatoes growing in them now), and its windows all intact and fitted with blinds. This villa was not his final destination today—that lay three or four minutes further on—but he had made up his mind to call in briefly while he was passing. In it lived a man who had helped him a great deal during the previous, difficult year, a man whom he had repeatedly disappointed, and yet who remained unfailingly kindly and helpful. A good, true friend, and quite selfless—one of life's rare gifts even in normal times, and how much more so today!

Doll had neglected this man criminally in recent months, acting as if this man, who continued to worry about him, no longer existed. Doll had made absolutely no effort to contact him. Now it was high time to go and show his face again.

Even so, Doll was sorely tempted to walk on to the next street corner, and the one after that, to see if the truck and trailer had arrived yet from the small town. And if the truck was there, then he would have to help unload the things and set them up indoors. In which case, he would have to skip this visit.

He stood there hesitating for a moment, and then told himself to get a grip: *Never mind the truck and trailer—you've put it off for long enough!* He pressed the bell button, and a moment later the garden gate buzzed. He pushed it open, walked through the front garden, and said to the maid: 'Is Mr. Granzow at home?' And as it had been a long time since he was last there, he added by way of explanation: 'Doll.'

'Yes, I know!' said the maid, sounding slightly offended, and disappeared inside the house.

Doll didn't have to wait long. He didn't have to follow the maid through into the writer's study, feeling anxious as he crossed the threshold and trying to read his host's expression. As so often, it was made easy for him, easier than he probably deserved ...

Granzow appeared at the door of his house, dressed in dark trousers and a pristine white shirt, evidently having come straight from his desk, with a pen in one hand and a cigarette in the other. And just like before, he cried: 'Doll! How wonderful to see you here again! Are you well again now? Are you living over there now? So you're waiting for Alma, who's coming with the truck that's bringing your things? I say again: wonderful to see you! Now you're starting to get somewhere, and it's all happening for you! But come on in, don't stand out there in the blazing heat. You do smoke, don't you?

Here, take one! And here's a light. Now sit yourself down and tell me how you are! What are you all up to?'

And so the conversation began to flow — no word of reproach, not so much as a passing thought. Nothing but kindliness, interest, and an eagerness to help. And then, of course, the moment came when Granzow leaned forward and cautiously inquired in a soft voice (as though he didn't want to damage something fragile): 'And how's the work going? Have you started to write again? Are you making good progress?'

'Oh well, Granzow …' replied Doll, slightly embarrassed. 'Yes, I've started to write again. I'm doing my stint every day, but that's just it: I'm just going through the motions. Like a schoolboy doing his homework. But I don't have the spark or the drive, the inspiration that is really the best part of all. And as for my day job, writing short stories for newspapers just to bring some money in … Well, yes, sometimes I do actually enjoy it again. But I'm not really getting anywhere. We're saddled with debt from the time when we were struggling. We can just get by each day, but there's nothing left over. And now there's the hire of the truck to fetch our things from the country, and that's going to cost thousands!' He looked quizzically at Granzow.

He had been listening to this litany of sorrows with his customary attentive concern. 'Ah yes, your debts!' he interjected. 'I've heard about them. I'm also told that you've started to sell off your books. You shouldn't do that, Doll! You've sold enough already. Far too much, in fact. It's time to stop!'

'But what am I supposed to do?' cried Doll in despair. 'It's all very well to say "Stop selling off your things!" I'd like nothing more. You know how I love my books. It's taken me fifteen years to amass my collection. Every spare mark I had went on buying more books.

But now I simply have to sell them. These debts are starting to make life very difficult!'

'I understand, I understand!' said Granzow soothingly. 'But I still wouldn't sell the books. Why don't you have a frank talk with a publisher?'

'But I'm already in debt to Mertens!'

'I'm sure that won't matter, Doll', said Granzow. 'Mertens is a reasonable man. Talk to him—he can only say no, and even if he does, you won't be any worse off than you are now. But he won't say no. Most likely he's only waiting for you to ask. Do you want me to have a word with Mertens?'

'Absolutely not!' cried Doll, appalled. 'I can't let you do all my dirty work for me, Granzow! If anyone is going to talk to Mertens, it'll be me!'

'So you will speak to Mertens?'

'Probably. Very likely. Don't give me that sceptical smile! I expect I'll do it, really I will.'

'And if you don't do it, then I'll do it for you. Anyway: no more selling off books and other things, Doll! Forgive me for interfering like this. But the other way really is better.'

'Fine', said Doll, his mind now made up. 'I'll speak to Mertens. You can't imagine what it would be like, Granzow, to be free from all these worries at a stroke! I never had debts before—it's just awful!'

'And then you'll be able to write freely again', Granzow went on. 'You'll see, one day you'll write the book that everyone is waiting for! I'm absolutely sure of it, and you'll do a great job!'

And he wouldn't be persuaded otherwise, despite Doll's sceptical head-shaking. Then they talked about Granzow's trip down to the south of Germany. They told each other stories, they chatted, they were still the same old new friends from before, even if there had been disappointments. They didn't have a lot in common, but there was one thing that united them every time: the belief that they had to work, for themselves and for their nation. And they loved their work—for them, everything revolved around this work, which never became just a day job for them.

Doll found himself out on the street again, still smoking one of Granzow's 'proper' cigarettes. He turned a couple of corners and stood at the entrance to the little street of villas where he now lived. There was no truck and trailer parked outside his house. So it was good that he had called in to see Granzow without checking first, good that he had made the effort—otherwise he would be feeling ashamed now that he had ducked out of it.

He walked slowly up to the house, unlocked the door, and went in. The children were living here alone now, looked after by an elderly housekeeper, but at the moment they were at school. The whole place was deserted and empty. Worse than that: it all looked untidy and squalid, covered in dirt and dust. Nobody was lavishing any care or attention on this house, which could have been a proper home. In the little girl's room the bed had not yet been made, even though it was now getting on for midday. Items of laundry, some clean and some dirty, were draped over the furniture or lying on the floor. An outsize teddy bear, as big as a six-year-old child, was sitting in the corner and gazing blankly at the visitor with its brown eyes.

He stood in front of the gaping wardrobe, trying to decide whether he should try and tidy up a bit. But he abandoned the idea with a sigh even before he had begun. Tidying up involved more than just stuffing the scattered laundry into the tangled mess inside the wardrobe. Tidying up meant cleaning the wardrobe from top to bottom, inside and out, along with all the other furniture, and then scrubbing the entire room, cleaning the windows …

So he just shrugged his shoulders. What would have been the point of tidying up, since there was nobody in the house with an interest in keeping it tidy? He opened the windows, just for the sake of doing something … Then he went upstairs to the top floor. *The boy's room is locked—and quite right, too! The lad keeps it tidy himself—and he doesn't want anybody poking about in there.*

The parental bedroom looked just as it did a week before, when Alma left to go to the small town. The bed was just as it was when she got up, with a few newspapers scattered around on the floor and a dirty ashtray, from which all the butt ends had been removed, leaving just the paper behind; a used washstand; and here, too, underwear and items of clothing scattered about on the furniture and on the floor, and the wardrobe gaping wide open.

It would be easy to blame the old housekeeper for doing nothing. But the few hours she was here each day were almost entirely taken up with shopping for food, waiting in queues, and cooking the meals. No, it wasn't the housekeeper's fault, but somebody else's …

Once again, just like downstairs in the children's room, Doll shrugged his shoulders, but here he didn't even bother to open the windows. He walked across to the other room, the one that he had planned to make into his study. Something had come up in the meantime; but the plan was still to turn this light, airy room into a study for himself.

He sat down at the desk and looked around the room. A few bookshelves had been hastily placed against the wall at random, only half-filled. The desk was still standing in the middle of the room, where the removal men had left it. The top section of a large bookcase was standing on the floor, like a second desk, and like the desk itself it was piled with books, the books that he hadn't been able to sell. Doll's gaze fell upon a large, lidded Chinese vase, a magnificent piece in purple, green, and blue, which stood on a tall, black pedestal in a corner of the room.

Doll greeted it with a wave of his hand. The vase was the only item of value they had managed to salvage from a catastrophic world war. It was the last of many precious things that remained in their possession, for no apparent reason — probably only because they were too feeble and lazy to carry it all the way out to an antique shop in the west end of Berlin. Otherwise they had lost practically everything that they cared about, he and Alma both, and what was left was more like a den than a house, a bolthole to eat and sleep in, but not a place to live, not a home.

And yet at one time it had very nearly been a home for them. Back then, after that first meeting with Granzow, when Doll received so much help from an entirely unexpected quarter, when they were able to move out of the half-wrecked room with its cellophane window constantly fluttering and twittering and into this house, leaving behind the dubious Mrs. Schulz, and Gwenda the actress, and all the doctors they had exploited; back then, when they had not wanted for encouragement, food, and fuel; back then, when Doll made contact with the publisher Mertens, and wrote articles for newspapers and started a novel — back then, they had thrown themselves enthusiastically into the business of making a home for themselves. Back then, this house had looked quite cosy and inviting …

So how come everything had started to fall apart again, and hard-won gains had quickly turned to losses? Sitting at his desk, in the dusty den, Doll pondered this as he gazed out onto the street, which lay shimmering in the heat …

Perhaps the first setback had occurred when Alma travelled to the small town to fetch the things they needed urgently; when they discovered that they had been robbed and plundered, that they had been reduced to poverty. Those small-town people had certainly taken their revenge on their hated mayor! During his absence, they had not left him a single sock or shoe, not a shirt or a suit, and not a frock for his young wife to wear—all they had left hanging in the cupboard were the oldest, shabbiest rags. He had found out once again, and this time to his own cost, how feral and depraved this country had become: people felt they had a perfect right to plunder and steal, since the war had robbed them of so much. Who was going to stop them helping themselves? The mantra 'Public need before private greed'—never actually practised—had been supplanted by a different one: 'Help yourself—and don't hold back!'

In the case of a man as hated as their former mayor was, they didn't need to be told twice. They had paid him back for that speech he made from the balcony of the town commandant's office, when he settled scores with the Nazis among them. They had not forgotten his interrogations, the house searches, the confiscations; every request he had turned down had been added to the list of his crimes.

Well, the Dolls had made the best of it, telling themselves: *What would we have done if the place had been hit by a bomb? Then we would have lost everything! At least now we have salvaged the furniture, or what was left of it after the little darlings used some for firewood, and some of the carpets and your books, which have survived more or less unscathed.*

So they had made the best of it. They had started to set up their new home, and he had started to work again—but maybe they still carried some inner trauma that had not gone away. There was nothing of the old fire and energy. *I'm getting old*, Doll kept on thinking. Not that he mourned the valuables they had lost: *What*

was bought for money before can always be bought with money again.
Nor did he care very much that he only possessed two pairs of
old socks, which had been darned a hundred times, and one very
shabby-looking suit.

None of this bothered him much. But what did bother him,
perhaps, was the discovery that evil continued to triumph, as it had
for the previous twelve years, that everything was actually getting
worse all the time. There seemed no possibility that this nation could
ever mend its ways. He often had the feeling that deprivation and
hardship were simply turning them into better Nazis than they were
before. How often did he hear the words: 'Oh yes, under the Führer
we had a lot more of this and a lot more of that …!' To all of them,
including many who had not been Nazis before, the years of the
Hitler tyranny suddenly seemed like some sort of golden age. The
horrors of the war, with the nightly bombing raids, husbands and
sons sent off to bleed and die, the defilement of the innocent—all
that had already been forgotten. They reckoned they had got a bit
more bread or meat back then: end of story. They seemed beyond
redemption, and sometimes it was almost unbearable to be living
among them; for the first time, Doll thought seriously about
emigrating—now, when the war was over!

But none of this was sufficient reason to sink into such a deep
state of apathy again, to destroy their hard-won gains, to give up
what they had struggled to hold on to. Perhaps the work also had
something to do with it, this work that had become more of a duty
than a pleasure: work that lacked any spark, any intuition, any love,
work that his heart simply wasn't in. He had always loved his work,
had seen it as the thing that gave his life meaning. And now he
watched himself just going through the motions, and the feeling
often came over him that he might never be able to work again like

before, that the old fire had gone out of him for good.

That's where they were now, and a thousand minor adversities, impossible to avoid in these times, had added to their troubles. He had even lost the ability to manage money sensibly, it seemed. Money was a constant problem: it never went far enough, and since it didn't go far enough, despite all their economies, why bother to limit their smoking? Why not smoke English and American cigarettes? What did it matter, after all?

And right on cue, his young wife's gallbladder trouble had started up again, whether due to some physical cause or just psychosomatically induced. When this complaint returned to the Doll household, so did the 'little remedies', and this time Doll made no protest; this time, it was a case of share and share alike. Now they abandoned themselves to their dreams, the world appeared in a rose-tinted glow, all their troubles were forgotten, and they were barely aware of feeling hungry or cold; they only got out of bed in order to go and fetch more 'stuff'.

But getting hold of money became increasingly difficult. Doll was not working on anything—so the big sell-off began. First the furniture went out the door, and then Persian rugs, pictures, and books. They were pouring their lives into a bottomless pit. Their strength, their courage, their hopes, their last possessions, they all went the same way—out the door.

They hid their passion cunningly enough from the world; when they were talking to Granzow, the work was making great strides. Doll talked the talk, coming out with one project after another; he invented the most amazing stories, and then promptly forgot about it all again as soon as he stepped outside Granzow's house. They lived only for their dreams now, each dreaming their own dreams alone, lying in their bed-graves ...

Until the day came when it had to stop, until everything had been sold, until they had lost everything they owned and run up a mountain of debt besides, until the body barely responded even to the strongest dosage, until they so hated their stupid, pointless lives that they just wanted out. But they didn't get out, any more than the rest of their nation did, though there was reason enough to go. They eventually ended up in hospital again—in his case, in that strange women's refuge at No. 10 Elsastrasse. She, young as she was, successfully overcame her substance abuse after a short course of treatment; now she was back in the small country town again, where she had gone some time before to collect the rest of their things.

So they would make another attempt to start out all over again—another attempt, and under much more difficult circumstances than before. They had squandered a great deal of capital in terms of friendship, trust, property, and self-belief.

He stood up from his desk in this dusty, threadbare room, where the remnants of his library gazed back at him accusingly. He stretched his limbs, stepped out on the balcony, and looked out over the sunlit greenery. *The trees haven't been through a war,* he thought to himself, *nor the shrubs or the grass. Life goes on.* It was not much comfort, but it was comfort of a sort. Why shouldn't he write another book that everyone would read, that would be a success? Soon—perhaps it was happening at this very moment, as he stood there on the balcony—the truck and trailer carrying the rest of his books and furniture would be rounding the corner. They would make a new start once again—and this time they wouldn't stray from their course just when the goal was in sight.

He suddenly felt cold in the sun. He couldn't bear to remain in this house a moment longer; it reminded him of a tomb where so many hopes lay buried. He hurried out of the house, passed through the red-and-white barrier again, and a few minutes later was sitting in a tram.

Right, he thought to himself with sudden resolve. *I don't want Granzow thinking I shirk every decision and leave everything to others. I need to know one way or the other, and before the truck arrives.*

Later he was walking through the heart of the destruction, seeing few people on these streets, which seven years ago were absolutely packed and could barely cope with all the traffic. Now he was able to walk down the middle of the road, with no need to worry about the cars. When one did occasionally appear, it crept forward cautiously to avoid the deep holes in the road surface.

Doll's progress was likewise slow. The sun beat down on the ruins (it was all quiet around here), and the smell of dust and burnt debris was everywhere still. Many Berlin locals had happy visions of the ruins being grassed over in next to no time. But we are a long way from the nearest tropical jungle here, and anyway the topsoil was completely smothered by the fallen masonry; nothing was growing as yet. You hardly ever saw so much as a green shoot …

Yes, my friend, Doll said to himself, *and why are you surprised, aggrieved almost? Things just don't grow that quickly from ruins—and that applies to you, too, especially to you! You're no spring chicken yourself, and just think back to a year ago, how damaged you were then! Don't you remember how you were lying in that huge bomb crater, which was the world, or at least Germany, waiting for help from the Big Three? So there! But I think you've pulled yourself together a bit since then. There's a little bit of grass growing on the ruin. Don't be so impatient—just keep on going the way you are!*

So he kept on going the way he was, and that way led him, just a few hundred paces further on through all this destruction, to a large, fairly well preserved office building—the former headquarters of the

German Labour Front. He climbed the stairs; nobody asked him what he wanted, he didn't need to fill out a registration form stating whether he was born, baptised, or existent—he was going to see a truly modern businessman.

He opened a door, and there he was, standing in front of his publisher Mertens—no desk clerk, secretary, or receptionist.

Ten minutes later he left the former headquarters of the German Labour Front. Granzow had been right: this Mertens was not a small-minded man. No faffing around, no protracted discussion, no words of blame. Just questions, a few moments of reflection, and then a 'Yes'.

Under his arm Doll was clutching a package—new titles published by Mertens and dedicated to him—and his wallet was now stuffed with banknotes. He no longer needed to make the gaps on his bookshelves bigger, yet the burden of debt had been lifted from his shoulders. Now all he needed to do was to keep working steadily, stay lucky, and all would be well again.

Although Doll knew of a small, little-frequented post office next to the tram stop near his house, he headed off through the streets of ruins, asking people the way to another post office. He couldn't wait to do what now had to be done. It was a much longer walk to this city-centre post office, through the streets of ruins, and the post office itself was still badly damaged and very busy.

He had to wait in line for a long time before he was handed a pen and a sheaf of money orders and transfer forms. Then he went to one of the desks, and started to make out the money orders. They were for large amounts, and it would take a long time, many months of work, to earn back the money. He thought of all the good things they could have bought for that money; their home would look like a human habitation now instead of an animal's den, if they had not squandered the money so senselessly on this wretched 'stuff', this trash that had made them ill into the bargain.

But this was just a passing thought. Doll now filled out the money orders with genuine pleasure, and with a profound sense of relief he crossed off the names of his satisfied creditors from the list he always carried with him. He couldn't pay them all today, but in a week's time he would collect the rest of his advance from the publishers—and then he could draw a line under all this business.

When Doll stepped out into the street again a good hour later, his wallet had shrunk back to its normal size, but his heart seemed to have grown bigger and stronger, because he felt so easy in his mind. He no longer noticed that there was hardly anything green growing on the rubble; in fact, he didn't even see the rubble any more. He was free from the heavy cares that had so long tormented him, and he now saw a way forward ... Suddenly he was in a hurry to get home. That dreary, filthy den—suddenly he was calling it 'home'.

And lo and behold, as he turned the corner and could see to the end of the villa-lined street, a scene of lively activity met his gaze. A truck and trailer were parked outside his door, he saw the children helping the men to carry things in—and good heavens, there they were, just taking his books into the house! The shelves would be full again despite everything, the den would become a proper home, they'd managed to do it again! He practically ran the last bit ...

He found Alma sitting in an armchair and smoking, giving out instructions to the removal men. She had used the time he was away to remove the traces of her dusty truck journey, and now she was looking fresh and youthful again ...

'I bet you're surprised', she called out to him. 'Yes, I managed to fill up the truck and the trailer completely. Now it's all here. We don't need to make another trip. We've seen the back of that dreary little place for good. All your books are here—are you pleased? Haven't I done well?'

He was very pleased, of course, and gave her a kiss. Then he quickly asked Alma if she could spare a cigarette for him, too.

'You can have a whole pack if you want it!' she cried. 'You poor dear, are you feeling desperate? Here—take one! And I've got something else for you: there's two bottles of schnaps in my bag! We should let the men have some, they've worked really hard. And don't pull a face because you think I've spent too much money. Schnaps is cheap out there—less than forty marks a bottle! I've also come back with all my travel money. More, in fact!'

'You have?' he said. 'How come you've still got all your travel money? And more than you took with you! Do they let people travel for free on the railways now? Do the hotels pay you for sleeping in their rooms?'

'Oh, that's easy!' she cried. 'I quickly sold off all the useless junk that wouldn't fit on the truck—old stuff that we'd never have used: mattresses, plain wooden furniture. And now let's raise a glass—to a better future! Cheers!'

They clinked glasses and drank the schnaps. She stretched herself luxuriously. 'Oh, that went down well after the long, dusty drive! Am I glad to have that behind me! We were working until three o'clock in the morning loading up the truck. We worked hard, I can tell you, and now you can give me a kiss to say thank you! I'm feeling so happy!'

He kissed her, this spoilt child, who was now ready to walk the way of hard work and austerity with him. He gazed at her as she sat there, smiling in all her joy and wholesome youthfulness, pleased with her achievements.

In the late evening Doll returned to the hospital to spend his last night there. Next morning he would move into the villa-lined street and start to make a new home for himself. He was well again, he felt the desire to work, and he believed in his future. And one cannot believe in one's own future without thinking about family and friends, the nation at large, and humanity in general. Believing now that he would get back on his feet again, he believed that Europe, too, would endure and rise again.

The apathy had finally left him, and he was no longer lying in that bomb crater. The strength he needed to climb up out of the crater had come to him mysteriously from within — not from the Big Three — and now he was at the top. He applauded life — the life enduring, forever sullied, but magnificent. The nations would sort themselves out again. Even Germany, this beloved, wretched Germany, this diseased heart of Europe, would get well again.

And as Doll made his way through the streets of Berlin at this late evening hour, he felt for the first time that peace had truly come. He walked past undamaged houses, past ruins, under the leafy treetops, and felt happy. At one with himself. At rest. Restored to health — and fit for a life of peace.

Life goes on, and they would outlive these times, those who had been spared by the grace of God, the survivors. Life goes on, always, even beneath the ruins. The ruins are of no account; what counts is life — the life in a blade of grass in the middle of the city, in amongst a thousand lumps of shattered masonry. Life goes on, always.

And maybe people will learn something, after all. Learn from their suffering, their tears, their blood. Learn reluctantly, hesitantly, or with relish. Learn that things have to change, that we have to learn to think differently ...

Doll, at any rate, was determined to be part of this learning process. He saw his path laid out before him, the next steps he had to take, and they meant work, work, and more work. Beyond these first steps, the darkness began again, the darkness that obscures the future for every German today; but he preferred not to think about that. In the last few years, people had learned so well how to live in the moment, from one day to the next: why should that lesson not be put to good use today? *Just get on with life and do your job*: that should be his watchword now.

A comforting late-evening breeze was wafting through the treetops. The breath of the big wide world was blowing upon him, the little man. He leaned against one of the trees for a while, listening to the wind whispering in the branches above. It was nothing, just the movement of air making the leaves rustle like that. Nothing. No more than that. But it sufficed. In the last few years he had never had time to stand under a tree and listen to its whisperings. Now he had time, for peace had come again—peace! *Know this in your heart, my friend: you are done with murdering and killing. Lay down your arms—peace has finally come!*

BRIEF BIOGRAPHY

1893 21 July: Rudolf Ditzen is born in Greifswald, the third child of Wilhelm and Elisabeth Ditzen.

1899 His father, a county court magistrate, is appointed a counsellor in the Court of Appeal in Berlin. The family moves to Berlin.

1909 His father is appointed to the Imperial Supreme Court in Leipzig. The family moves to Leipzig; he suffers a serious bicycle accident.

1911 Attends the grammar school in Rudolstadt, and is seriously injured in a suicide pact—made to look like a duel gone wrong—in which his friend Hanns Dietrich von Necker is killed.

1912 He is committed to Tannenfeld sanatorium in Saxony.

1913 Gets a job as an estate worker in Posterstein, Thuringia.

1914 Enlists as a volunteer in the German army, but is discharged a few days later as unfit for military service.

1915 Secures a position as deputy steward on the Heydebreck estate in Eastern Pomerania (until March 1916).

1916 Takes a job with the Chamber of Agriculture in Stettin, then joins the staff of a seed potato company in Berlin.

1919 He is re-admitted to Tannenfeld in August 1919, but soon leaves for Carlsfeld sanatorium in Brehna to be treated for drug addiction.

1920 Literary debut with the semi-autobiographical novel *Der junge Goedeschal* ['Young Goedeschal']; thereafter he adopts the pseudonym Hans Fallada. In November he takes a job as a bookkeeper on the Marzdorf estate in West Prussia (now Poland).

1921 Leaves Marzdorf in January. For the second half of the year he works as a bookkeeper on an estate near Doberan in Mecklenburg.

1922 From June to October he works as a bookkeeper on the Neuschönfeld estate near Bunzlau in Silesia (now Poland). Arrested in October for trading the estate's grain on the black market, he returns to Marzdorf for the last two months of the year.

1923 Publication of the novel *Anton und Gerda*. From the spring until October he is employed as a bookkeeper on the Radach estate near Drossen. In July he is sentenced to six months' imprisonment for embezzlement (deferred until 1924).

1924 Imprisoned in Greifswald from June to early November.

1925 Publication of three essays on social and political issues of the day in the liberal journal *Das Tage-Buch*. In the spring he goes to work as a bookkeeper on the Lübgust estate near Neustettin in Pomerania (now Poland); leaves Lübgust in July and takes a new job as senior bookkeeper on the Neuhaus estate near Lütjenburg in Schleswig-Holstein; in September he is caught stealing money from his employers again.

1926 Sentenced to two-and-a-half years in Neumünster prison for embezzlement.

1928 Earns a living addressing envelopes in Hamburg, joins the SPD (Social Democratic Party), and gets engaged to Anna 'Suse' Issel.

1929 Gets a job selling advertising space and reporting on local news for the *General-Anzeiger* in Neumünster; 5 April: marriage to Anna Issel; reports on the trial of the *Landvolk* movement agitators.

1930 Secures a position with Rowohlt Verlag; birth of son Ulrich.

1931 Publication of *Bauern, Bonzen, und Bomben* ['A Small Circus']; moves to Neuenhagen near Berlin.

1932 *Kleiner Mann – was nun?* ['Little Man – What Now?'] is published; he becomes a freelance writer. Moves to Berkenbrück in November.

1933 He is held in jail for eleven days after being denounced to the authorities; buys a house and smallholding in Carwitz near Feldberg; birth of daughter Lore.

1934–35 Publication of *Wer einmal aus dem Blechnapf frisst* ['Once a Jailbird'], *Wir hatten mal ein Kind* ['Once We Had a Child'], and *Das Märchen vom Stadtschreiber, der aufs Land flog* ['Sparrow Farm'].

1936 Publication of *Altes Herz geht auf die Reise* ['Old Heart Goes on a Journey'] and *Hoppelpoppel, wo bist du?* ['Hoppelpoppel, Where Are You?'].

1937 Publication of *Wolf unter Wölfen* ['Wolf Among Wolves'].

1938 Publication of *Der eiserne Gustav* ['Iron Gustav'] and *Geschichten aus der Murkelei* ['Stories from a Childhood'].

1940 Publication of *Kleiner Mann, grosser Mann — alles vertauscht* ['Little Man, Big Man — Roles Reversed'] and *Der ungeliebte Mann* ['The Unloved Man']; birth of son Achim.

1941 Publication of *Damals bei uns daheim* ['Our Home in Days Gone By'], *Die Stunde eh' du schlafen gehst* ['Before You Go to Sleep'], and *Der mutige Buchhändler* ['The Brave Bookseller'] (also published under the title *Die Abenteuer des Werner Quabs*).

1942 Publication of *Ein Mann will nach oben* (alternative title: *Ein Mann will hinauf*) ['A Man Wants to Get On'] and *Zwei zarte Lämmchen weiss wie Schnee* ['Two Tender Lambs White as Snow'].

1943 Publication of *Heute bei uns zu Haus* ['Our Home Today'] and *Der Jungherr von Strammin* (alternative title: *Junger Herr ganz gross*) ['The Master of Strammin']; at the invitation of the Wehrmacht, he undertakes fact-finding tours of the annexed territories of

Czechoslovakia and occupied France as a major in the Reich Labour Service; after Rowohlt Verlag is closed down by the Nazis and his general publishing agreement is cancelled, Fallada is left without any financial security.

1944 5 July: divorced from Anna Ditzen; during an argument he fires a shot from his pistol, and is committed to the Neustrelitz-Strelitz psychiatric prison, where the so-called *Drinker* manuscript with the 1944 prison diary is written (first published in 2009 under the title *In meinem fremden Land* ['A Stranger in My Own Country']); following his release he writes *Fridolin der freche Dachs* ['That Rascal, Fridolin'].

1945 Marriage in Berlin to the 22-year-old Ursula 'Ulla' Losch, who also has a history of morphine addiction; because of the ceaseless air raids they leave Ulla's apartment in Meraner Strasse (Berlin–Schöneberg) and move out to her wooden chalet in Klinkecken, on the outskirts of Feldberg; when the war ends, Fallada is made mayor of Feldberg by the occupying Red Army; in August the couple suffer a breakdown and are hospitalised; they return to their apartment in Berlin–Schöneberg, which is partly destroyed, partly occupied by others; first meeting with Johannes R. Becher, through whom he gets commissions to write pieces for the *Tägliche Rundschau*, and who arranges for him to move into a spacious house with a garden and garage in Eisenmengerweg (in the Pankow-Niederschönhausen district of Berlin), Fallada's last place of residence.

1946 Repeated admissions to hospital, including a spell in a private temporary infirmary specializing in female venereal diseases at 10 Marthastrasse, where Fallada is the only male patient; works on *Der Trinker* ['The Drinker'] (published in a reconstructed version in

1950/1953), *Nightmare in Berlin* (published in 1947), and *Alone in Berlin* (first published in 1947, although the book did not appear in its original version until 2011).

1947 5 February: Fallada dies in Berlin; he is cremated in a cemetery in Pankow, and his ashes are later moved to the cemetery in Carwitz at the instigation of Anna Ditzen.

EDITORIAL NOTE

The text of this edition is based on Volume 7 of the *Ausgewählte Werke in Einzelausgaben* ['Selected Works'], edited by Günter Caspar, Aufbau Verlag, Berlin and Weimar, 2nd edition, 1988. The 1988 text was in turn based on the first edition (Aufbau Verlag, Berlin, 1947), which contained two obvious slips that Caspar corrected: at the end of Chapter 8 the nurse talks of '16 February 1943', although she clearly means '1944', as mentioned at the beginning of Chapter 7. And towards the end of Chapter 12 there are two references to the 'Big Four', although this clearly refers back to Chapter 1 and the 'Big Three'. While preparing the new edition, Caspar also consulted Fallada's correspondence, the manuscripts, and other material relating to the novel, when the author's papers were still in the possession of the then copyright owner, Emma D. Hey (Braunschweig). Some of the material is now kept in the Hans Fallada Archive (Neubrandenburg/Carwitz), but the location of the manuscripts and typescripts, as well as the proofs for *Nightmare in Berlin*, is today unknown.

Günter Caspar assumed that Hans Fallada had read the proofs in full. But letters kept in the Aufbau company archive cast doubt on this. Based on three such letters (dated 17, 24, and 27 November 1946), it is safe to assume that he read 'the first 20 page proofs of *Nightmare*' as well as 'p. 21 to 127' ('page proofs 61 to 100 are missing'), and then returned them to his publisher (the first edition ran to 236 printed pages). The correspondence of the publishing director Kurt Wilhelm also contains a letter of 31 December 1946, in which he laments the fact that 'at the time of writing' he has still not received the corrected proofs back from Fallada. He reverts to the matter on 27 January: 'Our production department is still waiting for your proof corrections for *Nightmare*, and needs them very urgently now. Is it not possible for you to send me your copy of the proofs through an intermediary, as soon as possible after you receive this letter?' Wilhelm never received a reply to this request. Fallada died on 5 February 1947, in Berlin's Charité hospital.

As far as the preparation of the manuscript is concerned, it is clear from the correspondence that Fallada revised the text several times. On 27 September 1946, he wrote: 'Dear Mr. Wilhelm, with this letter my wife is bringing you the finished manuscript of my novel *Nightmare in Berlin*—unfortunately I am unable to come myself, owing to a bad attack of rheumatoid arthritis. / As you will see from a quick look through the copy, I have put a great deal of additional work into this novel, and I doubt if there is a single page that hasn't been revised, but the main thing is that I have cut the text substantially, probably by as much as a quarter. I hope that the book in its present definitive form is to your liking. [...] / Before the manuscript goes to print, I would like to look through it myself one more time, since all too often typing mistakes creep in that distort the meaning. I would also like to read the galley proofs myself.'

In October, further specific changes were agreed in an exchange of letters and sent on to Wilhelm by Fallada. The latter also expressed detailed views on the format and design of the book, took it upon himself to organise serialisation in the *Frankfurter Rundschau*, and announced his intention of placing the novel with three of his foreign publishers: Gyldendal in Copenhagen, Putnam in London, and Hökerberg in Stockholm: 'It would be really nice if you were the first German publisher able to announce the publication of a German book in a foreign country.'

What emerges clearly from all this is that even if Fallada was unable to deliver a full set of corrected proofs to his publisher before his death, he had meticulously prepared the text of *Nightmare in Berlin* for publication.

Dr Allan Blunden is a British translator who specialises in German literature. He is best known for his translation of Erhard Eppler's *The Return of the State?* which won a Schlegel-Tieck Prize. He has also translated biographies of Heidegger and Stefan Zweig, and the prison diary of Hans Fallada.